W9-AVM-132

SHADOW WALK

SHADOW
WALK

JANE WATERHOUSE

G. P. PUTNAM'S SONS

NEW YORK

G. P. Putnam's Sons
Publishers Since 1838
a member of
Penguin Putnam Inc.
200 Madison Avenue
New York, NY 10016

Library of Congress Cataloging-in-Publication Data

Waterhouse, Jane.
Shadow walk / Jane Waterhouse.
p.   cm.
ISBN 0-399-14305-X (acid-free paper)
I. Title.
PS3573.A812S53   1997   97-14765 CIP
813'.54—dc21

Printed in the United States of America

1 3 5 7 9 10 8 6 4 2

This book is printed on acid-free paper. ∞

BOOK DESIGN BY JULIE DUQUET

ACKNOWLEDGMENTS

Whenever I begin a book I'm reminded how little I really know about so many things. I'd like to thank the following people for helping to plug up the holes with helpful tidbits of information: Mary C. Evans, Liz Lobaugh, Mary Mater-Harris, Bill Acker, William Dorner, Dolly Kelleway, Gary Lotano, Paul Schlossbach, PLS.PP., and lifelong family friend, Robert Albrecht, for sharing his expertise on firearms.

On my research trip to Virginia, Gary, Waverly, and Scott Lee spoiled me with their southern hospitality. Forever friend Michele Armour provided software and steady encouragement.

I owe a particular debt of gratitude to my pal, Bette Spero, ace reporter and neighbor on the Jersey shore, who gave me a jumpstart on the plot; and Joe Sullivan, whom I will remember as the epitome of what a crusty journalist should be. A family man and raconteur, Joe always went out of his way—even for writers still wet behind the ears.

To my peerless editor, Christine Pepe, and my faithful champions at the Shukat Company Ltd.—Scott, Pat, and Maribel—thanks for patiently seeing *Shadow Walk* through to the end. Last but not least, I'd like to thank my mother, father, and my son, Baylen, whose love and support make all things possible.

For my sister Amy,
and Gary

PROLOGUE

BETWEEN THE IDEA

AND THE REALITY

BETWEEN THE MOTION

AND THE ACT

FALLS THE SHADOW

T . S . E L I O T
"THE HOLLOW MEN"

C ertain memories seem to exist apart. Like air bubbles in blown glass, they appear as tiny, perfectly delineated pockets of time embedded in the transparent window of our remembrances. Sometimes, within them, we can find clues to who we are, and what we're fated to become.

Or at least that holds true for me when I think of the last time I saw Lara . . .

OCTOBER 15, 1970
SPRING LAKE, NEW JERSEY

The building was unlocked, just as she said it would be. I cracked open the door and peered inside. Darkness curled forward on velvet haunches—poised, patient, ready to swallow me whole. Despite the chill air, a trickle of perspiration slid down my back, sopping the starch out of my white blouse. Out of my resolve. I wavered on the porch, trying to summon up enough nerve to go in.

From the distance, I heard the shush-shush *of tires scudding over fallen leaves. The macadam started to whiten.*

A car.

Best case scenario, some nosy do-gooder. ("Uh, everything all right there, young lady?") *Worst, one of the local cops on patrol. Either way, in a matter of seconds I'd be haloed like a trapped deer, paralyzing fear pinning me into place— into* this *place—a place I had no business being, a few minutes shy of midnight, on a school night.*

The headlights trawled closer, an ever-widening net of luminescence snagging whatever they came across. Severed tree branches. Chestnut pods scattered over the ground like small spiky helmets. The blue-black hedges. And me, caught dead-to-rights on the threshold, hovering like a shadow between the light and total dark. I watched the beams lap over my saddle shoes, then continue lasciviously up my legs until they nipped at the knife-edged pleats of my school uniform. Come on, Garner, *a voice in my head screamed.* Move, or you'll be riding home in a patrol car.

I threw caution to the wind and hurled myself into the predatory blackness inside. The automobile idled suspiciously at the curb. Fallout from its headlights sifted through the transom. I held my breath, waiting for the snap of a door. Would the police call my father in Manhattan? *I wondered.* Would he have to come down to the Spring Lake P.D. and bail me out?—*an appealing thought in a perverse sort of way, but ultimately farfetched; the hired help usually handled such domestic emergencies.*

Outside, the engine revved. Twin shafts of light crisscrossed the ceiling in a blaze of white, a sputter of red. Then nothing. Apparently the driver had lost interest. For a couple of minutes I stayed put, waiting until my night vision brought the marble staircase into hazy focus. I took the steps on all fours, feeling my way upward.

The lobby smelled of mildew, dead flowers, and rotting wood. I stood slowly. Clouds of must stirred in the air before settling back onto the rugs and furniture. After taking a few tentative steps, my knee hit something solid—the ticket desk. It wouldn't be much farther now. Moving more confidently, I searched out the padded vinyl double doors and pushed through, letting them close behind me with a wistful sigh.

Prologue

At first glance the theater appeared deserted. A single worklight hung from a metal noose, center stage.

Then I saw Lara Spangler.

She was on her knees, directly under the proscenium, drawing on the floor with a piece of chalk. The bluish cast of the bulb etched silvery highlights into her dark hair. She glanced up. "Thought maybe you'd chickened out." Her voice carried effortlessly over the rows of seats.

"Sorry." I started down the sloping aisle, feeling dizzy, as though the stage were somehow magnetized and I might be swept toward it like a packet of metal shavings.

"Run into any problems?"

"Just the usual." I shrugged.

Lara and I seldom discussed the defective inner workings of our respective families. In truth, an hour ago I'd narrowly averted disaster. The Jamaican woman who oversaw my father's Spring Lake home—and, parenthetically (I happened to be in it), me—had walked into the kitchen just as I was sneaking out.

"Back's h'aching like a tooth," Cilda Fields had said. "T'ink I'll mix me h'up a draught." Then, "What you doin' down 'ere, Ga'ner Quinn?"

"I'm hungry." Whereby God immediately punished me for lying with a slice of pie which I had to eat, insides heaving, while she went about concocting one of her evil-smelling brews.

The ingredients for Cilda's draughts arrived regularly, via parcel post, in lumpy brown-paper packages from a place in Brooklyn called Evangeline's. I pictured it: a narrow doorway in a block of shuttered storefronts, no name, no street number. A beaded curtain masked the back room where Evangeline sat, a yellow caul over one eye; around her neck, a talisman made from the shriveled paw of a monkey. All around were dusty jars. Chicken hearts pulsated in jewel-colored goo. Hacked-off rooster claws skittered against glass. The veiny irises of a young calf bobbed like pearls in syrup, and, on the topmost shelf, a pale embryo of an unborn child sucked its tiny thumb—

"Anybody see you come in?" Lara Spangler had stopped drawing.

"I don't think so."

"So everything's cool." She sprang to her feet. At her old school, in upstate New York, Lara had been a cheerleader; but her dad objected to the uniforms and made her quit. She said it was no big deal; she was "so past that rah-rah stuff, anyway."

"Careful." Lara offered a hand, pulling me up on stage. "Watch how you walk." I looked down at the chalk circle on the floor. "There shouldn't be any breaks," she explained, high-stepping in burgundy buckled shoes. "As long as the line is unbroken, the forces of evil can't get in."

At the center of the circle was a makeshift altar consisting of an open book, a knife, and a pair of black candles. For what seemed like the millionth time since sneaking out of my house, I realized what a big mistake I'd made, coming here.

"Got a match?" Lara asked.

I made a show of patting down my school uniform. "N-n-no," I stammered.

Lara shimmied a flattened pack out of the pocket of her skin-tight bell-bottoms. "Eureka." She smiled, kneeling down to light the candles. The wicks sputtered like Fourth of July sparklers before catching.

For some reason, when she'd first asked me to come, I hadn't quite pictured it like this—the circle, the candles, Lara with her paper-white skin and silver-streaked hair, her moonstone earrings and buckled shoes. The undigested piece of pie lurched in my stomach. I recalled the passages she'd read me from her book:

"The ceremony must be held in a secluded location, preferably a place with an air of mystery and romance."

Over our shoulders, the worklight cast a pale moon onto the painted balcony, one of the backdrops from the theater's production of Romeo and Juliet.

"The circle's power is magnified by the presence of a virgin."

I glanced down at my scuffed saddle shoes. "Maybe this isn't such a good idea," I said.

"Shh." Lara gently squeezed my arm. "Don't be scared, Garner. We're in the magic circle. Nothing bad can happen to us here."

I wanted to believe that, but I knew better.

For one thing, if Cilda Fields were to walk in, no circle—magic or otherwise—would protect me from the raging tempest of her island woman wrath. It might not be so bad for Lara Spangler, who was some vague sort of Protestant, a girl who went to public school; for a Roman Catholic and faithful recipient of the Blessed Sacraments, such sorcery would be considered nothing short of mortal sin. I was overcome by a miraculous vision—a celestial host of all the nuns I'd ever known, congregated in the vaulted heights of the auditorium, calling my name and beckoning me away, their shark fins flapping like the starched wings of angels.

Just then there was a sudden whoosh of air and the candles went out. "Holy Jesus," *I whimpered,* "what happened?"

"No need to freak." *Lara sounded calm, but her hands were trembling as she struck the last match.* "It's probably just the heat going on."

The theater reverberated with a wheezy rattle. "I don't think I'm up to this," *I said, nervously scanning the dark.*

"What are you talking about?" *Lara nudged my knee.* "You're Garner Quinn, remember? A perfect three"—*along with witchcraft, my best friend had recently become interested in numerology*—"bold and courageous. Destined for great things."

"You don't really believe that stuff." *The outright belligerence in my voice surprised me.*

"I have to," *Lara Spangler replied, deadly serious.*

"Well, I don't."

"You believe in us, though, don't you?" *she asked.* "In the sacred bond of our friendship?"

"Well, yeah," *I relented.* "I believe in that."

Lara tossed the witchcraft book aside. "I guess that'll have to be enough."

She picked up the knife. The black candles flickered between us. Holding up one hand, Lara jabbed the pointy part of the blade into her index finger. A tiny balloon of blood burbled out. Then she turned to me. "Come on, Garner."

I closed my eyes, wincing a little at the prick of the knife. We pressed our bloody fingertips together.

"Now, and for the rest of our lives," *Lara said,* "we'll always be friends."

"Always," *I echoed solemnly.*

"No matter where I go, I'll take a part of you with me. Wherever you lead, a part of me will follow behind like a shadow," she whispered fervently. "And no matter what happens to either of us, we'll never forget this night."

"Never."

"Never, ever," we repeated, our voices momentarily intertwining before they wafted out of the circle, and disappeared into the balcony like so much smoke.

I NEVER DOUBTED for a moment that the special kinship Lara Spangler and I shared would last a lifetime. But I was only fourteen, and just beginning to learn how quickly life could change—how absolutely and completely—in the space between drawn breaths.

Less than a week after we sealed our promise, my father sent me off to a private boarding school in New England.

And a few days after that, Lara's father killed her.

PART ONE

EVERY JOURNALIST WHO IS NOT
TOO STUPID OR TOO FULL OF HIM-
SELF TO NOTICE WHAT IS GOING
ON KNOWS THAT WHAT HE DOES IS
MORALLY INDEFENSIBLE. HE IS A
KIND OF CONFIDENCE MAN, PREY-
ING ON PEOPLE'S VANITY, IGNO-
RANCE, OR LONELINESS, GAINING
THEIR TRUST AND BETRAYING
THEM WITHOUT REMORSE.

JANET MALCOLM
THE JOURNALIST AND THE MURDERER

1

SUNDAY, MAY 18
TWENTY-THREE YEARS LATER...

IN THE SPRING of my thirty-seventh year, I came dangerously close
to copping a Spangler.

I remember the exact moment it happened. I was sitting on a drop cloth
in the great room, staring up at a wall of spanking new sheetrock. It had
been one of those picture-perfect days that occasionally crop up in early
May. A breeze blew in from the open window down the hall. Outside,
waves tickled the back of the stone seawall, but I couldn't see them.

My beachfront estate was located on the secluded tip of a narrow peninsula off the Jersey coast. Once it had boasted a million-dollar view of the
Atlantic; then the panoramic glass wall got shattered, under circumstances
I preferred to forget. I'd kept it boarded up all winter long until my
fourteen-year-old daughter Temple complained that it was like living in a
crack house. I told her she watched too much TV.

The next day I called Ben Snow. Ben's a retired carpenter who
sometimes does odd jobs for me. Together we drew up plans for an
addition—a sort of enclosed veranda which would act as a buffer
between our living quarters and what I'd come to regard as the cold,

cruel world outside. Most evenings, around twilight, I came out here to survey the day's work.

I can't say what made this particular night any different. Maybe it was the sound of the tickly waves on the other side of the sheetrock. Maybe it was the gypsy breeze, with its after-tang of split pine and fresh paint—pleasant scents, which normally generated a sense of hope, but instead left me curiously depressed. I gazed up at the cathedral ceiling, feeling suddenly claustrophobic, the beams like a ten-ton weight on my chest.

And that's when it first crossed my mind. *Get out of here, Garner,* came the phantom whisper. *Why don't you just cop a Spangler?* And the fact that I could think such a thing, however fleetingly, made me realize how low I'd sunk—what a cold, hard, callous person I'd become.

Of course, by then, the term "to cop a Spangler" was part of the local vernacular. Time had sanitized it of blood. Divorced it from the memory of those five corpses—Lara, her two brothers, mother, and grandmother—arranged precisely on the ballroom floor. After a couple of decades, the horror which gripped my hometown of Spring Lake with the sudden force of a riptide had ebbed to a nagging undertow. What stuck in most people's minds wasn't that a bland, colorless man as Gordon Spangler had so cold-bloodedly annihilated his entire family—but that *he'd actually gotten away with it.*

A "Spangler" came to mean the ultimate disappearing act. A spectacular swan song, a big-time crash-and-burn. To pull a Spangler was to shuffle off one's outer coil as matter-of-factly as you'd shuck an ear of corn. It was the A-Number One act of abandon, the razor-sharp cleaver that severed every binding tie. The unsettling, yet strangely liberating notion that—yes, dammit, maybe it *was* possible to start over. To begin a new life.

Which, on that balmy May evening when I was thirty-seven, was something I desperately wanted to believe. Even at the expense of the promise I'd made, all those years ago, to my friend Lara.

. . .

TO SET THE record straight, this had absolutely nothing to do with killing my family. On the contrary, in dreams I saw us huddled in a small, battered boat: Temple, Cilda Fields, and me. And there was only one oar, and I was feverishly paddling it, trying like hell to get away from a dark and dangerous shore.

What I wanted to kill was my career.

I wanted to snuff out GARNER QUINN, true-crime writer, in bold print, above the title. And while I was at it, I wanted to squelch all her flashy little brainchildren—those bestsellers which had multiplied with jack-rabbit alacrity into paperback deals . . . motion pictures . . . public appearances . . . movies-of-the-week.

In the new life I imagined for myself, my name appeared only in the white pages of the phone book: microscopically small, in ordinary upper-and-lower-case letters, one in a sea of undistinguished Ps and Qs. I would look, and act, and talk, like the other moms in the super-market—women who'd never once skipped a teacher's conference to interview some psychopath on death row, who didn't need to scrub the stink of violent death off their hands before sitting down to dinner.

It's difficult to say when things started going wrong. I think at some point during the book on Jeff Turner, I lost my head for true crime. Then after the book on Dane Blackmoor, I lost my heart.

When I called my agent Max Shroner to explain this thing about losing my heart and head for writing, he very pragmatically said, "So do it for the money."

Max has represented me for more than fifteen years, which is the longest continuous relationship I've ever had with a man; but sometimes he just doesn't get it. "I don't need money," I told him.

He then asked if I knew how much it would cost to send my daughter through college, not to mention the years of financial support before she actually got a job, and then again, when her first marriage fell apart. Spewing figures gleaned from personal experience and factoring in the rate of inflation, Max painted a bleak picture of what I had in store—rationing tins of cat food, saving the Fancy Feast for Cilda, my longtime friend and keeper; plugging leaks in the roof with old dust jackets; using the glowing reviews as insulation against the cold.

"It could happen," he said.

"I'll take my chances."

On the other end of the line, I'd heard him lighting up a cigarette. "You'll go crazy with all that time on your hands," he predicted, inhaling deeply.

"I'll manage."

I'd already begun to fill up the empty spaces with what had come to be known as my Projects. Besides the addition to our house, I was in the midst of renovating the Spring Lake estate my father had left me in his will. I'd also bought a mountain bike and was teaching myself Italian. Mr. Dane Blackmoor—world-renowned sculptor, self-professed scoundrel, and the man I'd almost fallen in love with—had abruptly left the country, saving me the protracted pain of one of those energy-sapping, ego-battering relationships I'd been majoring in since college. I could now devote myself, day and night, to my teenage daughter. Spring had come, summer would follow. I was comfortably well-off, reasonably good-looking, and only thirty-seven.

I had it made.

It occurred to me that people probably had said the same thing about Gordon Spangler before he went off the deep end—a man with a lovely wife, three promising young children, a nice home, a good job. I did the arithmetic and figured out that, in 1970, he would've been just my age.

2

LOOKING BACK, I can't help wondering whether I brought it all on—as if my casual invocation of Spangler's name that night had somehow conjured up his dormant evil and triggered the chain of events which followed. I remember being gripped by a premonition of danger so strong, it propelled me out of the dark, empty great room into the safety of my well-lit kitchen.

They were both there, exactly as I'd left them—Temple, on the cordless phone, talking to her father; Cilda Fields, at the table, pretending not to listen. Later Cilda would recount the entire conversation between my only child and my ex-husband for me, word by word, as though she'd been an active participant, and not eavesdropping over a cup of tea.

"That is *so* cool." My daughter was giggling.

So much for premonitions, I thought, sardonically. This feeling of impending doom was only a logical response to Andy's regular Sunday-night call.

It was one of life's little ironies that, just when I gave up my career to become a full-time mom, my former husband should suddenly resurface. After a gap of thirteen years—during which time our child had been weaned, potty-trained, and ushered into puberty—Andy decided it was now time to try his hand at being a father.

And, to my surprise, Temple seemed all for it.

I yanked open the dishwasher and began to put away the clean dishes, making as much noise as humanly possible. Although I hadn't been invited to play a part in this budding relationship of theirs, I damn well wasn't going to be ignored.

"She's fine," my daughter said, raising her voice a little.

I slammed a cabinet so hard it sounded like a discharged gun. At the table, Cilda took a slow sip of tea, managing to look both superior and sorry for me.

"I don't know. I'll ask." Temple put a hand over the receiver, searching my face, hopefully. "Dad wants to know if I can spend next weekend at his place."

The wine goblet I was holding had some water in it. I stuffed a dish towel into its glass mouth and twisted. "Nope. That's mine," I said, adding petulantly, "We're going to take a ride out to the Amish country, remember?" In addition to my Projects, I had a long list of Day Trips and Family Vacations.

Temple's face darkened. People said she looked like me, but her expression now—the pout puckered with disappointment, the curtain of thick lashes veiling those mile-a-minute thoughts—that was one hundred percent Andrew J. Matera. "Darn," she sighed. "I wouldn't ask, except it's kind of a special occasion."

I crossed my eyes. "Aren't they all?"

"Mo-homm," Temple beseeched.

She lowered her voice to a stage whisper. "Daddy and Candace are getting *engaged*. They're throwing a huge party at this cool Russian nightclub, and they really-really-really want me to come."

I left the wine glass on the counter. Took a bottle of chardonnay out of the refrigerator, and poured while I did the math. On one hand, a bunch of dour-faced men with scraggly beards and straw hats, Cilda Fields, and me. On the other, a smoke-choked speakeasy, filled with barrel-chested peasants, tossing back vodka and dancing the mazurka.

"All right," I muttered. "But I get the next two weeks in a row."

"Thank you!" Temple did a victory dance with the phone. "I can go," she told her father. I slapped the icetray against the sink, knocking cubes out like teeth.

"Oh, she doesn't have to do that," Temple was saying, coyly. I strained, wishing I could hear more than just a low rumble coming out of the receiver. "Well, it depends"—Temple smiled—"usually a size five."

Through the steam rising from her teacup, Cilda's eyes flashed like warning signals in a fog. *They were buying her a dress. Something red and slinky—suitable for belting shots of Smirnoff, tossing the empty glasses against walls, and shouting "Nostrovia!" Was I just going to sit here and take it?*

It didn't appear I had a choice.

Before turning away, Cilda tossed me another silent I-told-you-so for having made the mistake of marrying *t'at h'awful man* in the first place.

3

"WELL," I SAID after Temple had hung up the phone, "it seems a toast is in order." I raised my glass. "To Andy and Candi."

"Candace," Temple corrected in a weary tone.

That bugged me even more.

Typically, the females my ex-husband went for had small vocabularies, large breasts, and names that ended with the dotted letter i. I'd considered myself the exception, an anomaly—Andy's one brief but daring foray into the realm of good taste.

Enter Dr. Candace Kressler. In her mid-forties, with a face more aptly described as interesting than pretty, she was a well-respected clinical psychiatrist who had a thriving private practice and a seat on the board of a major New York hospital. At first I figured her interest in Andy must be professional—sooner or later, I told myself, Kressler would publish a case study, something about the classic narcissistic male in action, and my poor ex would be history. But this engagement was troubling.

Even I wouldn't go so far in the name of research.

"She's really nice," Temple piped up.

"I'm sure she is," I replied, adding to myself, *Nice and nuts.*

Temple hopped up onto the counter and started kneading my shoulders. "We can go to see the Amish people the weekend after next," she said in a conciliatory tone.

I shook my head, intent on feeling sorry for myself. "That's Memorial Day. Too many tourists." As if people like us fell into another category.

The telephone rang. Temple jumped for it, probably thinking it would be Andy again, reminding her to pack Rollerblades, or asking what kind of take-out she liked better, Mexican or Chinese.

"For you." She held out the receiver. "It's a *man.*"

Cilda sat up straight in her chair. Seeing the two of them exchange hopeful looks, it suddenly hit me. In their misguided innocence, they believed that one little call from a member of the opposite sex might be enough to rescue me from the self-imposed house arrest I'd been living under these last few months.

"This is Quinn," I said curtly.

"Pissed off already, GQ?" said the voice on the other end. "Before you even know who's calling?"

"You sound like somebody who probably pissed me off in the past."

"So sue me," the man said, "everybody else does." That was the giveaway.

"TJ Sterling, as I live and breathe." I picked up my wine glass, heading for the privacy of the empty great room. Although I had no interest in talking with this guy, Cilda and Temple didn't need to know that.

Sterling sounded drunk. "Yeah, well, the way I hear it, the air you're breathing is pretty rarified these days." A short strangled sound echoed over the line, a laugh, or perhaps just a cough. "Hey, might as well eat, drink, and be merry, 'cause tomorrow all of us die, right?"

I lowered myself onto the drop cloth. "Gosh, I'll have to write that down." For some reason the sight of the bare sheetrock suddenly angered me. "So, TJ," I said, cutting to the chase, "to what do I owe this honor?"

"Relax, GQ." The initials were a dig on his part; over the years I'd steadfastly refused to call him "Tom" or "Tommy" as did the people who professed to like him. "I'm not going to ask you to testify as a character witness again—that is, unless you want to." He laughed again. "Lord knows, you got the time, I got the lawsuit."

"Time's a problem for me lately." I didn't tell him I had too much of it. With Sterling, you had to nip these things in the bud.

"No prob." From the other end of the line I heard the gentle clink of ice cubes. Another pick-me-up, surprise, surprise. "The real reason I'm calling is, I'm planning to be in your neck of the woods this weekend. I was hoping we could get together for dinner."

His offer caught me off guard. Sterling took advantage of this by quickly adding, "If I recall correctly, there's a decent French place in Rumson. But, hey, I'm not picky. Why don't you call it?" I detected a note of urgency in his voice, which made me instantly uncomfortable. TJ Sterling wanted something, and what was worse, I'd have to spend a couple of hours in his company before he told me what it was.

"Aw gee," I said, "I've already got plans for this weekend."

Cilda and Temple had drifted out of the kitchen. I put up a hand and waved them away.

"Look, Garner." TJ lowered his voice. I wondered who it was he wanted to keep from overhearing. "I wouldn't bug you if it wasn't important."

Yeah, I thought. *Important to you.*

He seemed to read my thoughts. "It concerns a certain . . . uh, area of common interest." The notion was ridiculous. We both wrote true crime, but after a promising beginning, Sterling's shoddy journalistic practices had landed him in a netherworld of quick-turnarounds, fly-by-night exposés, and exploitational tell-alls—one small step up from the tabloids.

"I don't know what all the secrecy's for, TJ, but I'm afraid it's a waste of time where I'm concerned. I've given up the true-crime biz."

Again the clink of ice against glass. When Sterling spoke again, it was almost in a whisper. "Yeah, well, after you hear what I have to say, you just might reconsider, Garner. Because I know where he is." His breath drummed in my ear. "I've found Gordon Spangler."

I DON'T REMEMBER much after that, only that we settled on a time, and agreed to bring our own cars. I hung up, feeling weak in the knees.

"You're going out to dinner." Temple's perfect white smile flashed in the darkness.

"Yes," I managed to respond. "Maybe your father will buy me a new dress."

4

SPRING LAKE, THE town where I grew up, boasts two miles of pristine beaches and the longest stretch of old-fashioned, non-commercial boardwalk in all of New Jersey. Legend has it that the land was once an Indian playground, but in the early years of the twentieth century it became the watering hole for wealthy families of Celtic origin who built their grand estates along the ocean, or around the fresh-water pond from which the town took its name. Spring Lake became commonly known as "The Irish Riviera," and its inhabitants' allegiance to both the old country and their town can be plainly heard in this local blessing:

> *Health and long life to you,*
> *Land without rent to you,*
> *A child every year to you,*
> *And may you die old,*
> *Young in Spring Lake.*

Personally, I'd always found the sentiment rather scary.

The morning after TJ Sterling's call, I dropped my daughter off at school and embarked on a leisurely thirty-minute drive, heading south. Following the coast down Ocean Avenue, I passed through Long Branch, into Deal and Allenhurst, and edged along the boarded and abandoned shorefront of a faded Asbury Park; then I made a loop around Ocean Grove, connecting with the water again at Bradley Beach. Each tiny community was another bauble in the gaudy necklace of the Jersey shore—pearls strung alongside paste, battered glass beads next to sparkly diamonds. A brick gate set Spring Lake off from the others, as if this place deserved its very own setting.

Less than half a mile later I was pulling up to the beachfront mansion that I would always think of as my father's house. In truth, Dudley had made only occasional pit stops here, on his way to, or from, someplace else more interesting. It was one of several residences left to me in his will, and I'd planned to sell them all as quickly as possible; but after walking through it with a real estate agent, I was shocked to see how shabby the place had become. Unoccupied for years, it had the feel of an abandoned hotel. I imagined the ghosts of Dudley's friends lurking behind upstairs doors, hovering over the bedposts, as ethereal and transparent as mosquito netting.

"Charming." The realtor had wrinkled her nose.

The drawing room, with its bracketed ceilings and wood paneling, suddenly seemed just plain dark. A Steinway once played by Rachmaninov stood in the corner. I went over to it and wrote my name in the dust.

"You know, if you put some Andersen windows in here," the intrepid real estate lady had commented, "it'd up your price by at least fifty thou'. I know a contractor who works wonders with old gems like this."

I didn't care about the money, but something about redoing these rooms, taking a sledgehammer to the walls, and turning the whole place upside down, had appealed to me. The more the contractor proposed, the more I wanted done. Weeks turned into months. A quick sale no longer mattered. This was one of my Projects. I wouldn't be happy until I'd erased whatever it was about this house that made me still feel—at age thirty-seven—like a lonely little girl.

The workers were on the job again today. Through the gap in the front gate I spotted a flatbed truck and a van. I didn't feel like stopping to check on them, nor did I want to be caught spying. I pulled away from the curb without a backward glance.

5

I CONTINUED DOWN Ocean Avenue, my rearview mirror reflecting nothing but empty road. Memorial Day was still weeks away. Only the year-round diehards had braved the Spring Lake boardwalk today—nannies wheeling preschool children; elderly men leaning on canes; the inevitable bare-chested jogger, scowling into the wind. The ocean slapped the shore, and drew back again, sullen and angry. I rolled up my window, feeling chilled to the bone.

Then the Raleigh-Eton Hotel came into view. *Here it is,* I thought. *The straw that broke Gordon Spangler's back.*

It looked like a wedding cake made by a baker gone berserk. The vanilla cream facade was stripped in places, laying open a chocolate-brown nubble inside. Windows rose in layers, dripping filagree crowns and gingerbread balconies, peeking out from dormers, or under gables. In the center of the slate roof sat a cupola, as intricate as a lace doily, and easily the highest point for miles.

I parked the car on the boardwalk side and trotted across the street, with my hands jammed deep in the pockets of my wool blazer and my hair flying wild in the ocean breeze.

The huge wrap-around porch that had once boasted dozens of fan-backed wicker chairs and potted palms was now empty. On the patchy lawn a sign proclaimed "LUXURY CONDOS COMING SOON!", but the salt air had taken its toll on the paint and someone had scrawled "LUXURY CONDOMS" in large bubble letters over the developer's name. A more ambitious hand had added mustaches, and detailed—if not exactly to scale—genitalia, to the elegant silhouettes of a man and woman in evening dress, clinking cocktail glasses on a balcony overlooking a moonlit sea.

After a string of bright prospects which had prematurely dimmed, fabulous opportunities that didn't quite pan out, and jobs that it seemed he wasn't really suited for, Gordon Spangler had come here, to Spring Lake, and this sprawling, magnificent, ridiculous white elephant of a hotel.

I'd only been a kid at the time, but I remembered all the talk. The wealthy family who'd purchased the Raleigh-Eton in the early sixties and subsequently ran through a big chunk of change trying to restore it to its former glory had given up and gone back to Ireland. They sold the property to a group of hotshot New York investors calling themselves Coastal Star Development, Inc., who proposed parceling the hotel into high-end resort condominiums.

The project was plagued by controversy, legal red tape, and money problems from the start. Everyone in Spring Lake seemed to be against it, although reasons divided along economic lines. The wealthy decried the "nouveau riche riff-raff" that such a complex would attract. Poorer folks who'd depended on the Raleigh-Eton for their bread and butter found that—after years of carrying luggage, cleaning rooms, and waiting tables—their jobs were suddenly obsolete.

I never connected Lara Spangler to this brouhaha over the Raleigh–Eton, nor did I think much about what her father did there. She mentioned he'd been hired as an engineer for Coastal Star, that they'd moved to New Jersey from Utica, New York. Before that, she said they'd lived in a half-dozen places, mostly in the midwest. I remember her ticking off cities on each finger—*Grand Rapids . . . Indianapolis . . . Des Moines . . . Cincinnati . . .*

To me, it sounded so wonderful, all these places outside of Spring Lake.

THE SKY HAD turned cloudy. As I headed back to the car, a startle of color on the ground caught my eye. A tiny circle of crocuses was poking defiantly out of the dirt. I picked one and put it in my buttonhole. Then I turned around one last time.

The old hotel was so huge it dwarfed the surroundings. From this angle it looked lopsided, almost menacing—like a vast, crushing weight ready to topple down and crush whatever happened to be in its path.

6

I MADE THE first right after the Raleigh-Eton, traveling west toward the center of town. A camera crew had set up camp on the lake. Two professionally adorable children were striking poses on the wooden bridge while a gaggle of ad executives stood on shore flapping their arms, trying to get the local swans to swim into their shot. I turned onto Second Avenue and followed it all the way to the pond.

Wreck Pond formed a natural boundary, separating Spring Lake from the neighboring community of Sea Girt. Once I reached the water I veered north, driving slowly, looking for landmarks. Surprisingly little had changed over the years. Neatly kept Victorian- and Craftsman-style cottages still lined both sides of the road. Through the willows, Wreck Pond shimmered like scraps of fallen sky.

The street sign to the cul-de-sac where the Spanglers had once lived was conspicuously missing. Blacktop gave way to gravel, spitting out from under my wheels with a barrage of pistol-cap pops. Up ahead I saw the rusted remnants of a magnificent wrought-iron fence. Whole sections of grillwork had been pried away, so that it seemed to yawn toothlessly over the horizon.

For a moment I considered turning around, but my foot kept gentling the gas pedal, as though not a part of me. The sign on the gate once said "Holly Hill," until Spring Lake's roving graffitti artists had paid a visit with their spray cans. It now read "HOLY HELL." Below the name, they'd put the number "666."

I parked the car, leaving the keys in the ignition.

A swath of cottony quiet enveloped the world outside. No birds sang, no squirrels skittered. Although less than a mile from the ocean, Holly Hill seemed remote and landlocked. Overgrown holly and honeysuckle wound a prickly parapet around the property, blocking the closest houses from view.

Suddenly I felt afraid—ridiculously afraid—as though Spangler might actually be crouched behind the gate, a still figure, wrapped in leafy camouflage, patiently waiting. I shook off the feeling and marched up to the pillared posts.

"Gordon," I called softly, "I'm home."

A tumble of charred blocks loomed through the fence, like a poor man's Stonehenge. This was all that was left of the house where Lara died. Less than a year after the murders, Holly Hill had been torched. The arsonist was never found. I'd read newspaper accounts, but they hadn't prepared me for the utter devastation.

The foundation looked as though it had been shattered by a bomb. Gordon Spangler's manicured lawn was thigh-high with weeds, the flower beds thatched with dead tree limbs and debris. Vandals had pilfered most of the Belgian block walkway. I upended one of the remaining bricks with the toe of my sneaker, dispossessing a family of fat quicksilver bugs which slithered away, seeking new cover. A horrific image flashed through my mind: *five bloated corpses teeming with maggots . . . what Lara's face must've looked like . . .*

I forced myself to focus on this scorched site, trying to rebuild the house in my imagination—framing walls, adding windows and doorways—until memory took over, transporting me back . . .

ON A GRAY autumn afternoon in mid-October of 1970, I visited Holly Hill for the first and only time. I'd come directly from school, running the whole way down Second Avenue, until my shoes were damp and muddy and the tail of my blouse hung out over my uniform. At the wrought-iron gate, I stopped to bunch my uncontrollable avalanche of hair into an elastic band. Every night I rolled it in Campbell's soup cans, to no avail. Never would it be silky and straight, like Lara Spangler's.

I loped down the brick sidewalk, bookbag slung over one arm, the other struggling with the ponytail. My first glimpse of the Spanglers' house caught me by surprise—it didn't seem possible that Lara could live in such a dreary place as this. The columns were peeling and in need of repair. Battered shades hung at half-mast in all the windows. Black felt had been tacked over the casements in the cellar. A gutter yawed limply off the roof, which appeared to be molting shingles. The general deterioration seemed at odds with the well-tended grass and shrubbery.

I approached the porch gingerly, testing each step to make sure the rotted wood would bear my weight before going on to the next. With a rich kid's carelessness, I wondered why Mr. Spangler didn't just hire a few people to fix up the place.

The doorbell was rusted. Its urgent trill echoed my own growing nervousness. From inside came the sound of people talking. Not the cheerful *"I got it, Ma!"* kind of patter you heard on television sitcoms. These voices were tense and anxious. After a moment, they lapsed into silence. I had the distinct impression that someone was staring at me, yet not the slightest movement ruffled the drawn shades. The deafening quiet made me want to dash down the splintered steps and fly back to town, not stopping until I reached the safe haven of the library—which was where I'd told Cilda I'd be, anyway.

But a familiar voice whispered in my ear: *You're Garner Quinn, aren't you? Bold and courageous, a solid number three . . .*

I took a deep breath and rang the bell a second time. Silence persisted for another thirty seconds; then I heard the echo of footsteps. Lara opened the door a crack. "Hi, Garner." I could tell she wasn't surprised.

My eyes drifted over her shoulder into the dim interior of the house. "I was just checking to see if you were okay," I said. "Mr. Corio said you dropped out of the play."

She shrugged. "Yeah, well, you know, it was taking up a lot of time."

I could guess what that meant. Of late, things had been pretty strained on my home front as well. My absent father had gotten it into his head that I'd be better off in boarding school and nothing I said could convince him otherwise. On Dudley's last weekend home, Cilda had marched into his study and shut the door. When she came out a half hour later, her brown eyes were shot with red and swollen like sponges. "Man's got a 'ead as thick as a church door" was all she said.

I longed to tell my friend this, but something in her face stopped me.

The front door yanked open wider. "Hello," said a round-faced boy with Lara's same blue eyes and grave half-smile. This would be the younger brother.

He ducked under his sister's arm. "I'm Gordy. Who're you?"

"My name's Garner."

"Can't she come in?" the little boy asked Lara.

"Oh, sure," she said, stiffly motioning me inside. "For a minute."

The first thing I noticed was that the house was really cold—really cold and really bare. Vivid splotches of color on the bleached wallpaper hinted of mirrors and paintings recently removed. A knot of electrical wire dangled from the plaster rosette on the ceiling, as though the chandelier had been summarily yanked and carted away. Plastic runners crisscrossed the floor. To the right, a room was cordoned off with vinyl accordion doors.

"Take your shoes off," called a querulous voice. "Don't track mud in here."

Through the pleated gap I saw a woman of about seventy—bone thin, blue-haired, nicely dressed—sitting on a shabby plaid sofa. A teenage boy was curled up on the rug in front of her, watching television with the sound turned off. I remember thinking how odd they looked, just sitting there, in front of the silent, flickering picture.

"Garner's not staying, Grandma," Lara said.

"Why not?" Gordy wanted to know. "Why can't she stay?"

"That's okay, I have to be—" I faltered, then, in an undertone asked Lara, "You're sure about the play? You won't change your mind?" She'd been cast in the title role of George Bernard Shaw's *Saint Joan*. The director had chosen the play specifically for her.

Lara gave me one of those "I'm so *past* that" shrugs. "Don't be sad, Garn," she said, "I would've probably made a mess of it, anyway." In the empty hall, with her grave smile and glistening eyes, the only thing Lara Spangler seemed to be missing was a suit of armor and a stake.

"Larie!" came a hoarse cry from upstairs. "What's going on down there?"

"Mom's not feeling well today," Lara said quietly, and I understood. My own mother, whom I barely knew, shared the same sickness. These women would never feel well, as long as they still had the strength to hold a bottle.

"Call me," I said. "Maybe we could get together in town."

"Or you could come back to visit," Gordy suggested. "Couldn't she, Lar?"

"Sure," his sister replied, without conviction.

Halfway down the rickety front steps, Lara called my name. She leaned over the railing as if to hug me good-bye. "Meet me at the theater, midnight tomorrow," she whispered. "The door'll be open. I have a key."

"Midnight?" I fiddled with the strap of my bookbag. "Gee, I don't—"

"It's important, Garner." Lara stared directly into my eyes and gave me a little push, like, *just go.*

When I reached the gate I turned for a last look. Lara was standing on the front porch with Gordy clutching her sleeve like a security blanket. For some reason my eyes gravitated toward the basement windows. One of the black felt curtains had been drawn aside. A man's face was centered in the glass. Although it was too far away to see him clearly, I could feel Mr. Spangler's glare.

7

"WHAT'AYA DOING THERE, young lady?" A woman in a bright red coat and matching tam strode toward me dragging an old black dog on a leash. Her legs were bare and shapely, and she wore neatly rolled bobby socks with Hush Puppies, which made her shriveled, sun-wizened face seem rather a shock.

"This is private property," she warned. "No trespassing allowed."

"Sorry. I didn't know—"

"Hah!" She spat out a venomous laugh. "If you didn't *know,* you wouldn't be here, now would you? Nobody comes here without *knowing.*"

The mongrel began enthusiastically slobbering on my hand. "I meant to say, after all these years, I expected someone would've bought this land and put up another house."

"There been those who tried." Again, the nasty cackle. "One had a heart attack and died the day he signed the papers. Then a young couple from up Fort Lee put a bid in. Got hit by a truck on the turnpike going home. Had to fish body parts out of their car with one a them metal jaws. People started to get spooked, thinking the place must be cursed."

"Is it?" I asked, trying to keep her talking.

"S'been a curse to me." The woman scowled. "Kids partying all hours of the night. Gawkers snapping pictures. Carting away bricks like they had hundred-dollar bills hid inside. For a while there we had witches coming through, too, chanting and singing, trying to wake the dead. *Pah.* If you ask me, they should leave the dead alone. Haven't they suffered enough?"

"I guess you live nearby."

"Down the block." She hitched a crooked thumb. "Seen you drive past."

The dog nuzzled me. He had cataracts and psoriasis. I crouched, scratching behind his ears. "Good boy. Good old boy." He closed his eyes and whimpered, in doggie ecstasy.

"He likes you." The woman relaxed her hold on the leash. "Don't you, Elvis?"

I scratched Elvis some more. "Were you here when the house burned down?"

"I was here for the whole shebang," she chortled. "When they moved in, when he killed them, and everything after. Frankie and me—that was my dog before Elvis, a good old chocolate Lab—we used to see him out here mowing the lawn. Cutting the grass in his shirt and tie. Coulda been a hundred degrees, that tie never came off."

She shook her head at the memory. "He was a queer one, all right. But polite? Always a good morning, or wave hello riding by in the car. Not like the wife. Never saw her but two or three times the whole year they was here. Up in that room, day and night, with the shades pulled down." Her voice dropped to a confidential level. "She drank, you know."

Elvis had settled into a drooling, itchy lump of contentment at my feet. His mistress continued, clearly on a roll. "And the old woman! Boy oh boy. There was a royal pill if you ever saw one. Invited her for coffee, you know, to welcome her to the neighborhood? She sat at my kitchen table with her mouth screwed into a knot and her back so straight you'd think she had a broom stuck up it. She was allergic to dog hair, she said. Very cold, very German, if you know what I mean."

She narrowed her eyes at me. "You're not German, are you?"

"No."

"Hah, not with that complexion," she crowed. "My husband was Irish, too. White as a snow drift by the time he was twenty, but not a wrinkle on him the day I put him in the ground. Me, I'm Hungarian, both sides. You know, like the Gabor sisters?"

Elvis lifted his head hopefully, ready for another ear massage. I obliged, letting the moment pass in silence, before steering the conversation back. "A shame the firefighters weren't able to save the house."

Once again the woman lowered her voice. "Ask me, they were glad to see it burnt. Wasn't the first time they got called out, and the police, too. A big headache the place was. Soon as the news about the murders hit the papers, all the vandals and vultures started swarming. By the time the wife's sister come down for the funeral, there was hardly nothing left inside. They took all the good silverware, even the towels off the rack. Carried off the family photographs and left the empty frames sitting there on the mantel, the sister said. Bunch of scavengers!—stealing school pictures of those poor dead children."

I turned away, ministering to Elvis's many itches. "Did you know them?" I asked, in an offhanded manner. "The kids?"

"You're not a reporter are you?" The woman was suddenly suspicious.

"Me?" I said. "Good Lord, no."

"Because I already gave my story to the papers a million times."

"I was just curious."

She lapsed back into a familiar tone. "Well, I can tell you, the little one—that was Gordon, Jr.—he was a real rip. Broke my garage window. *He* brought the boy over, the father did. Made him apologize. Paid cash for the repair, too—though from all that came out later, it was probably with the old woman's money, not his." She jangled the dog's leash.

"The older boy kept more to himself, like his ma. And the girl, well, if you ask me, Lara had them all beat. She used to always fuss over Frankie. Feed him M&M's and teach him tricks. Look, Mrs. L, she'd tell me, he can say 'candy'—and wouldn't you know that dog would get up on his hind legs and go *caa-rfff!*, just like that? She acted in plays. William Shakespeare and whatnot, over at the theater. You should've seen the write-ups! Of course, *he* didn't approve."

The walnut-shell face bobbed under its festive red tammy. "After she died, rumors started going around about how she was into that there black magic. I say too bad she wasn't a witch. Maybe then she coulda put a pox on him and saved herself."

I remembered Lara's face when I asked if she really believed in the occult. *"I have to,"* she'd said. But, in the end, it had proved to be a sword of paper.

A whisper of sadness crept into the woman's voice. "I suppose she'd be about your age now, or even older."

I stood up, not trusting myself to stay another minute. At the sudden withdrawal of my hand, Elvis threw back his head and began to howl. "Once he's made a friend, he doesn't want to let go," the old lady said. "Poor dumb animal." Her loneliness was palpable, part of the forlorn landscape of toppled stone.

"It was nice talking to you," I said. The dog strained against his collar.

I stooped, allowing him to slather me with hot, wet parting kisses. Then, on an impulse, I took the crocus from my buttonhole and tucked it in a crack in the foundation while Elvis and the woman watched.

They followed me to the gate. "You know, from the first I saw you"—she huffed and puffed, trying to keep pace—"I kept saying to myself, don't she look familiar? . . . and just now, it come to me—"

I reached the Volvo, a split-second too late. The woman wagged an accusing finger. "Didn't you used to be Mr. Quinn's daughter, the writer?"

"Yes," I said, opening the car door, "I used to be."

8

MY FATHER HAD the wits of an old Tammany Hall politician. He knew the value of having people indebted to him, and his shrewd beneficence earned him a reputation as a much kinder man than he actually was. Detective Sergeant Gerald T. Donovan owed his career to Dudley, who—as a favor to the widow Donovan—had pulled a few strings to get her baby boy a spot on the Spring Lake P.D. I knew that was partly why Donovan seemed so agreeable when I asked to meet on such short notice.

He suggested a coffee shop on Third, known for its great rye bread and baseball memorabilia. I found him in a back booth—a granite mountain of a man in a nylon running suit, nursing a cup of coffee. "Well, if it isn't the Jersey shore's most famous daughter." He stood as I slid onto the seat across from him.

"Good to see you, Gerry," I said, embarrassed by the greeting. "I appreciate you fitting me in like this."

Donovan waved me off. "You kidding? It's dead as a doornail this time of year."

The waitress came over to take our order: a roast beef on rye and a shake for me, three fried eggs and a double side of bacon for Donovan. "The power protein diet," he said, patting his gut, "twenty-seven pounds in six weeks."

"Congratulations," I told him, not really sure whether he'd gained or lost.

"See you're sprucing up over at your dad's." Donovan tasted his coffee, and added a second packet of Sweet'n Low. "Could that mean we'll be welcoming you back to town?"

"Just making a few minor repairs before it's put on the market, I'm afraid."

"Too bad. Your dad always said he hoped you'd move in with your little girl, once he was gone."

Since Dudley's death, I'd heard similar remarks from casual acquaintances and complete strangers. *Your pop was so proud when you won that big award. . . . He just loved showing off that picture of you in* People *magazine . . . Said you were a regular chip off the old—*

At first it angered me that my father had offered these precious bits and pieces of himself to the Gerry Donovans of his world when, rightfully, they should've been mine. Now it just left me with a hollow ache, like a hunger that wouldn't go away.

"A great man, your dad." Donovan was looking at me curiously.

I glanced around the empty room. In a few minutes the lunch crowd would arrive, most of them locals who knew the detective and would no doubt stop to say hello. I decided to put my cards on the table. "Listen, Ger, the real reason I'm here is to pick your brain."

"Pick away," he chuckled. "What little's there is yours for the asking."

I leaned forward. "Gordon Spangler."

Donovan whistled. "Now that ain't a name I'll ever forget."

"Do you keep in touch with the FBI about the case?"

"Maybe more than they'd like."

"And, in all these years, nobody's ever gotten a bead on the guy?"

"Not anything that turned out to be real. Oh, in the beginning there were sightings on a pretty regular basis. One month we'd hear Gordon Spangler was living somewhere down in the Okefenokee swamp. The next he was logging wood out in Oregon, or working as a forest ranger in Yellowstone Park.

"It got to be a joke. Every time one of the boys went on vacation, we'd get a postcard, you know like, '*Having a ball here in Disneyland. Traveling's so much easier without the kids. Your friend, G. Spangler.*'" Donovan laughed, the way I'd seen a hundred other cops laugh with the cases that really got under their skin.

"Think he's still alive?"

"Absolutely. I can feel him out there—just about taste and smell him, too. Only thing, I can't *see* the bastard." The detective smacked the table with his big fist. "Yeah, he's alive all right. As my sainted mother used to say, stinkweeds never die."

The waitress returned with our food. Donovan dug into his eggs as though he'd never eaten food before. I waited until his fork slowed to normal pace before asking, "Did you ever come up with a profile projecting the kinds of places or jobs—the situations he'd be drawn to?"

Gerry stopped eating. "You writing another book, Garner?" The broad smile almost masked his sudden wariness. "Is that what this is about?"

"No," I assured him. "No book."

"Because that one fella did a whole big thing on it a few years back—"

"TJ Sterling."

"Good old Tom." Donovan handled the name carefully, as if it were a sharp-edged implement.

"I was over in Nam at the time of the murders, but from the moment I made the force, it became a thing with me. I tell you, I immersed myself in those files. Knew 'em frontward and backward. So when Sterling came around asking about the case, I thought, cool. You know, anything to keep it in the public eye and maybe catch the sonofabitch. And old Tom, he seemed like a stand-up guy." Donovan laughed at his own naiveté.

"So a coupla nights we head on over to Reggie's bar, and we're drinking, and he's buying, and then *I'm* drinking, and he's still buying, and I'm spilling my guts, giving him all the inside dope . . ."

I knew what was coming: TJ Sterling's version of journalistic date rape.

Gerry went on bitterly, "A year later, I read the book. He's made the Spring Lake P.D. out to be some flannel-mouth Mayberry, with me as a drunken Barney Fife and Chief McGlynn a retarded Andy Griffith."

"Sterling's an ingratiating asshole," I said.

"You got that right. But you can see why I'm a little gun-shy." He hastened to add, "Not that anything you'd write would be like that. My wife's read every one of your books. You got more than just talent, Garner—you got integrity, like your old man."

I accepted the compliment, and its underlying irony: Dudley was one of the most extravagant liars of all time, and I'm not much different.

I said, "I'm not writing a book, Gerry. You have my word on that. Lara Spangler and I were . . . friends."

"Oh, yeah, I forgot." Donovan signaled for another coffee. "The theater over in the community center, right? You two did shows together."

I waited until the waitress had gone. "Lara did the shows. I helped out backstage."

If Gerry was to trust me, I knew I had to go the extra mile. "A few days before the murders," I said, "I went away to boarding school." I

4 4

didn't tell him that my father exiled me, had sent me packing because I reminded him too much of my mother. "I was hundreds of miles away when I heard what happened. I don't think I ever really dealt with . . . the loss."

I shrugged. "Call it a midlife crisis. I just feel the need to go back, I guess. To try to make sense of things."

Gerry Donovan's tough facade turned to mush. "You don't have to say another word," he said.

The other booths were beginning to fill up. Our waitress plunked down the check on her way to another table. With practiced ease I palmed it, shrugging off the detective's protests. "You should really talk to Chief McGlynn," Donovan said as we headed out.

"Over at headquarters?"

"Nah, Frank's retired now." We walked outside and stood on the sidewalk together. "But whatever you want to know about Spangler, he'd be the guy to ask. He was the first detective on the scene."

Gerry took out a roll of Tums and began peeling off the foil. "If you're not in a hurry, I could call and tell him you'd like to stop by."

"That would be great."

"Only thing, I wouldn't mention the Sterling book if I were you. That oily sleaze made a big thing of how Frank tossed his cookies all over Spangler's dead mother." Donovan popped a fistful of antacids in his mouth. "But I'm telling you, Garner, I went through Nam, and no lie, the first time I saw those crime-scene photos? Man oh man, I'm not sure if it'd been me I'd a done any better than poor Frank."

I stood outside while Donovan called ahead for me on his car phone. When he emerged, smiling broadly and flashing a thumbs-up, I felt a flutter of guilt—a side effect of having told the truth, but not the whole truth.

By the time he wrote out the chief's address, though, it had passed.

9

RETIRED CHIEF OF police Frank McGlynn lived in a modest split-level in Spring Lake Heights. If the house was plain, the lawn had been do-dadded up enough to stop traffic. Tulips, in an array of astonishing colors, wound through a fairy terrain of birdbaths, balsa-wood cutouts, and whimsical garden statuary. I walked up the cement path, past an honor guard of Disney's Seven Dwarfs.

"Come on around back," a voice called through the open garage.

I found the chief on the rear patio, holding a garden hose nozzled with Miracle-Gro. He was in his sixties, small and wiry, with the kind of shrewd squint and pugilistic stance that made me think of Jimmy Cagney, in one of those old gangster movies.

"Have a seat"—he motioned toward a set of white plastic garden furniture—"while I finish up here." I watched him water his flowers, wondering how Gerry Donovan had characterized my visit. A few minutes later McGlynn shut off the outdoor spigot.

"Sorry about your old man. He was one of a kind, that's for sure. Not like these slimeball dial-a-lawyers they got today." The chief wiped his hands on his corduroy trousers. "You want instant coffee? A Budweiser?"

"No thanks. I don't know what Gerry told you—"

He sat at the plastic picnic table. A furled yellow umbrella sprouted from its center like a corn dog on a stick. "Said you were looking for answers in the Spangler case."

"Yes."

McGlynn's crinkled blue gaze turned hard. "Well, honey girl, you've come to the wrong place. I don't have any answers for you. Don't have a single one."

My heart sank. *I should've known from the moment I drove up,* I thought. It was obvious that Frank McGlynn had been working overtime to banish the shadows of the past with these brightly painted cartoon characters in his sunny little suburban garden of Eden. He leaned forward in the plastic captain's chair, and wrestled a bulging leather wallet from his back pocket. "Lemme show you something."

From behind the clear window containing his driver's license, McGlynn produced a folded piece of newsprint. "There's the only one with the answers. Go on, take a look."

The paper was so yellow and brittle, I had to open it carefully for fear it would disintegrate. "5 SLAIN IN HOUSE OF HORROR," screamed the headline. Below it was the impressive facade of Holly Hill, its shoddiness all but erased in the grainy black-and-white exposure. A picture of a man wearing a dark suit and tie filled the far-right column. His clothes, and the thick black frames of his glasses, appeared to date the photograph to the early sixties, but it was difficult to tell for sure. Gordon Spangler had never been the type to keep abreast of trends in fashion.

I stared at him—this unremarkable man, not particularly attractive or notably homely; his face neither smiling, nor serious, as though he'd long ago given up hope of making any kind of strong impression at all. His eyes were focused a millimeter away from the camera lens, giving him a look that might be shifty, or simply shy. The accompanying banner read, "Local Businessman Kills Wife, Mother, Children."

"I've carried that around for twenty-five years," Frank McGlynn said. "I'll carry it around till the day I die, if I have to." He took the article, and put it back into its sheath, behind his license. "See, missy, I want answers, too. And I'm gonna have 'em, I promise. This world or the next, don't matter. That cold-hearted snake's got some big explaining to do before I'll ever rest in peace."

Overhead, the sky was still overcast and cloudy. The leaves had not fully budded on the trees. Stocking-capped gnomes peeked through the forsythias, their mischievous faces still as stone. In the gathering gloom, the tulips seemed unnaturally colored, artificially bright.

"You were the one who found the bodies?" I asked softly.

McGlynn's squint-eyed, pugnacious face darkened. "There were two of us went in at first," he said. "Ernie Waldmier and me. Joe Corio—he was the drama coach over at the recreation department back then—he waited outside with two of the kids from the theater.

"December fifteenth, nineteen hundred and seventy." McGlynn's dentures clicked softly as he recited the date. "Ten days before Christmas.

"Corio'd been calling the department for a week. He was worried something happened to the girl. Spangler had written notes to all the kids' teachers, saying how they'd be out of state for a while visiting a sick relation, but somehow it didn't sit well with Corio. He started driving by the house, trying to see what was what. He had us send a guy over, to check things out, but there were no signs of trouble. The bastard had stopped the papers and told the post office to hold the mail." He shook his head in grudging admiration, acknowledging Spangler's forethought.

"A few days later, Corio's on the horn again. Claims there's a broken window in the basement and sounds coming from inside the house," McGlynn said. "I think Joe kicked in that glass himself, though he always denied it. It was pretty clear he had a thing for young Lara." He added quickly, "I'm not saying sexual—from what I could tell, Corio looked to be a happily married man. More like a fascination. She had a kind of magnetic effect on people. But I guess you knew that."

I nodded, unwilling to share what I knew or did not know about Lara Spangler. After all the years spent writing true crime, I found it difficult not to play my thoughts close to the vest. It was a habit so ingrained in me that I'd perfected a diversion—a complete toning-down of self that allowed me to blend into any background. I recalled the photograph of Gordon Spangler, and I realized that he, too, had understood the advantages of protective coloring. It was an unsettling thought.

"I'd made detective sergeant the spring before," Frank McGlynn went on, "so I went through the window first. Right off, I got a bad feeling. Spangler had a combination office-bedroom set up in the basement. Just a cot and a desk, some filing cabinets. There was a fancy fish tank in one corner. All the fish were floating, belly up.

"And of course, I recognized the smell," he sighed. "I'd never known anybody to be murdered in this town, but people died, and every so often you'd get one that'd been hanging around for a few days. So I knew what we were dealing with."

McGlynn winced. "Though after six and a half weeks, it's like nothing you ever . . . seeps into your pores and just stays there. Weeks later, you're still trying to wash the stink away."

"He'd left them upstairs?"

The chief squinted toward his candy-colored tulips, and spat. "In the infamous 'ballroom.' All we had to do was follow our noses and ears."

"Your ears?"

"He'd kept the radio on, tuned to one of them religious stations. We could hear it blaring all the way up the basement steps." McGlynn slipped a hand inside his jacket and patted down the pocket—the telltale tic of an ex-smoker under stress.

"They had one of them folding doors that runs on tracks closing the room off from the hallway," he said. "Ernie opened it, and I walked inside.

"The bodies were on the floor. Estelle Spangler was face up, with a yellow checkered tea towel over her eyes. She was still laying on the plastic runner he used to drag her from the kitchen. We figure she'd been reading the morning paper when he came up and shot her from behind with his trusty Austrian Steyr. *Bang.* We found a bowl of Cheerios and a cup of coffee on the kitchen table. You feel like stretching?"

I said sure, and we began a slow turn around the backyard. "The boys were on Boy Scout sleeping bags, perpendicular to their mother. He'd arranged it so one of her hands was kind of draped over each of them. They had their coats and scarves on. The older one, Robert, usually got home from school around two-thirty. Best guess, his father was waiting for him. Probably had just enough time to pull the kid into the ballroom by his ankles, and clean some of the blood up before young Gordy arrived at three."

McGlynn stooped to right a stone cherub that had toppled among the daffodils. "The girl was the only one not lying on her back. She'd stopped by the theater after her last class, so it must've been after four when she came home. Maybe he didn't have as much time as he needed to set things up, or maybe she suspected something the minute she walked in. However it went, she ducked away before he could shoot her in the head. We found a bullet lodged in the plaster molding.

"The second shot caught her right above the shoulder." Neither of us looked at each other, concentrating instead on McGlynn's pretty flowers bobbing in the breeze.

"She went down. He pulled the trigger again, shooting wildly, catching her in the thigh. Unable to walk, that little girl crawled down the hall on her hands and knees, trying to get away. But Daddy didn't give up. She was only a few feet away from the front door when he pounced on her. Grabbed the necklace she had on from behind, and started choking her. Choked her so hard the chain broke and the little moonstone beads spilled all over the floor. And when she still resisted, probably begging and pleading for her life, her father took her neck between his hands and squeezed until the skin turned blue, and all the blood vessels in her eyes burst, and her tongue lolled out of her mouth like a dying pup.

"Then, when it was finally over, he slid her back up the hall to the ballroom, and carefully arranged it so the top of her head was under Estelle's feet—the two females in a straight line, with the boys at right angles to their mother."

The old chief picked up a stick, using its tip to trace a simple design in the dirt.

"It was a cross, you see," he said. "I didn't notice it right off. Walking in on something like that, your mind can't fathom it all at once. So you notice crazy little things—how the dish towel on the woman's face is the same yellow check your wife has . . . and that the kids' bodies are so swollen it looks as though they got water balloons under their coats. And the stench. The stench in there was like a great humming noise, you know, one of them high-pitch frequencies you can't hear, but it's driving you crazy just the same? Even with the damn radio blasting, I kept thinking, *Please, God, just shut off the smell.* Poor Ernie, he turns to me and says, *Can you hear it? That's the sound of the maggots feeding . . .*"

McGlynn suddenly threw the stick. "The ballroom was pret' near empty, except for a metal folding table and some chairs along one wall,

5 1

but there were orange and black streamers Scotch-taped all around, with cardboard pumpkins and silhouettes of witches on brooms. Halloween decorations, and there it was, mid-December."

"He killed them on All Saints' Day," I said.

"November the first." He nodded grimly. "A month and a half later, we're standing there, and this choir starts singing on the radio. Never forget it as long as I live—'The Hallelujah Chorus'—you know, them deep voices booming—'and He shall reign for ever and ever' and then, the women—'Hallelujah! Hallelujah!'

"And that's when I look down and it come clear to me. The cross. The black and orange crepe paper hanging limp off the walls. *Ten . . . fucking . . . days . . . before . . . Christmas.*" Frank McGlynn wiped something from the corner of his squinty blue eyes.

He paused for a moment. "I radioed for backup, and Ernie and me split up. He searched the rest of the first floor, while I went upstairs.

"See, we expected there'd be two more bodies—the old woman's and Spangler's. I scoured every inch of the second floor, where Estelle and the kids' bedrooms were . . . Nothin. It was eerie."

We walked slowly across the yard, heading back toward the patio. "His mother had an efficiency apartment in the attic. Bedroom, bath, sitting room, a small kitchen—but not a sign of her anywhere. There was some knitting and a Bible on the Barcalounger. A place setting for one at the kitchen table. Two pieces of stale bread were sticking out of the toaster on the counter. I could smell sour milk . . . it smelled sweet compared to the other, that death smell."

McGlynn gripped the back of a plastic lawn chair, but did not sit. "To the right of the landing I noticed a closet. Somebody had stuffed a rolled braided rug against the bottom runner, like to keep out drafts. I kicked it aside and opened the door."

His cock-of-the-walk stance collapsed in on itself suddenly, making him look smaller, more fragile than he'd seemed at first sight. "She fell out on top of me—a hundred-and-twenty-pound woman blown up like the Goodyear blimp. The back of her head had been shot away, and the front didn't look like it had much of a face anymore.

"I lost my footing, fell over the rug. Her housecoat had come loose. My arms were flailing a mile a minute, trying to break free of her. Somehow I got tangled up with the sash of her robe, and her tit brushed across my neck, hard, and gray, and cold as a peeled potato . . . *Christ.*" The chief squeezed his eyes shut.

That's when the tough guy cop had heaved his guts out, all over the *corpus delicti*—one of those small but gripping details that a crime writer like TJ Sterling would make good use of on the printed page. Not long ago, I'd have done the same thing myself. But in this whimsical, Crayola-colored garden, the sight of Frank McGlynn leaning on his flimsy plastic lawn chair, his jaw clenched in anguish, looking so beaten and haunted, that thought made me ashamed.

1 0

HEAVY DRAPES IN a nubby flame-retardant fabric sealed McGlynn's house in permanent twilight. I sat at the imitation Duncan Fife dining-room table, across from a china cabinet filled with dusty crystal and a few pieces of Belleek. On the sideboard, a framed photograph of the McGlynns on their wedding day showed a Brylcreemed sharpster standing next to a hatchet-faced woman who looked old enough to be his mother. The only other picture in sight was a painting of the Virgin Mary.

I could hear Frank in the kitchen, taking dishes out of the dishwasher, crossing the linoleum in his stockinged feet. With exaggerated care, I lifted the photocopy from the file. The handwriting which covered the page was uniform in size and perfectly legible, from top to bottom. Each line flowed with ruler-straight precision. Not a single undotted i or uncrossed t betrayed the writer's state of mind. Taking it slowly, one sentence at a time, I began to read Gordon Spangler's letter.

addition to these considerations, I have been deeply concerned about state of their souls. *This past summer, I was summoned to police idquarters to pick up Robert. The incident is still too painful and ibarrassing to recount, but let me say that a small amount of marijuana was involved. Recently even Gordon, Jr., has shown signs of disobedience, sloth, and insolence. I believe the children have been negatively affected by my wife's illness and the fact that she has not been to church in 12 years.*

Since moving to Spring Lake, my daughter Lara also refused to attend services. I have seen the devil influencing her at every turn. Although I forbid her to wear short revealing skirts, she continued to flaunt her body in tight jeans, and on the stage. She listens to Satanic records and reads books on astrology and witchcraft. I suspect she has had sex with boys.

It became apparent that if I were to save their souls, I had to act quickly. At first I considered the day of our Saviour's birth to embark them on their journey, but things began unravelling and I settled upon All Saints' Day. It wasn't easy especially since Lara had invited her theater friends to a Halloween party, but after that show of pagan revelry I was more committed than ever to free them from the Devil's insidious grasp.

Estelle went peacefully. I don't believe the boys even knew what hit them. Lara posed more of a difficulty. She struggled a lot and I had to hurt her, which I felt sorry for, but at that point I couldn't have let her live, especially knowing what had happened to the others. It would be too awful, and besides this way I knew she was saved.

I thought about killing myself, but decided that then God would send me to Hell for the sin of suicide, while my beloved family would go straight to heaven. Once the bodies were in place I prayed over them, and felt that I had done right.

Please tell Estelle's family, her mother, sister, and my brother-in-law Ken (who I will always consider a friend) that I am sorry to have caused them pain. I have also left a letter for my minister asking for absolution.

To Whom It May Concern, it began—

    By the time you read these words, you wil.
which has fallen upon me to render. Try to see p.
take comfort (as I do) that they are all in heaven
    In recent weeks it became clear that this dire path wa.
to take. My wife Estelle's failing health confined her to t.
weak and debilitated body. Bereft of support from my spouse,
ble for the day to day running of the household, the food, clothin.
back and forth of the children, cleaning, repairs, shopping, finan.
    This last area (finances) was particularly stressful in light of
termination of my position as chief engineer for the proposed Rale.
condos. I do not hold my former employers at Coastal Star Dev.
responsible for my actions. In fact, I apologize for any negative public.
may incur on them. (Note to Chip Ewell: the WWII books I borrowed a
in the bottom drawer of the filing cabinet. Thank you Chip, I found them
highly informative.)

    My financial situation since leaving Coastal Star left me in a constant state of worry and depression. The $5000 I borrowed against the house is gone, as is my mother's bank account. (Which she didn't know, and if she had found out about would have killed her.) I had hoped to be able to make a modest living selling life insurance, but my progress in this area was disappointing. One problem is that I have been told I need to develop my interpersonal (people) skills.

    I did not want my family to have to face the humiliation of bankruptcy, losing the house, not to mention a lower standard of living. I have always tried to provide them all the amenities (clothes, gifts, jewelry) and didn't want to see them suffer. Also, my mother being elderly, I did not think it would be fair for her to face having to go back to live with her sister in Grand Rapids, who she doesn't get along with.

(Note to funeral director: you should bury all five in matching coffins, and see that they are laid to rest together. The headstone is to be inscribed with the following: "In righteousness I will see Your face" (Psalms 17:15). Also, if at all possible, violets should be used in the floral arrangements. (I realize this may depend on when the bodies are found, seasonal availability, etc.) Lara loved violets.

I set the thermostat on its lowest level before leaving to slow the rate of decomposition down as much as possible. Hopefully, the pipes won't burst. I have no wish to cause the heating company any undue problems.

(Note to police: the Steyr is in the locked left hand drawer of my desk. The key is in the envelope marked "Keys" on the filing cabinet.)

Very sincerely,
Gordon Spangler

P.S. I had to leave Mother in the upstairs coat closet. I would have had an awful time dragging her down three flights of stairs.

I turned the stacked sheets facedown on the waxed surface of the table so I wouldn't have to look at the neatly ordered lines of penmanship. A few minutes later, Frank McGlynn entered from the kitchen carrying two bottles of beer.

"Need a glass?"

I shook my head. He set a coaster out for each of us and sat. For a while we drank, saying nothing.

"I'll let you in on a secret," the chief said at last, "something I haven't ever told another soul." He rolled the twist-off cap in his palm. "There've been a couple of times in my life when I swear I could feel him. Feel him watching me."

"Spangler?"

"The first was at the funeral." McGlynn grunted. "Jesus, what a day that was! The whole town showed up just about. All the kids' school friends. Joe Corio and the theater crowd. People from that church of theirs. And there musta been a hunnerd reporters.

"Bill Flynn from over Flynn Brothers was the undertaker, and let me tell you, he didn't relish getting that business. Five bodies, in the shape they was in? Let alone there being no money to bury them with." The chief's voice was bitter. "For all of Spangler's careful instructions, he left out one small detail. He'd drained his bank accounts of all but sixteen dollars."

He shrugged. "So Billy and me pulled some fancy maneuvers, passed the hat, sold what furniture was left in the house. Wasn't much, though. Spangler'd already stripped the place of any valuables." I remembered the empty hall, the tangle of wire where a chandelier had once hung.

"Anyhoo—" The chief took a swallow from his beer. "Then the day comes, and we're heading over to the gravesite and Flynn, he's sweating like an ox, a complete bundle of nerves. *Frank,* he says, *I got this feeling that Spangler's out there somewhere, waiting to see if they get buried the way he wants.* Now I don't say a word, but I had the exact same feeling. And Marty Kovatch, he was chief then, he musta too, because he stationed ten of us all around the cemetery, to watch."

"But nothing happened," I said.

"No." McGlynn took another sip of beer. "Yet if you asked me was Spangler at that funeral, I couldn't tell you no. If you've ever been out there, you'd of seen the trees all around, and the way the plots sit, at the bottom of the hillside. The whole time that Lutheran minister was speaking, I just kept looking up, and Billy did, too. And when they lowered the caskets, strike me with lightning if the pastor didn't take out a handkerchief and wipe his forehead, his hands shaking to beat the band."

"You said there were other times you sensed Spangler's presence?"

The chief nodded. "At Ernie Waldmier's funeral. And then—though I can't be sure of this—eight years ago, in the hospital, after my first bypass. The last was the day I buried my Ruth." He tried to spin the bottle cap, but it rolled, landing on the brown nylon carpet.

Poor guy, I thought. *In his fear and loathing, he's confused Spangler with the shadow of death.* "Sounds as though he spends a lot of time in cemeteries," I joked.

"Yes." McGlynn's reply was serious. "He likes quiet places where he can hide."

"Why have you told me all of this?"

"Helps to talk about it," he replied. "Most of the others are gone. Ernie, and Billy Flynn, and Chief Kovatch. Joe Corio had a coronary a few years back. Fifty-two, they said he was. Every so often Gerry Donovan and I get together, and rehash the whole thing, step by step. I guess you could say I sort of infected him with it . . . the Spangler bug."

I tapped the photocopy of the letter. "This has never been publicly released. What makes you so sure I won't write about it?"

The old man smiled. "For one, I knew your father." *Ah, yes, Dudley. That icon of trustworthiness and honesty.*

"For another"—he leaned across the mahogany table—"I went through every nook and cranny in that house, Holly Hill. And in the daughter's room I found a packet of letters, and what looked like the beginning of a play by a young writer named Garner Quinn."

I felt the blood rush to my cheeks.

"I didn't think you'd be the type to exploit a friend." McGlynn's voice was gentle and teasing, punctuated by the soft clacking of his dentures, like the slow tick of a clock.

I felt like a one-day-dry alcoholic who'd just been congratulated for staying on the wagon. I shifted in my chair. "I've got to be going."

I pushed the papers in his direction. "It was kind of you to take the time—"

"Don't pay it no mind, girlie," McGlynn said, lapsing back into irascibility. "Most days I got more time on my hands than I know what to do with." I knew the feeling.

He walked me through the parlor, out the front door, and down the sidewalk to my car. "You should see the place at Christmastime." He gestured toward his plywood and plastic wonderland. "People stop their cars and take pictures. I got a life-size Nativity, and wooden soldiers, and Santa and all the reindeer. About a thousand lights in different colors, and speakers, piping out the songs of the season."

I opened the door to the Volvo, anxious to be on my way.

"Not that *Messiah,* though." Frank McGlynn lowered his voice, as if Gordon Spangler might be here, among the gnomes and terra-cotta bunnies—a watchful but motionless figure all but hidden by lilacs.

"Nope, that one's ruined for me. Hearing those voices sing 'Hallelujah'—I tell you, it's enough to make my blood run cold."

MIKE'S BIKES WAS located on Route 70, a couple of miles from Frank McGlynn's place. A glance at my watch told me I had time for a quick stop before picking up Temple at school. I pulled into the empty lot and parked in front of the building.

A sign in the window said, "CLOSED UNTIL MEMORIAL WEEKEND," but the door was wide open. Vending machines softly percolated against the wall near the entrance. From the back of the shop came the whiskey warble of Janis Joplin singing "Me and Bobby McGee." I walked down the aisle between racks of rental bicycles, and pressed the service bell on the counter. "Hello . . ."

"Didn't you read the sign?" yelled an impatient voice. "We're not open for business until—" A man came out of the back room, carrying a wrench. The annoyance on his face evaporated the second he saw me. "Oh, hey, Garner, sorry. I didn't know it was you."

At forty, Mike Kenah's once impressive upper torso had begun its downward slide into a beer gut. His long, silver-blond hair was thinning, and the broken capillaries on his nose were a microscopic roadmap to all the area bars and taverns. Time had not been kind to the Spring Lake Community Theater's Romeo, circa 1970.

"Hope I'm not interrupting, Michael. I was just in the neighborhood."

Kenah tossed the wrench onto the counter, his smile igniting a small flicker of teen idol charm. "Slumming, are we?" He said this each time we ran into each other in town.

"Taking a trip down memory lane's more like it."

"Lemme turn off the tape." Kenah disappeared into the rear of the shop, and a second later, Joplin stopped, mid-*la-di-da*.

"I had a long talk with Chief McGlynn today," I called, adding when he returned, "It got me thinking about Lara."

Mike ran a hand over the top of his head, where a thatch of hair had once grown thick and wavy. "Join the club. Doesn't a day go by that I don't."

We became mired in a sudden, sticky silence. It was almost as if Lara had walked into the room, catapulting us into one of those eternal, adolescent triangles—the boy . . . the girl . . . the girl's best friend. I said, "I guess the last time you saw her was at the Halloween party?"

Kenah sauntered over to the soda machine. "Yeah. And how weird was that."

"I don't know. I wasn't there."

"Oh, right. You went off to sleep-away school," he said snidely, pulling a fistful of change from his jeans. "Wanna Coke?"

"Sure."

The machine choked up two cans. Mike tossed mine, then sat. He patted the scoop-backed vinyl chair next to his. "Take a load off, Gar."

We drank for a while without talking, then I said, "Tell me about that night."

"You writing a book?"

"No." The response was automatic by now. "Just curious. You and I never spoke about it." In fact, I'd only seen Mike Kenah once or twice in all these years, and during those chance meetings, neither of us had even mentioned Lara's name.

"I guess you heard about the fight."

"Only from what I read in Sterling's book," I replied, truthfully.

"Yeah, well, Sterling didn't know shit," he said, stretching out his legs. "I was married back when he interviewed me, and my ex was the jealous type. If I so much as mentioned Lara, she went ballistic. So I had to soft-pedal around a lotta stuff."

I steered him back to that Halloween. "Was it a big party?"

"About fifteen, twenty kids." Kenah shrugged. "There was a lot of back-and-forth over whether Lara would even have it. I pretty much figured once her old man yanked her outta the show, they'd call the whole thing off. But then she stops by the theater and says no, she's worked it out.

"The whole gang of us raided the costume room that night before going over. We rang the bell, half-stoned, you know, decked out like a bunch of fools. Lara answered the door. She didn't have on a mask or anything, just this short black dress, and dark stockings, with one of those ribbony things around her neck—"

"A choker."

"Yeah, only on her it looked like Tiffany diamonds. I could tell something was up, though. She seemed real quiet. But they had the ballroom all decorated, and there were chips and sodas, and the record player was going."

"Were her parents around?"

"The old man and the two brothers sat on the staircase in the hall the whole time, watching."

"Did Spangler seem angry?"

Kenah shrugged. "Not angry, but definitely not happy, either. Especially with the music. Though, looking back, how bad could it've been?—The Doors . . . Santana . . . a little Hendrix? Hell, that's tame compared to what kids listen to these days, right? But Spangler just kept staring behind those dorky glasses of his. You could feel the strain—like we were invited, but we weren't really welcome, you know? I remember a few of us sneaked outside to smoke a little weed, to relieve the tension—"

"Did Lara go?"

"Yeah. Why? Does that offend your puritanical sensibilities, Quinn?"

"I thought maybe that's why Spangler threw you out."

"Spangler threw us out," Kenah replied, testily, "because we wanted to dance, so we dragged a couple of chairs over his precious floor and—according to him— gouged the wood. *That's* why he threw us out."

Kenah drained the last of his Coke and tossed the can into a bin, muttering, "Fucking nutcase . . . I mean, if you knew that in less than twenty-four hours, your whole family was going to be dead—that you were going to fucking *kill* them—would you be having a temper tantrum about a goddamn scratch, on a goddamn oak floor, in a goddamn house you were planning to run away from anyway?"

It took Mike Kenah a minute to collect himself. "Here's the thing I didn't tell that Sterling guy," he said finally, once again running a hand through his nonexistent hair. "I almost asked Lara to run away with me that night."

"What do you mean—run away?"

"Back then, kids could drive down to Maryland and get married without a blood test or anything, remember?" He laughed sadly.

"After we messed up the floor, Spangler said we had to leave. I sort've hung back, waiting for Lara to walk me out. She got as far as the door, then she stopped, under the porch light—" Mike's hard-drinking, middle-aged face melted, and I caught a glimpse of the young boy who'd kissed Lara on a make-believe balcony three lifetimes ago. "Christ Almighty, Garner. You know how she was—"

"Yes."

"I should've done it. I wanted to. But I remember saying to myself, hey man, don't do anything you might regret in the morning." He repeated the words, scornfully, *"Don't do anything you might regret . . ."*

I didn't tell Mike Kenah what I thought—that Lara Spangler would never've gone with him, even if he'd asked. "Funny how things turn out," Kenah said; then, as though reading my mind, he added, "How *people* turn out."

He kicked the spokes of the bike closest to him. "And now I rent bicycles. And you're a big-time famous writer. And Lara's dead. Hell . . ." He shrugged, looking in equal parts angry and defeated. "Who ever said that life was fair?"

11

THE NEXT MORNING I drove Temple to school as usual, then swung back home for my second cup of coffee. "Think I'll bring it over to the office," I said to Cilda, casually, as though it hadn't been months since I'd done such a thing. "I've got reading to do."

Cilda didn't bother to reply. She didn't have to. After a lifetime together I could read the slightest flicker of her eyes. *'Bout time, Ga'ner Quinn. Stop mopin' over that big man Blackmoor breakin your 'eart, and all them other t'ings can't be changed. Get h'out from h'under me feet, and do somet'in wit' yourself, and you a grown woman* —all this, with just a flare of her nostril and a tiny lift of one brow.

I picked up my coffee mug, my *New York Times,* and a tote bag of books. "If that contractor calls—"

Cilda waved me off. "You t'ink I don't know where you goin t'be?"

She was right, of course. My office—a gabled cottage, complete with slate roof and dark storybook charm—stood less than five hundred feet away, connected to the house by a stone path that also led to the guest quarters, the seawall, and the beach.

"Don't bother with lunch," I called, hefting the tote onto my shoulder. Cilda's lips tightened, just a millimeter. *"What?"*

"Didn't say anyt'ing," the old woman replied smugly.

I UNLOCKED THE door, and walked inside. It smelled damp and salty, the way that summer houses do, when they're opened up after a long winter. The fluorescent lights wavered halfheartedly before sticking, and so did I. A slender needle of fear prickled the skin at the back of my neck, traveling swiftly down my spine.

It's just a room, I told myself, *an empty room.*

The desk that had once belonged to my assistant was bare. I set my mug down on the blotter and dropped the tote. Everything looked the same, but different. The small refrigerator hummed efficiently in the corner.

Crossing to the filing cabinet, I pulled out the drawer marked "S" and began thumbing through the files. *Shawde . . . Slater . . . Snow . . . Spangler . . .* I stopped for a moment, before resuming. *Spring Lake . . . Stein . . . Sterling . . .*

I brought TJ's file back to the desk, but couldn't seem to get comfortable. After a few minutes, I gathered everything, shouldering through the door that led to my office.

It seemed larger somehow. The yawing pyramids of books now stood in orderly piles. Vacuum tracks candystriped the carpet, and on the desk, last year's school picture of Temple had been replaced by a more recent shot. I ran my finger across the glass. Not a speck of dust. *Well, what did you expect?* Temple taunted me from the silver frame. *Cilda has to do something while I'm at school, and you're off acting busy with one of your dumb old Projects.*

I leaned back, scooting my chair up against the wall. TJ Sterling's file was about a quarter-inch thick, filled with clippings, mostly; a few book reviews; several postcard book announcements; and a stack of letters from Hirsh, Haller, Minnock, Attorneys at Law. Just picking them up gave me a bad feeling.

I reached into the tote bag and pulled out Sterling's book on Gordon Spangler.

The hardcover had been published in 1985, this paperback version a year later. On the cover, a silhouette of a man carrying a gun cast a long, dark shadow over an actual photograph of Holly Hill. TJ's name ran in red over the title—

BEHIND CLOSED DOORS
The Untold Story of the Gordon Spangler Murders

The pages sounded like the ruffled wings of a bird when I fanned through them. There was even something lightweight about the way the book felt in my hand. As with all of Sterling's more recent efforts, it had been researched and written in a hurry. The days of six- and seven-figure advances were long over for him. After a brilliant debut, TJ Sterling found himself having to hustle for every last buck.

Still, *Closed Doors* was a cut above the other garbage Sterling had cranked out during the past few years. I could tell that Gordon Spangler had gotten to him, the same way he'd gotten to Chief McGlynn, Gerry Donovan, and me.

I turned to the photo section. *"32 Rare Shots, Including Previously Unpublished Views of the Crime Scene!"* the blurb raved. It didn't take me long to find what I was looking for—a picture of the cast and crew from the Spring Lake Community Theater's 1970 production of *Romeo and Juliet*. A radiant Lara Spangler stood front and center, holding hands with her director, Joe Corio, and her tall, blond Romeo,

Michael Kenah. I was in the last row, my face a blur, obscured by a tangle of unruly hair.

Sterling had noticed my name on the playbill and called to fish around. "How come you never told me about your glory days in the *the-ah-tah,* GQ?"

"I don't know what you're talking about," I'd hedged.

"You and Gordon Spangler's girl acted in plays together."

"I didn't act," and I thought, *Oh shit.* "It was a project for my English class."

"Funny. I heard you and Lara were close."

"She was sixteen, I was fourteen," I scoffed. "She went to public school, I went to private. She played leading roles, I schlepped scenery in the wings. She dated guys, I went to confession. We lived on completely different sides of the tracks. Does that sound like the makings of a beautiful friendship to you?"

"Guess not." TJ probably guessed I was lying, but there was nothing he could do. None of his usual manipulations would've worked on me. I'd been wise to his game for years.

Sterling's first book, *Buying the People's Choice,* exploded in the face of a complacent, pre-Watergate America. Fresh out of Yale and clearly going places, the young journalist had been granted permission to cover a key senatorial race from inside the camp of a flamboyant, wealthy Texan with his sights set on the White House. A scant six months after the election, TJ's account of the campaign touched down on the best-seller's list and took off running.

His book painted a searing portrait of a ruthless demagogue so paranoid that he tapped the phones of his staunchest supporters, and had once paid a huge sum to have a security company ferret out the tiny transmitters he believed the CIA had put in his golf balls. Sterling gave his readers a behind-the-scenes glimpse at the multimillion-dollar

Madison Avenue packaging of this near lunatic into the folksy, egalitarian people's choice for U.S. Senate.

While the senator's staff publicly condemned the book, privately they pointed fingers at each other, trying to figure out how this genial young man had gotten close enough to beat them at their own game. The answer was simple: like vampires in folklore, journalists like Sterling only enter when invited. They count on the unchecked egos of their subjects to open doors for them. That rich Texan had relished the idea of an eager cub reporter recording his dramatic rise to power; and so it went.

There was a clean-cut NFL quarterback who provided his barroom buddy TJ with a season pass to party with the pros—that relationship resulted in a locker-room tell-all chronicling the married athlete's many affairs, his abusive treatment of women, and his addiction to cocaine. Not long afterward, a Pulitzer Prize–winning novelist made the mistake of befriending an awestruck Tommy Sterling, only to find his closely-guarded homosexuality graphically uncloseted on the pages of his protégé's next book, *Queen's English*.

Hello? Do we see a pattern here? Clipping after clipping told the same story. Sterling infiltrated his subjects' ranks armed only with his boy-next-door smile and the innate guile of a master spy.

TJ and I met in 1982, at a fund-raiser at the New York Public Library. By then his star had already begun to wane, while mine was steadily rising. "Golly gee," he'd said upon being introduced, "if it isn't the Nancy Drew of true crime."

"And which Hardy boy are you?" I'd inquired politely.

Our initial wariness stuck. Oh, sure, we spoke the same street machospeak used by cops, lawyers, writers, and the actors who play them on TV, but underneath our banter was a smoldering undertone of sexual tension. Minus the sex.

Clearly I wasn't Sterling's type of woman. His first wife, Maureen, seldom spoke and appeared to be in a perpetual state of pregnancy. Every Christmas another tow-headed mini-Mo would be added to the family line-up on their cards—sullen, rabbity-faced little girls, with pipe-cleaner arms and tiny clenched fists, swimming in yards of taffeta and crinoline—

Season's Greetings from the Sterlings
Ariel, Alyssa, Madison, Mo, & TJ

The marriage came to a bad end a month before Maureen gave birth to baby girl number four. This is what I heard—while appearing as the featured celebrity at a southern writers' conference, TJ had fallen madly in love with some young woman attending his lectures. The girl was rich, beautiful, and barely over the drinking age. Quiet little church-mouse Mo didn't even try to compete; she just hired a high-powered divorce attorney and took the philandering louse to the cleaners.

That next year Sterling became embroiled in a major lawsuit, one which would bring him to the brink of financial ruin, and nearly pull the plug on his entire career. The suit—for breach of contract, libel, and fraud—was filed by Edward Finch, a convicted murderer serving out consecutive life sentences for raping and killing several little girls.

EDWARD FINCH WAS the subject of Sterling's true-crime classic, *Shake Hands with the Devil.*

In 1971 *Forbes* magazine cited Finch as one of a new breed of entrepreneurs, a self-made man who'd been instrumental in the revital-ization of Baltimore's harbor district. But when a state trooper pulled the prominent businessman over on a DWI, his routine search led to a grisly discovery—the battered corpse of a ten-year-old parochial schoolgirl in the trunk of Finch's car. Finch insisted he had no idea how the body got there. The Buick was a company car, he said, regularly driven by a number of his employees. He'd been set up, he protested. Framed.

The community scrambled to support him. As a major contributor to the local economy, Big Ed's fan club stretched from the PBA to the Chamber of Commerce. Even when skeletal remains of two more little girls were found buried on his property, many of his friends remained loyal. One of his TKE brothers from the University of Maryland suggested calling the investigative journalist TJ Sterling, who listened to the tale and promptly agreed that it had all the makings of a great book.

Shortly afterward, Sterling and Finch entered into an agreement. "The subject promises to give exclusive access to the writer, *blah, blah,* and absolves said writer of legal liability, *blah, blah, blah*"— I've used similar contracts myself. But Finch's lawyer tacked on a murky addendum: *"The writer agrees to present an honest and truthful account of the case as it unfolds while at the same time maintaining the essential integrity of Mr. Finch's personal story."*

Those words would prove to be his legal undoing. And because of them, a few years later, I found myself in the unenviable position of having to come to TJ Sterling's defense.

ON THE MORNING I was set to testify on his behalf, Sterling intercepted me on the courthouse steps. He'd aged ten years since the last time I'd seen him, and in the morning sun, his face was haggard and puffy. "Thanks a million for coming, GQ." He pumped my hand until it hurt. "Times like this, you find out who your real friends are."

"No problem." In truth, my decision to jump on Sterling's bandwagon had more to do with my revulsion for Edward Finch than anything else.

"I'm Caroline," said the tall, slender woman standing next to TJ. The second Mrs. Sterling was striking in a classic, horsey-set sort of way, with a small chiseled face, emerald baguette eyes, a lush, unpainted mouth, and the longest legs I'd ever seen. I could only imagine the impact she must have made at that writers' conference—sitting in the front row while TJ lectured, crossing her shapely thighs, and leaning forward to hang on his every word.

Sterling circled his arm around her waist. "Sorry, honey. This is

Garner Quinn, the writer friend of mine I'm always talking about? GQ, let me introduce my beautiful bride."

"It's been over a year, Tommy," Caroline said in her soft, petulant drawl. "When are you going to start referrin' to me as your wife?"

About the same time he starts taking you for granted, sweetie, I thought to myself. But TJ protested, "Never!" and gallantly held open the court-house door to let us womenfolk pass through.

The minute we were inside, however, he locked ranks with me, letting his bride trail a few paces behind as he launched into a tirade about the total unfairness of Finch's suit. "This is the week my attorney brings out the big guns." Sterling rattled off the names of some distin-guished writers who were scheduled to testify on his behalf. "Not that anybody on the fucking jury's ever read a book in their lives—"

"Thomas." Caroline tapped him on the shoulder, with a gentle warning. "Someone might hear you."

"So what? It's true, isn't it?" he said, shaking her off. "That's why it's so great you're here, Garner. Even those illiterate imbeciles will have heard of you."

"You flatter me."

Just then a reporter snagged Sterling for a comment. I hung back with Caroline, hoping not to be recognized. "You'll have to excuse Tom," the young woman said in an undertone. "This has been just awful for him. The stress, the strain—not to mention the financial burden, so soon after the divorce. It's a travesty. A man like that, killin' those young girls, and then havin' the nerve to turn around and sue poor Tommy, just for writin' the truth."

"Finch is a scumbag," I agreed.

I didn't bother to add that *poor Tommy* had brought this lawsuit on himself. For almost two years, he'd played the part of Big Ed's faith-ful sidekick. During the trial, Finch gave him the run of his luxury townhouse and the keys to his Mercedes. They watched pay-per-view every night in Finch's state-of-the-art media room. They took jogs together every morning. They sat in bars and ogled women. After the good days in court, they got plastered; when it started turning bad, they cried in their cups.

And through it all, Sterling engaged his pal in a running game of truth-or-dare—*What do you think goes on in the head of a guy who kills girls like that, Eddie? Me, I always had a thing for those little plaid uniforms—forget Victoria's Secret. What turns me on more is a pair of white cotton panties, ha, ha. How about you? You know, I cheated on my wife when she was pregnant. What's the worst thing you've ever done?*

"If only it wasn't for those damn letters." Caroline tossed her honey-blond hair.

"What letters?"

"Oh, some old notes Tom wrote Finch in prison," she sighed, as if it were beyond her understanding.

And, with a sinking feeling, I realized that TJ Sterling had failed to learn the very first precept of writing true crime. *Never try to manipulate a manipulator.*

"THEY'RE DEADLY," TJ's attorney, Alan Hirsh, admitted when I asked him about the letters over lunch. "Poison. I'm talking lethal, toxic, disastrous. A frigging smoking pen." He adjusted his tie. "Between you and me."

"And Finch's lawyer read them to the jury?"

"Nah, Jessica Ludacer's too smart for that. She had Finch do it himself. Eddie, as you know, is a passionate believer in his own cause." Hirsh opened his briefcase and slid a piece of paper across the table to me. "Picture what a field day he had with this."

I recognized TJ's distinctive writing, a mix of printed capitals and straight up-and-down script.

Hey Buddy,

I'm in a state of shock. How those stupid SOBs could look at the evidence and come back with that guilty verdict is beyond belief. I'm beginning to think you were right—maybe it is a "stick it to the rich white guy" mentality we're bucking. That's an issue Ray should pursue on appeal. Just hold on, pal, you're going to beat this thing yet.

Listen, I realize you must be bummed out and the last thing you probably feel like doing is writing out the answers to the questions I gave you last week. I wouldn't bug you if I didn't think it was important. To you, to the case, to the book. To all of us, big guy.

Another thing—Kyle says that Newsweek *reporter came to see you again. Hope you made it clear this time. I mean, we've fucking shed blood together these two years (not to mention our contract, because you and I both know the relationship we've built goes far beyond that). Man, the worst thing about that bogus verdict, besides the obvious injustice, is that your friends (and I'm right there in the front of the line, bud) are left without the pleasure of your company on a daily basis. And—as a friend—I'm telling you, it doesn't help our cause to tell ANYTHING to reporters because (so I'm a cocky SOB, you already knew that) NOBODY will be able to write your story the way that I will. So tell Mr. Newsweek to take a hike, huh?*

By the by, dinnner with your mom was great. She's disappointed and angry with the jury (as we all are), but she's a FIGHTER who knows the truth will eventually out. Keep your chin up Eddie boy . . .

Tom

P.S.) Could you finish the responses to those questions by my next visit? Appreciate it, kimosabe.

"You like that," Alan Hirsh said after I'd finished reading, "they got a hundred and twenty-some-odd more."

"How could Sterling be so stupid?"

"He's an arrogant prick." Hirsh shut his briefcase. "That doesn't mean a psycho like Finch deserves a dime for crying psychological rape to some bleeding-heart jury, though." The attorney stood. "Not to make you nervous, Ms. Quinn, but you just might be my last best hope."

I'VE LOGGED IN a lot of trial time, most of it as an observer. Taking the witness stand at Sterling's trial was a whole different ball game. When I promised to tell the truth, my voice sounded as strained and stilted as Andy's had, saying his vows on our wedding day. I tried to ignore Ed Finch, sitting at the plaintiff's table in his starched shirt and club tie, looking like he'd never jaywalked, let alone murdered a little girl.

Alan Hirsh asked me to explain who I was and what I did for a living. I spouted off the no-frills, back-of-the-book bio. Hirsh's follow-up was a blatant attempt to score points with the jury. "And do I understand your latest book will soon be a major motion picture"—he appeared to struggle with memory—"starring, um . . . ?"

"Tom Cruise." A ripple of excitement passed through the jury box. These people might not read books, but they obviously knew their movies.

"Sounds like a hit already." Hirsh smiled. "Ms. Quinn, as a nonfiction writer you're familiar with the type of agreement made between Edward Finch and Mr. Sterling?"

"Yes. The contract I have my subjects sign is very similar."

"In your experience, does that contract in any way limit your right to tell the story in your own way?"

"Absolutely not," I said vehemently. "People looking for a white-wash, someone to make them look good—I tell them to go hire a publicist."

A couple of the jurors snickered. "What if your view of the story changes?" Hirsh pressed. "If, for example, you start out believing in a subject's innocence, but the evidence points you in another direction?"

"A writer's first obligation isn't to the subject," I said, "it's to tell the truth. And Mr. Sterling did that. He fulfilled his contractual obligation by presenting the facts as he saw them. In the process, he wrote a fine book. He can't be held liable simply because Ed Finch doesn't like being portrayed as a vicious murderer—"

"Objection!" Jessica Ludacer protested loudly. "Mr. Finch is not on trial here, your honor!"

"Sustained," said the judge.

Alan Hirsh wagged his head as though I were a bright, but incorrigible child. "Ms. Ludacer is correct," he told the jury graciously. "You've not been called to decide whether Edward Finch is a murderer. Fortunately, that's already been determined beyond a shadow of a doubt—"

"Objection," cried Ludacer.

"Withdrawn." Hirsh crossed back toward me. "In your work, Ms.Quinn, are you always completely candid with the people you interview?"

"Not always."

"Do you share your innermost feelings with them?"

"No," I said.

"Have you ever lied to a subject?"

"No," I said. "But I haven't always told the whole truth, either."

"Really?" Hirsh reacted with mild surprise. "And why is that?"

"The type of people I deal with"—I looked directly at Finch—"are manipulative sociopaths who lie as a matter of course. Sometimes you have to play along with their lies and deception, as a means to a greater end."

Jessica Ludacer stirred in her seat, on the verge of objecting, but before she could, Alan Hirsh said, "Thank you, Ms. Quinn. You've been very enlightening."

Ludacer rose, flashing the horizontal creases in her wrinkled linen suit at the jury like smiles. "Let me see if I can get this straight, Ms. Quinn. You're suggesting that Mr. Sterling—now tell me if I'm paraphrasing correctly—'participated in the lie' of Mr. Finch's innocence, as 'a means to a greater end'?"

"Something like that," I said, sensing trouble.

She spun on me. "And what end is that?"

"Well, if you're a writer, the end is a book." The moment I said it, I realized how shallow my answer sounded.

"A book." Ludacer considered this. "So you lie to a subject for the sake of a book."

"I don't lie." I tried to keep my voice even.

"Oh, that's right." The attorney smiled knowingly at the jury. "How did you put it?" She glanced down at her notes. "You just 'don't always tell the truth.' Isn't that like being a little bit pregnant, Ms. Quinn?—I mean either you tell the truth, or you don't."

"Objection." Hirsh stood. "Is there a question hidden among all that innuendo?"

"As a matter of fact, there is." Jessica Ludacer walked slowly toward me, in wrinkled linen, with lipstick on her teeth; but none of that mattered—I knew she was someone to be reckoned with.

"How much did you make from the sale of your last book?"

"Objection. Ms. Quinn's earnings have nothing—"

"I'll allow it," came the overruling.

Ludacer stood there, expectantly. "I don't know, exactly," I said truthfully.

"I guess you have agents and business managers who take care of that for you." The attorney twisted a flyaway lock of hair. It was all an act, and yet, if you were a juror, you'd have to root for her. "Would it surprise you to know that it was in the area of four million dollars?"

"No." The amount seemed suddenly crazy, obscene.

"And the movie sale—that would be extra? The picture deal with *Tom Cruise*?" This time the dropped name didn't get the jury smiling. "Yes."

"How much did you pay the subject for that particular book"—once again she checked her notes—"um, Mr. Howard Beech?"

"I don't pay my subjects."

Now it was Jessica Ludacer's turn to act surprised. "Nothing?"

"No."

"Four million"—the attorney used her hands as scales, weighing thin air—"versus no dollars at all. Hmm. Certainly puts your comment about having to play along with lies"—she referred to her clipboard—"as a means toward 'a greater end' into a whole new perspective."

The derisive laughter from the courtroom almost drowned out Hirsh's faint objection. "Just a few more questions, Ms. Quinn," Ludacer said with a thin smile. "Do you socialize with your subjects?"

I hedged, aware of TJ Sterling, a few feet away, leaning forward in his seat. "I'm not sure what you mean."

"Do you attend sporting events or other recreational activities with the people you write about?"

"No."

"Do you go jogging with them?"

"I don't jog."

"Do you pal around with them? Become their drinking buddy . . . their chum?"

As much as I disliked TJ, I didn't want to do this to him. "Every writer has his own manner of—"

"Yes or no, Ms. Quinn," Ludacer admonished.

"No." Sterling slumped back in his chair.

"Have you ever lied in a letter to a subject?" she asked, adding pointedly, "I don't mean one of your soft, fuzzy lapses in truth—I'm talking about a hard, pointed, knowing lie." The child killer Ed Finch nodded, his eyes flashing with moral outrage.

"No, but—"

"Thank you, Ms. Quinn. That will be all."

"It was probably the only way he could've gotten to the truth," I protested, so lamely that Jessica Ludacer didn't even move to strike the comment from the record.

THE JURY FOUND for the plaintiff. TJ Sterling was ordered to pay Edward Finch $500,000 in damages—a relatively conservative figure when you consider that one of the jurors felt the author should've handed over every penny earned from *Shake Hands with the Devil* for "grossly misleading Mr. Finch in a cynical attempt to make money."

Even in the litigiously overwrought world of publishing, the case caused ripples. TJ's career, which had never quite lived up to its early promise, took a real nosedive. He began churning out material— sensational exposés that were, for the most part, sloppily researched, carelessly written, poorly reviewed, and read only by the diehard fringe fans of true crime.

For my part, I studiously avoided those places where I might run into him. My personal aversion had soured into gut-sinking guilt, a sense that I had let down a fellow comrade-in-arms. The gossip I heard was divided along two lines. One camp reported that Sterling had gone bankrupt and was drinking heavily. Another put forth a more hopeful version—he was teaching at a prestigious university, he had something in the works, a hush-hush project, which was going to be huge . . .

I told myself I didn't care either way. I had my own life to live.

But now it appeared I would have to deal with TJ Sterling again. I turned the paperback of *Behind Closed Doors* over, weighing it in my palm before tossing it aside. Was it possible that TJ had really seen Gordon Spangler? If he had, why did he call me? Information of such magnitude could breathe life into Sterling's moribund career, and the TJ I knew had never been too keen on sharing.

For a while I played solitaire with his books, turning the dust jackets over to reveal a full suit of TJs—arranging them categorically, chronologically. The face broadened or hollowed, lines appeared, hairline receded with the changing times, but the man himself remained unreadable. With his regular features and pale, almost lashless eyes, he seemed to have been designed for deception.

I stayed there until the afternoon sun faded, alone in my strangely silent office, at my oddly empty desk, counting up the reasons TJ Sterling had to hate me, and wondering whether this Gordon Spangler sighting wasn't simply a hoax.

1 3

NO MATTER HOW I tried to prepare myself for the meeting with Sterling, when Friday evening finally rolled around, I felt vulnerable and on edge.

"Nice car," said the young man as I pulled up to the "VALET PARKING" sign.

"Thanks." My old red 190 was full of dings and rust spots, but one look at the monochromatic rows of black Mercedes sedans and silver Lexuses, and I understood why the kid might appreciate a change.

This swanky restaurant suddenly seemed a poor choice for a rendezvous with TJ. If I'd been thinking straight, I would've suggested somewhere more low-key—one of the fish eateries in the Highlands, or some noisy Ocean Avenue dive—places where a person didn't have to check a car, or be expected to sit through a four-course meal.

"Ah, Ms. Quinn." The maître d' looked up from the reservation list. "Your friend is enjoying an aperitif at the bar. Whenever you're ready, we can seat you."

"It'll only be a minute," I said, knowing it would be in my best interests to cut TJ's happy hour short.

The bar sparkled like a tiny store of semi-precious gems, all smoky topaz and amber light, medallioned garnet and emerald bottles. Sterling stood when he saw me, splattering some of his drink on his striped tie.

"Well, will you get a load . . . ? Hot damn, GQ, you look fantastic!" Inspired by the continental decor perhaps, TJ kissed me on both cheeks.

"Thanks."

He'd put on a few pounds, which suited him, and his straw-colored hair was shot through with gray. Although he didn't appear as haggard as he had at the trial, his skin was unnaturally flushed, and—despite the bar's comfortable temperature—heavily beaded with sweat.

"I mean it." TJ engaged the support of the bartender. "Doesn't she look great?"

"Yes, she does," he responded politely.

"Ab-solutely fan-tastic. What'r'ya drinking, babe?"

"Nothing right now. Listen, they're holding our table—"

"Say no more." TJ peeled two twenty-dollar bills from his billfold, and tossed them on the bar. He'd never struck me as a big tipper. I wondered if he could've run up that much of a tab just while waiting.

"I'm not kidding, Garner." Sterling pressed me against his navy blazer. His breath smelled forty dollars' worth, easy. "You look like a fucking teenager. Come on, what's your secret? You got some kind of picture hanging in your attic?"

"Clean living." I used the narrow door as an excuse to shrug off his embrace.

"More like good genes," TJ snickered. "Your mom was quite the knockout, wasn't she? Sorta the Frederique of her day . . ."

I had no idea who that was, nor was I prepared to make small talk about my mother. Thankfully, just then the maître d' caught my eye. "We're ready." I smiled.

He led us to a corner table, a discreet distance from the regular Saturday-night patrons—middle-aged husbands sporting country club tans, their wives in pearls and Talbot plaid. One of the local land barons was there with his dowager wife, both so stiff and pale they might've been part of a taxidermy exhibit. Next to them sat an aging Don Juan and a fluttery nymphet, all rhinestone nail art and big hair.

"Can I get another one of these?" TJ held up his cocktail glass.

"Another kir," the waiter said. "And for the lady—?"

"Just water for now."

"And the wine list," Sterling called after him.

I attempted to steer the subject away from booze. "So, as we natives say, what brings you down the shore?"

His pale eyes turned wily. "Oh, you know, coupla birds and a stone." He let me stew for a minute while he drained the last of his kir. "Actually, I was up in Connecticut, seeing the kids." I tried not to show my surprise.

He produced a picture from his wallet—the four little Sterlings arranged around some white wicker porch furniture. The eldest daughter had progressed into a stage of generic prettiness; the others still looked pinched and rabbity, their sullen, secretive mouths locked behind a barbed-wire fence of braces.

"Ariel had one of her dance recital things going on. And can you believe, Maddy's graduating? Goes to Vassar in the fall." Sterling squirmed in his seat, putting back the photograph. "Jesus! Makes me shit dollars just thinking about it. Anyhow, the visit worked out great 'cause, as it happened, I had to be in the city, anyway. Man, could they get any slower around here? How long does it take to fix a drink, for chrissakes?"

I'd seen TJ drunk before, but never quite so talkative and jittery. "Nice place, though. Lotta ambience. Did I tell you I fired my agent?" I shook my head. "What'd'ya hear about this guy, uh—" He patted his navy blazer, bringing out a leather daybook, and flipping through it until he found the right name.

It was no one I'd ever heard of. "Yeah, well, you ever leave Shroner"—he patted the little book in his pocket—"he's the man. Auction to film deal—the *man*."

I was about to ask what exactly it was he had to bring to the block, and if Gordon Spangler figured into it, when the waiter returned with our drinks. TJ listened raptly to the chef's specials, interrupting with questions, and agonizing over the right bottle of wine. By the time we ordered, the moment had passed.

"How's Caroline?" I asked.

"Fantastic," he said, "just great."

"You're still living in Virginia?" I buttered a piece of bread with a nonchalance I didn't feel. *Was that where you saw Spangler,* my mind screamed, *or was it all a lie? And, if it's true, why tell me?*

"Yeah, we're over in Cheswick Forest, just outside of Charlottesville," TJ was saying. "Ever been down that way? Lotta actors, lotta writers. You should visit sometime, look around. Caroline's father's big in real estate. He could set you up good."

The sommelier brought the wine, which Sterling pronounced passable. He'd ordered the escargots and poisson des huîtres, both of which he attacked with enthusiasm while I picked at my salad. "Counting calories?" He didn't wait for an answer; in Sterling's mind, women were always dieting, or having their period.

"I could afford to take off a few pounds myself," he said, sponging up garlic butter with the doughy part of his bread. "Too much southern-fried home cooking."

"I heard you've been teaching," I said, again trying to change the subject.

Sterling's frown was fleeting, a momentary inversion soon mastered by his usual self-deprecating grin. "Yes, consider me just the latest legend to stroll across the UVA Lawn. Ole Tombo Jefferson, Woody Wilson, Edgar the Opiate Poe, and me—the once and future journalist king.

"I'm on sabbatical now, though, so—" He lifted his glass. "Up the Rotunda."

In a series of fluid motions, the busboy took away our empty plates and the waiter presented the main course. Sterling ordered another bottle of wine.

"This veal is fantastic." He talked with his mouth full. "Despicable as the French are, you have to admit they can cook—what, don't you like yours?"

"I'm not hungry." I hadn't eaten much these last few days. Thoughts of Gordon Spangler had begun to occupy my every waking moment. Like a secret love (*or that other fluttery, stirred-up feeling—the one I got at the start of each new project, each new book*), it consumed me—eradicating hunger . . . intruding on sleep . . . invading dreams. I was miserable, but I felt more alive than I had in months.

I put down my knife and fork. "Cut the crap and tell me, TJ. What do you know about Spangler?"

Sterling cast a lingering look at his veal chop and sighed, "You really wouldn't be here if I hadn't mentioned his name, would you?"

My heart sank. *It* was *a lie*, I thought, *a ploy to get me to come.* "Okay, TJ," I said bluntly. "Just tell me what you want from me."

His mouth drew up in a battered little smile. "Is that what you think, Garner? That I have some big favor to ask?"

"What other reason could there be for this dinner? We've never exactly been best friends."

"Well, maybe not best—" He stopped, and something in his tone of voice made me pause, too. For the first time I realized that TJ Sterling *did* think we were friends. He'd probably really liked Ed Finch, too—and the rich senator, and the writer, and the quarterback, and all those others he'd used and betrayed. I suddenly pictured him as a nerdy ten-year-old, hanging around with the cool crowd, desperately wanting to be liked, but unable to stop himself from tattling to the teacher—then wondering why nobody wanted to play with him anymore.

"I want the truth." I grabbed his hand as it reached for the wine. "Did you really see him?"

Sterling looked straight into my eyes. "Yes."

"You're sure?"

"I'm sure."

Across from me the stuffed old gent in dusty dress clothes was using a knife to push peas onto his fork, scraping them against the china until it hurt my teeth. "Oh, God" was all I could say.

The waiter appeared with a second bottle of wine and went through an elaborate uncorking ritual. He filled my glass. After he left I drank it down thirstily. "Who else have you told?"

"No one."

"You haven't notified the authorities?" I couldn't believe my ears. "Are you nuts?"

TJ glanced around the room as if FBI agents might be lurking even here, among the country club set. "Shh," he warned softly. "All in good time, Garner, all in good time."

"What the hell's that supposed to mean?" I demanded in a whisper.

"It means, I have to lay some groundwork first." At some point in the last few minutes, Sterling appeared to have sobered, while my senses had started spinning, making me feel intoxicated, out of control. "That's why I was in New York."

"And while you were *laying groundwork*," I spat the words out, "how do you know Spangler hasn't already bolted again?"

"He's not going to bolt," TJ said confidently. "He's quite content where he is."

My mouth dropped open in astonishment. "You've been *spying* on him?" He didn't answer, just swirled his drink. "God, TJ, don't you realize how stu—" I checked myself. "—How potentially dangerous that could be?"

"Give me some credit," Sterling said, annoyed. "I was staking out stories before you got promoted from grade school, honey."

I sat in confounded silence as the busboy cleared our plates. TJ ordered Remy Martin and coffee for both of us. "What makes you think I won't call the feds the second I get home?" I finally asked.

"Two reasons. First, there's a code between writers like us. A kind of honor among thieves," he responded coolly. "Second, you owe me."

"Owe you? For what?"

"I got royally screwed in that breach of contract trial and you know it. Nothing I said or did to Finch was any different than what you, or Wambaugh, or Mailer, have done a million times. Drop the virgin act, Garner." He stretched his legs out with a comfortable sigh. "I heard about your last book. What happened, you played up to the wrong guy, and the boundaries blurred a little, didn't they? You go in all nice-nice, and pretty soon you're over your head and things start to get hairy. Well, big fuckin' deal. It's all part of the job, GQ. At least I admit it."

I reached for my bag, tossing whatever bills I found in my wallet on the table. "Thanks for dinner." The chair teetered dangerously as I pushed it back. "Before you get back in your car and drive south, have another drink on me."

"You don't have to get all huffy." Sterling jumped to his feet. "Come on, GQ, I was just picking with you." He put his hands around my waist to hold me back. Over his shoulder, I could see the waiter wheeling a dessert cart toward us. I sat down, not wanting to make a scene, and—if the truth were told—reluctant to leave without learning more.

"I still don't get it," I said honestly. "Of all the people in the world, why tell me?"

Sterling took a sip of brandy. "Partly because I've always suspected you of holding out on me. I think you knew Lara Spangler better than you let on. And I figured if my hunch was correct, you'd have more than just a casual interest in seeing her old man brought to justice."

"Me and a hundred other people."

He regarded me curiously. "Play it that way if you like. But say I'm on the verge of making the whole thing happen. I've got all the little ducks"—he used his index finger to shoot out a word at a time— "lined . . . up . . . in . . . a . . . row. Only I need your help to pull it off."

1 4

HERE IT COMES, I thought. *Watch your back, Garner. Guard your flanks. Keep your head.* "So what's the favor, TJ?" I asked.

Sterling shifted uncomfortably in his chair. "All right. I'm not gonna bullshit you, GQ. Things haven't been so good for me these past few years. I mean, you probably know better than anyone about lawsuits— Christ, your own father hauled you into court, didn't he?" He looked to me for some sign of bitter understanding, but I gave him none.

"Anyway, after the amount of the Finch settlement hit the papers, every litigious-minded loon who'd made so much as a footnote in one of my books suddenly wanted to sue. And my publisher, who'd split the damages with me, started factoring legal costs into my next advance." He'd finished the Remy, and was eyeing the snifter I hadn't touched. I pushed it toward him.

"Luckily, the teaching job came along." He raised the glass. "Up the Rotunda, huh? Still, it's a long way from where I started—" TJ's voice grew thick with emotion. "Damn." He took several swallows of the brandy.

"Caroline tries, but she doesn't get it." He leaned forward in his seat, earnestly. "In fact, you're probably one of the few people who actually realizes what it's like—to go over to the other side, the dark side, the wild side. To be part of it, and yet not a part of it. To be able to rifle through the drawers and closets of someone's mind, and ferret out their secrets—*whoooh!*" Sterling seemed to succumb to an inner rush. "You know how it gets in your blood."

I said, "A lot of things that get in your blood end up killing you."

"You think you've got it beat, but you don't," TJ said with a cold knowingness that sent a chill down my spine. "If it is a sickness, you're infected just as bad as me. It's what brought you here tonight. You just had to know."

"Is Spangler in Virginia?" The words tumbled out angrily. "In Charlottesville? Where did you see him?"

Sterling held up a hand. "Uh-uh-uh. First things first. We have some business to settle. Don't look so glum, Garner, it's only a small favor, a trifle really—"

"What?"

"I need you to help pave my way back to the upper echelons of the publishing world. Talk to your editor—leaving out the specifics, of course. Just tell her it's big."

"I don't know how that would help you," I said.

"You underestimate your name value," Sterling said with a tight little smirk. "I dropped it once during my interview with Herr Slickmeister the agent and he almost creamed himself."

"And what do I get for my pains?"

"Access to Spangler." TJ qualified this. "Not for the purposes of researching a book—that falls exclusively to me. But I'd see to it you had some time alone, just the two of you, to ask those questions you've been dying to ask."

For a split second I let the thought of that overwhelm my better judgment. I saw myself walking down a long corridor, hearing the prison sounds and smelling the prison odors that, in my line of work, were so familiar. I watched the guard turn the key, with glistening knuckles big as ball bearings. I listened to the metal clang of the door sliding into place behind me, I saw Gordon Spangler stepping out of the shadows . . .

And that's when it hit—a premonition in hindsight; at the time, a muscle-clenching fear. I looked at TJ Sterling sitting across from me with his barroom tan and canary-feather grin, but instead of feeling angry and repulsed, I was afraid.

"Okay," I said, "I'll speak to my editor, whatever you want. But only if you promise to bring the law in on this. Right now—tonight," I pressed, with a new sense of urgency. "We can drive back to my place. You can call from there."

"Forget it, Quinn," he cut me off. "It's my terms, or nothing."

The ancient couple at the next table were long gone—he clinging to a silver-topped cane, she to the metal jungle gym of a walker. The first set of Rumsonite wives and husbands had given way to the next, men and women in plaids either more or less subdued, but otherwise virtually the same.

"You're playing with fire."

"I can handle it," and here he smiled. "Or is that what you're afraid of?"

"I'm afraid," I said testily, "that you'll smash your car into a guard rail on the way home. Or the booze will kill off so many of your brain cells, you'll forget where you saw him. Come on, Tee'j," I wheedled. "Just give me a hint. A crumb."

"A crumb? Oh, all right," Sterling said with a playful sigh. "He's in Virginia."

"In Charlottesville?"

"You're warm."

"Around Charlottesville, then?"

TJ made a noise like a game-show buzzer. "I'm sorry, that's all the questions we have time for today."

Our waiter came with the check.

"My treat." Sterling pushed the crumpled bills on the table back to me. "You can get the next time. Oh, and bring your gold card, Garny, because I'm gonna have a lot to celebrate."

WE STOOD OUTSIDE as the preppy valet jogged off to get my car. "I'm going to call the feds," I told Sterling.

"No, you're not."

"Try me."

"Do I look worried?" Under the harsh outdoor lights, TJ's face was a placid mask of serenity.

"You know, for years Caroline kept telling me it would all work out, but I didn't believe her. I thought I was washed up . . . finished. Oh, I went through the motions—teaching my little classes, trying to write, the usual schmooze. But half the time I felt like a fucking zombie, like I wasn't even there. And then, just as I hit rock bottom, it happened. *I saw him.*" His voice dropped in an awed whisper. "And it was as though the scales dropped from my eyes—I mean it, Garner—all of a sudden *everything changed.*"

Sterling's body lurched unsteadily, but whether from alcohol, or something else, I couldn't say. "This is gonna sound corny, but I think of it as a kind of . . . well, a gift from God. A second chance, to start over, maybe do things right this time. I mean, it can't be a coincidence. There has to be a reason why . . . why it happened to me.

9 3

"This has changed my life, Garner." He took my hand and held it. "Let it ride for a little longer. I'm gonna bring the bastard in, you'll see."

The young valet pulled my Volvo to the curb, and jumped out. "Come home with me," I told TJ.

"Can't, babe." He released his hand to box my chin. "Places to go. People to see."

I turned toward the car. The valet, who'd been watching, rushed to open my door. "Enjoy the rest of your evening." He smiled flirtatiously, as though hoping I might extend an invitation to him. I handed him a five-dollar bill.

Before pulling away, I leaned across the front seat and rolled down the passenger window. "Three weeks and I'm calling."

TJ Sterling stuck his hands in his pockets and stepped nonchalantly off the curb. "Three weeks," he said, smiling, "and you'll be reading about me in the papers, GQ."

In the end, it turned out to be more like three and a half.

LESS THAN A month later I was sitting down on my daughter's bulging suitcase, watching as she struggled with the clasps. "But what will you do here all alone in the house?" Temple's brow dimpled with concern.

"I'm a big girl," I said. "I'll manage."

Secretly, I was enjoying her guilt. Since she'd first broached the subject of spending summer vacation with her father, I'd been going through an inner struggle of Shakespearean proportions. Daily I shifted from jealous wrath to piteous grief, railing at the heavens one moment, thirsting for revenge the next.

Not wanting to burden Temple with my angst, I turned to my rock and support, Cilda Fields—only to be told that she'd be glad to have two months off, *t'ank you very much.* Her niece Emma would be getting married in Jamaica this July. Mercedes and Deon—Cilda's eldest daughter and only son, who both lived in Brooklyn—were planning to go for the wedding. If she called right away Cilda said she might be able to book a seat on the same flight.

Well, I'd thought, *thou hast comforted me marvellous much.*

Things had reached an emotional head on the day of Temple's eighth-grade graduation. Andy came, with his Trident smile and hearty handshake, working the crowd in the Country Day gymnasium, joshing with other parents as if he'd known them for years, while I, who *had* known them for years, hung back, reticent and tongue-tied. In my mind, I heard them whispering, *Isn't he wonderful? So sweet and charming! And much more sociable than* her . . .

Candace Kressler, M.D., Ph.D., never left Andy's side. Temple had been right. This was no way, no how a Candi. The woman exuded strength and self-assurance. Her blunt-cut pageboy, well-tended, unpolished nails, and deep, contagious laugh all communicated a pleasing straightforwardness.

It was a crushing blow, not being able to dislike her.

As the eighth graders filed down the center aisle, Candace touched Andy's arm, and cried, "There's Temple!" Then she leaned over to whisper to me, "God, look at her—it's like Audrey Hepburn, with the cast of 'Welcome Back, Kotter.' "

The laugh caught in my throat as Temple glided by in a white sleeveless dress and her new pixie haircut. She stole a small, sidelong glance in our direction, before continuing on, toward the front of the gym. It was the sight of her walking away—so slender and proud, shoulders set, chin high—that released all the choked-back emotions I'd been trying to hide. Without a word, Candace handed me a tissue.

They were all headed somewhere, I suddenly realized, *every last one of them.* These fresh-faced children, clutching their diplomas. Peter Pan Andy, grown up, and about to take a nice new bride. Temple—my only child, my little girl. Even Cilda. They were face-front, moving forward, while I just stood, marking time and going nowhere. Going nowhere at all.

"YOU SURE YOU packed enough?" I asked my daughter.

"I'll only be there until the wedding," Temple reminded me. "Just a little over a month."

I looked doubtfully at her single suitcase and minuscule backpack. "Well, if you need more, let me know and I can always send—"

"Chill, Mom." She hoisted the pack over her shoulder, shaking me off when I tried to pick up the other bag. "You haven't changed your mind about coming?"

There had been some discreet inquiries about whether or not I'd like to go watch Temple play bridesmaid at her father's wedding. "No." I trailed behind on the staircase. "I'm going to be up to my ears with stuff around the house."

Yeah, right, the empty great room seemed to yawn, *a regular three-ring circus you got going here, Quinn.*

In the back of my mind, of course, I was thinking about Gordon Spangler. It had been over three weeks since my dinner with Sterling. As I promised, I was letting things ride. Still, I couldn't help being annoyed that the messages I'd left on TJ's answering service hadn't been returned.

Temple set the luggage down near the front door. "I know!" She clapped her hands together. "Why don't you take a trip somewhere? You could go to Paris! It would be awesome. Sightseeing. Visiting all those old churches and museums—"

"Have you lost your mind? Why would I want to go all by myself to Paris?" She looked crestfallen. I hugged her, knuckling up her short dark hair. "Don't worry about me so much. I'll be fine."

From outside came the sound of car tires on gravel, and the one-two toot of a horn. We gave each other a quick kiss. I stood on the steps, acting brash and happy, while Andy threw the suitcase into the trunk of the Jaguar and Temple strapped herself into the passenger seat.

"I'll take good care of her, Garn," Andy promised.

Temple had put on sunglasses so I couldn't see her cry. "Have a good time," I called, but she didn't answer. Andy sat behind the wheel and put it into gear.

I stood there, waving, as the car traveled up the drive. It wasn't until it pulled out of the gate and became just a dribble of silver, speeding through the gaps in the pine trees, that I relaxed my hand and let my shoulders sag.

I went back into the house, trudging like a sleepwalker down the hall to the kitchen. Early-morning sun streamed through the windows. In my backyard, the Atlantic was playing a frisky game of tag with the seawall. It was one of those spring days when the ocean appears so much finer than the sky, like a skirt of deep sapphire silk sewn to a plain cotton sash. I walked over to Mr. Coffee and poured myself a cup.

Cilda had been gone for only two days, but already the creeping disarray that seemed to follow me had begun to assert itself. The tiles had a marzipan glaze of sugar and spilt milk. Yesterday's mail littered the counters, the contents of envelopes unceremoniously yanked like so many trouser pockets turned inside out. Even the ladderback chairs were unruly, pushed this way and turned that, instead of their usual obedient stance, flush to the old pine refectory table.

I sat down in Temple's place, ridiculously saddened by the sight of the bowl of half-eaten cornflakes, and the smudge of chocolate lip gloss rimming the juice glass. After spending so many weekends with Andy in Manhattan, Temple had recently made a point of commandeering the *New York Times* before I could get to it. Today's Arts and Leisure section lay next to her place mat, folded in such a way that there could be no doubt as to what she'd been reading.

"Old Blackmoor Magic Has Paris Under Spell," ran the headline. My heart lurched as though it had been electrically jumpstarted.

Paris. Dane Blackmoor had gone to Paris. It seemed an awful long way for someone to go to avoid making a commitment. I scanned the opening sentence—"Sculptor Dane Blackmoor has had more comebacks than an alley cat has lives . . ."

I brought the photograph over to the window, as though instead of newsprint it were some new denomination of treasury bill, containing a secret, hidden image, which was apparent only when you held it up to the light. But, of course, it was just Blackmoor, in a white shirt with his sleeves rolled up, paler and thinner, his eyes a little sad. Or was that the optic trick, the thing that might or might not be there?

"You could go to Paris," Temple had suggested. Suddenly I saw her spur-of-the-moment bright idea for what it was: a misguided attempt to put me in geographic proximity with the man I loved, a man who'd made it clear he wanted to disappear from my life.

"Fat chance," I said out loud. I ripped the page in two, and I kept on ripping until the article was only a pile of shredded paper on the kitchen floor. After the rush of childish anger subsided, I felt immediately ashamed. I picked up the ragged ribbons and tossed them into the trash. Then I walked back to the table, planning to throw the rest of the paper into the recycle bin.

As I was stacking the sections, another headline caught my attention. I sank into my chair. "No, it can't be," I whispered.

I read it again, taking each word one at a time, desperately trying to color them with different meaning—

TJ STERLING SHOT TO DEATH

But the smaller print underneath I found even more baffling—

Controversial Author Committed Suicide, Say Police

PART TWO

THE SUREST WAY TO BE MISSING—

AND TO STAY THAT WAY—IS TO

BECOME A VAGUE RESIDENT IN

THE WORLD OF THE EVERYDAY.

PART OF THE ORDINARY MOB, YOU

ARE EVERYBODY, AND THEREFORE

NOBODY.

ANDREW O'HAGAN
THE MISSING

FRIDAY JUNE 18

HE TOOK LUNCH from a quarter after eleven until twelve noon.

At precisely eleven-ten, he rose from his desk and put on his suit jacket. The brown bag with his name printed neatly on the flap waited in its usual place, on the middle shelf of the office refrigerator. He placed it in his briefcase, then headed directly for the washroom where he lathered his hands with antibacterial soap brought from home.

He never used the toilet. It was a unisex restroom, as signified by the side-by-side silhouettes of a man and woman on the door. All the Lysol in the world couldn't mask the fuggy female smells of discarded tampon shells and soiled sanitary pads; of blotted lipstick kisses left on crumpled tissues in the trash; Trident bubble-gum wads and lingering clouds of designer perfume. Most horrible of all was the hair—long, silky strands, so different from a man's, clinging in curliques to the walls of the sink, or those other ones, dark and springy, coiled like wire, left behind like some obscene hieroglyph on the plastic seat. It made him physically ill—and yet, one had to wash one's hands.

He ate alone in his car, summer and winter, with the windows rolled up. It was one of those things about him: he seldom felt discomfort from heat or cold. Sometimes he just stayed in the lot behind the office. On certain days, however— special days like this one—he would drive to another location, and find a secluded place to park.

Once there, he spread a paper napkin on the passenger seat side and set out his food. The small carton of milk went in the upper right corner, a piece of fruit in the upper left. The sandwich he placed in the middle—Mondays it was bologna; Tuesday, ham; Wednesday leftover meatloaf; Thursday bologna again; and Friday, sliced egg. After he was finished, he read the newspaper or he worked with his numbers, making small, precise notations in his notebook.

Today, of course, was different. The problem that had nagged him for months was finally solved. He looked out the window, the shadow of a smile wreathing his lips. For an instant, he experienced a feeling of absolute invincibility—an exhilarating rush that puffed out the nether regions of his body, filling up all the empty spaces, and satiating him far more than food, or sex, or (the thought popped into his head, unbidden) even prayer ever could.

He put the egg sandwich back into its square of waxed paper. He'd save it for later, perhaps as a before-bedtime snack. A reward for a job well done.

It bothered him, though, not being able to eat as usual. He didn't like it when emotions—even good emotions—interfered with his daily routine. He wasn't comfortable with feeling invincible. If truth were told, he wasn't comfortable with feeling much of anything at all.

To stave off this thought, he opened his notebook. How many other cars were parked, up on the hill? He began to count, relaxing as the numbers bracketed him in their ordered equation. There was such a profound elegance to numerical figures, an unencumbered clarity, so lacking in the outside world. Every digit had a distinctive character of its own. And while he loved each of them, some seemed to him more powerful than others.

He looked out the window, at the peaceful valley beyond the hill. It was a lovely location. Stone paths wound like mosaics under the trees. He noted with satisfaction the oblong patch of overturned earth, and the people down there, around it.

One, two, three, four, five, he counted, pausing, as always, to acknowledge that, yes—five might be the most powerful number of all.

1

A FLAT CANOPY of Wedgwood sky stretched over the rolling landscape. The trees were broccoli-shaped, fat green crowns on slender stalks. From the southern stretch of horizon rose the pale bluish outlines of what Virginians called mountains, but which looked more like hills to my outsider's eye. This scene of bucolic splendor seemed an ironic place for the mortal remains of someone as worldly as TJ Sterling to spend all eternity, and yet his wreath-draped casket was winched up and at the ready, a few moments away from being lowered into the spring-softened earth.

Directly across from me, Caroline Sterling, in dark sunglasses and black silk, leaned on the arm of a handsome man with a mane of silver hair. Like an origami, Caroline's long, graceful limbs had folded in on themselves; she appeared fragile and on the verge of collapse.

Of the over fifty mourners, the majority were affluent, middle-aged WASPs—TJ's neighbors, I assumed, or former colleagues from the university. A group of college kids clustered together, shifting awkwardly in their clunky Doc Martens and earth sandals. One girl, in particular, caught my eye. Dressed in a flowery summer print, with carefully accessorized Aigner pumps and pearls, she sobbed continuously into a wadded Kleenex. This sniffling grief and china-doll sweetness made the girl's buzz-cut bald head and double-pierced nose seem strangely anomalous.

Sterling's first wife, Maureen, and her four daughters sat in the second row of metal folding chairs, under the vinyl canopy, having discreetly left the front and center seats empty for the family of wife number two. A slender man with acne-scarred skin and kind eyes hovered near them. The instant Mo saw me, her rabbity face softened into a radiant smile. I smiled back, marveling at the unpredictability of life—that she should be here, so flushed and revitalized, while the husband who'd once dominated her lay still and unmoving in his satin-cushioned cell.

An Anglican clergyman walked over to the head of the casket. Tall, dark, and bearded, with bony appendages and voluminous black vestments, he bore a rather unfortunate resemblance to the Grim Reaper of Death.

"Man, that is born of a woman," his voice swelled dramatically, "hath but a short time to live, and is full of misery. He cometh up, and is cut down, like a flower; he fleeth as it were a shadow . . ."

Fleeth, as a shadow. The words sent a sudden chill through me.

I scanned the other faces, wondering if this text had affected anyone else. But, aside from Caroline and the girl with the shaved head, who were both crying, I saw only stoicism, tinged with slight embarrassment—an understandable reaction at a funeral where the deceased is thought to have not so much passed away, as opted for immediate express checkout. Even Bill Tyree, the Albemarle County detective I'd spoken with on the phone, hung back, looking chastened and uneasy, as though not wanting to intrude.

"Unto Almighty God," the priest continued, "we commend the soul of our brother Thomas James departed, and we commit his body to the ground; earth to earth, ashes to ashes, dust to dust—"

Caroline moaned, the kind of low bleating sound that a wounded animal might make. The man with the silver hair ushered her toward an empty folding chair. Under cover of the broccoli-sprigged trees, I caught Bill Tyree's partner, Leedon Whitley—who resembled a younger, trimmer Denzel Washington, and knew it—copping a quick eyeball rove of the cemetery perimeter.

I wondered what he expected to see.

Cars were parked on both sides of the hill above us. A few people sat inside their vehicles, apparently having chosen, for whatever reason, not to attend this graveside service. If Sterling's death had been a homicide, Tyree and Whitley would have had a battalion of plainclothes cops on hand, keeping track of all the comings and goings. But his death had been ruled a suicide, and the only one who seemed to be watching was a young movie-star lookalike in a knockoff Armani suit.

The clergyman raised a bony hand in benediction. "I heard a voice from heaven, saying unto me, *Write*." He let the word echo for a moment in the still air before adding with somber finality, "From henceforth blessed are the dead who die in the Lord."

Write? What the hell did that mean? A voice from heaven saying, *write?* A sharp-edged memory jabbed me—TJ shooting out words with the tip of his pointed finger— *"I've got all the little ducks lined up. But I need your help to pull it off . . ."* Only TJ was dead now, his mouth sewn into a phony little smirk, forever mute. He couldn't relay messages to me through the scripture readings of some Anglican priest, any more than he could send signals in tea leaves, or levitate tables at séances. The Albemarle police believed he shot himself, and the chief medical examiner of the Commonwealth of Virginia had confirmed it. Who was I to question their findings?

You're Garner Quinn, a voice in my head sang. *Questioning is what you do.*

—What I *used* to do, I corrected myself.

A representative from the funeral parlor had stepped forward to address the crowd. "Mrs. Sterling wishes to extend her heartfelt gratitude for all your sympathy and support during this difficult time. She asks that you return with the family to Edenfield, the home of her parents, Mr. and Mrs. Ford Childress—" He directed a somber little bow toward the silver-haired man sitting next to Caroline.

I felt a tap on my shoulder. "Care to share a ride?" asked Detective Whitley. I could only guess how many hours a day he spent in front of the mirror, practicing that megawatt Denzel smile.

"I have a car," I demurred.

"Know where you're going?" Whitley hooked a thumb toward Detective Tyree. " 'Cause we gotta put in an unofficial appearance, anyway."

"I could follow your car," I said vaguely, my attention focused on the canopy, where a steady stream of people were offering their condolences to the young widow. To my dismay, Whitley slid a hand under my elbow.

"I was thinking maybe you and I could drive together," he said.

"Ms. Quinn! Ms. Quinn!" I turned to see the bearded pastor running toward us, his cassock billowing like a cloud of smoke. "Oh, I'm so glad you're still—" He closed a skeletal hand around mine. "Wyatt Tunn-Beecher. Father Wy."

"Fine service, Father," said Leedon Whitley.

The clergyman blushed. "Thank you. It's so difficult when—" He shot a glance toward Caroline, then rallied. "Still, I didn't want to miss this opportunity. I'm such a fan, Miss Quinn, I've read everything you've ever written."

"Thank you," I said, trying to be gracious, "and, please. It's Garner."

"Garner." He gargled my name with unabashed delight. "Do you think I might—Garner . . . could I *possibly* have an autograph? I wouldn't trouble you *now*, if I were going back to Edenfield." He'd started to chew on the wiry ends of his mustache. "But *unfortunately*, I have an afternoon wedding to perform."

People were leaving the gravesite, walking slowly up the hilly path to their cars. I hedged, "I'm afraid I don't have a—"

"Not to worry." Father Wy's slender hands disappeared into his cassock. "I'm sure I have something . . . yes, look, right here." It was a Mass card, imprinted with TJ Sterling's name. And Leedon Whitley just happened to have a pen.

"Wonderful." The clergyman offered his prayer book for me to lean on. "I can't tell you—Garner—how thrilled . . ." On the flip side of the card a gloriously robed and beatific Jesus opened his arms in a gesture of forgiveness and compassion. I said a silent *Hail, Mary* and, using Whitley's pen, scrawled my name over Him.

"Thanks again," Tunn-Beecher said, backing away, "you've made my day."

"While you're at it"—Leedon Whitley flashed his bad-boy grin—"Tyree's got an ole parking ticket for you to sign." The guy had way too much attitude.

"Careful you don't sit on that, Detective," I said, handing back his ballpoint. The rent-a-pallbearers were passing out printed maps. I took one and gave it a perfunctory scan. "You know, I think I can manage this by myself," I told Whitley.

"Fine," he said with a laconic shrug. "I just thought, the way you grilled my man Bill on the phone, maybe you wanted to take a peek at the file, satisfy that powerful curiosity of yours."

I stopped in my tracks. "Sterling's file?"

"Only thing"—a small petal had fallen from a magnolia tree onto my blazer; he brushed it off my shoulder—"one of us gotta be there, either Billy or me." On the crest of the hill, Detective Tyree glowered down at us. Whitley gave him a friendly wave. "On account of it going against policy—"

I tossed the keys at him. "You drive," I said.

2

WHILE DETECTIVE WHITLEY went to get the file I leaned up against the hood of my old 190, taking inventory of the people who passed. I wondered how they had fit into TJ's life, and if any of them—knowingly or not—held a clue to Gordon Spangler's whereabouts.

"Garner?" called a voice. Maureen Sterling sidled up shyly, a mini-Mo in tow.

"Maureen." I smiled down at the little girl. "And let me guess. You must be—"

"Ariel," she said.

"The dancer." Her wary eyes grew round. "Your father told me how much he'd enjoyed your recital the last time I saw him."

It was a small lie, but it seemed to please her. "I did *Kokomo,*" she said, "and the *Somewhere* ballet, on point."

"Wow, that's pretty impressive."

"Richie's got juice boxes in the car, honey," Maureen told the girl. "Tell him I'll just be a minute."

She watched fondly as Ariel scampered away. "You look great, Mo," I told her. "How've you been?"

"Well, I finished my degree in Special Ed.," she said, adding shyly, "and I think I might be getting married again." I followed her gaze toward the Chevy Blazer where the man with the kind eyes waited patiently behind the wheel.

"I'm happy for you, Maureen," I said, meaning it.

"Thanks." Again, that surprising smile transformed her face. Then it passed. "Poor TJ, huh?"

It was the opening I'd been waiting for. "He stopped to see me on his way back from your place. I had no idea—" I let her fill in the blank. "Did he seem depressed to you?"

"With Tommy it was always hard to tell." Mo sagged against the hood, as though suddenly tired. "He drank too much, but that'd been going on for years. The only thing—" She shook her head, and shrugged.

"What?"

"It sounds dumb," she said, "but he acted a lot *nicer.* Like right before he left, he all of a sudden turns to me and says, I realize now how much shit I put you through, and I'm sorry. Then he goes, You're a good person, Mo, you deserve to be happy—" Her voice quivered. "It was the first time he apologized to me since back in college."

"But there was nothing else? Nothing to indicate he might—"

Maureen smoothed the pleats of her skirt. I could tell what she was thinking: I just didn't get it. "Twenty-twenty hindsight. I think he wanted to make amends, that's all." Already she was looking past me, at the car where Richie sat, surrounded by her daughters.

"Are you going to Caroline's parents'?"

"No," Maureen laughed. "I did my bit. We came, we said good-bye. Now it's time to go home. I'm glad I saw you, Garner. You were always real kind to me."

I hoped that was true, but for the life of me, I couldn't remember. "Maureen," I ventured one last question, "did TJ mention anything about a project he was working on? A new book he had in the works?"

"Tommy always had some big idea or another running around in his head, but he never talked much about them to me. I mean, you knew him, right? He was so damn *smart*"—again, she fought back tears—"like a genius, almost. He probably figured I would never understand . . ." Her eyes drifted toward the fresh grave on the bottom of the hill.

"Take good care of yourself, Garner," Maureen whispered when we hugged good-bye. I watched as she made her way to the blue Blazer, taking light, nimble steps, like a woman who's just had some huge weight lifted from her shoulders.

3

"NOW," LEEDON WHITLEY said after I closed Sterling's folder. "You mind telling me what's going on?"

"I don't know what you mean."

"Don't give me that." The detective drove with studied disinterest, the way he did everything else.

"No, really—"

"Listen here. If Dr. Kevorkian pays a visit to my grandma tonight, odds are I'm gonna be out shopping for caskets in the morning." He put on his blinker to pull into the passing lane. "Same thing applies. If Garner Quinn starts asking questions about one of my cases, I gotta figure there's some pretty heavy shit waitin' to hit the fan."

"Not necessarily." I opened up the file again. "I'm just confused, that's all. The last time I saw Sterling he didn't seem like a man on the verge of killing himself."

"Maybe the pleasure of your company," Whitley said, "temporarily uplifted him."

"Yeah, and maybe I should've caught a ride with Tyree," I

muttered. The landscape streaking by looked plush and ribbed, like rolled-out sheaths of wide-wale corduroy in shades of hunter and emerald green.

Detective Whitley ignored my remark, turning the steering wheel with one lazy finger, coaxing my Volvo up to seventy. It occurred to me he'd really bought into this Hollywood cop routine. With the looks, the lines, and the attitude, all Whitley needed was a high-speed car chase. *But not,* I thought, watching the speedometer climb, *in my car.* I said, "What about the gun?"

"An old Austrian Steyr, registered in Sterling's name."

The same kind of gun Gordon Spangler had used to kill his family. "Not your run-of-the-mill firearm," I commented casually.

"Apparently, the man was a collector of sorts. According to his wife, he liked to familiarize himself with a weapon before he wrote about it— thought it made his books more authentic. She said the Steyr figured into some case he worked on a while back. He kept it in his desk. Not only that, the paraffin test was conclusive. Sterling fired that gun himself.

"Add to that the fact that the only other fingerprints found in his office belonged to his wife, who happened to be in Charleston at the time of the shooting, and the cleaning woman, who was in Blacksburg, attending her son's wedding. Plus those other little details, like the door being locked, and no sign of forced entry. Oh—did I neglect to mention that no less than a dozen of Sterling's close friends testified to his state of mind?"

He took his hands off the wheel to flip through the pages on my lap. "See where it says—'depressed'. . .'unusually agitated' . . . 'erratic behavior'. . . . 'manic'. . ." Whitley let the Volvo veer to the right while he stared at me. "What you flappin' them goldy eyes like that for?"

"Watch where you're going, please."

"You don't believe what's down there in the report?"

"I don't believe Sterling had a dozen close friends," I replied. "Enemies, maybe. He had them by the score."

Whitley smacked the steering wheel. "Damn, you are one pigheaded woman!" He pointed to another paragraph. "I suppose it won't impress you that his blood alcohol tipped the scales at point three-five?"

"Sounds like pretty much an ordinary evening for the guy I knew."

"Yeah, well, he didn't wake up from this particular hangover," the detective countered.

I wouldn't admit it to Whitley, but after looking at the police photos, I'd been shocked by the sheer degradation of Sterling's final moments. He'd been found at his desk, amid a mountain of crumpled paper, half-filled bottles of booze, and dirty glasses, facedown in a mucky pool of vomit, liquor, and blood.

Still, there were just too many coincidences . . .

"We're not talking about a man who drank himself to death, Detective," I said, doggedly. "If I remember correctly, a bullet was involved."

"A bullet that came out of a gun that *he* fired," Whitley retorted, then his voice thickened with innuendo. "Hey, I don't know where you're coming from in all this, whether you and he were—"

"—professional acquaintances. We knew each other professionally."

"Yeah, well, if you ask me, you seem to be having an unusually hard time accepting that your professional acquaintance Mister TJ Sterling had some pretty powerful reasons to consider blowing out his brains."

Whitley lifted his hands from the steering wheel again, ticking off each point. "One, he was mortgaged up to his eyeballs. Two, everybody and his brother was out to sue his ass. Three, he had a high-rent wife and a grabby ex to support—and that's not counting whatever else he had going on the side. Four, he had no real job. His career was in the toilet—"

"Would you mind just driving the car?"

The detective took control of the wheel with careless grace. *"And* he was an alcoholic," he went on blithely, "—an alcoholic has-been nobody wanted anymore. Damn, I lost count. What number we up to now?"

I pretended not to hear. Whitley turned off the highway onto a private road. Rolling pastures spilled away in every direction. I'd lost track of Tyree's squad car miles ago. "I didn't see anything here about a suicide note," I commented, changing the subject.

"Yeah, well, maybe you should have your eyes checked—no, next page, near the bottom. He left a poem, all balled up on the desk."

I'd missed it the first time through. Now I read TJ Sterling's last words aloud, *"If thou regret'st thy youth, why live?"*

The line sounded vaguely familiar. I took a stab. "One of the Romantics? Byron or Keats . . ."

"Shelley. Tyree ran it through the computer."

A huge Federal-style manor house with several soaring brick chimneys came into view. Beyond it I spotted at least two barns, a corral, and some stables. Edenfield, it appeared, was a classic Virginia horse farm. Somehow it didn't surprise me that Caroline had been born with a silver riding crop in her hand.

Whitley didn't react to the surroundings. I wondered if he'd been here before. "Way I figure it, the 'regret' shit was just Sterling's way of apologizing for the times he fucked up in the past," he explained. "He didn't see the point of going on like that, so he killed himself."

His interpretation made no sense to me, but I didn't feel like arguing anymore. I directed my attention out the window. This silence seemed to rile Detective Whitley more than my questions. He pulled into an empty parking space on the circular drive, just behind Tyree's squad car, and switched off the engine. "Okay, one more time," he said, his voice crackling with frustration. "You mind telling me what's going on?"

"Nothing." I handed the file folder back to Whitley, and got out of the car. The group of students I'd seen at the funeral were peeling out from the confines of a bright orange BMW. I watched as, one by one, they filed up the brick walkway.

"Wait up." The detective sprinted toward me. There was no trace of the Denzel Washington grin on his face now. He looked totally pissed.

"Nothing's going on," I repeated, impatiently.

A few feet away, a middle-aged man was zap-locking his Camry. He nodded solemnly, the way people at funerals are wont to do.

Whitley grabbed my arm. "Hey, you owe me."

I shook him off. "I don't owe you anything."

The man with the Camry stiffened, his eyes suddenly sharp and alert. It took me a moment to figure out why—what he saw, or *thought* he saw, was a young black guy hassling a white woman. Of course, the reality was vice versa. I smiled reassuringly at the Camry man, who shot one more backward look of concern before disappearing into the house.

"Listen, Detective," I said in a conciliatory tone, "I appreciate you letting me see that file, I really do. And you're right. All the evidence points to suicide."

"So?" Whitley asked.

"So I'm paranoid," I told him. "Comes with the job."

"Mine, too."

"Friends?" I offered a hand to shake.

Whitley declined to take it. "The jury's still out," he said.

A black maid in livery opened the front door. She told us that a buffet was being served on the rear patio, and that extra chairs had been set up all over the house. In the living room, people perched on damask sofas balancing china plates heaped with fresh ham and fried chicken. They looked up at Whitley and me as we passed.

"Nice, huh?" he whispered under his breath, taking in the early-

American furnishings—the tasteful, if predictable, botanical and eques-
trian prints, the custom window treatments. "Very tallyho-and-all-
that."

Detective Tyree was standing at the door to the patio, a drink in one
hand, a double helping of food in the other. He had the small, neckless
head and gelatinous musculature of an ex-jock, and while some of
Whitley's slickness had rubbed off, on this guy it looked plain oily. "Y'all
enjoy the ride?" Tyree asked with an implied leer.

I replied, "Yeah, it was a barrel of laughs." I turned to his partner.
"Thanks for the info, Detective. And now, if you'll both excuse me, I'd
like to give my condolences to the widow."

I found Caroline Sterling sitting in the study, surrounded by a half-
dozen clubby-looking people. "Garner." She wobbled a little as she rose
to her full, statuesque height. "I'm so glad—oh Lord, I'd meant to ask if
you needed a ride. Forgive me." She started to cry. "I'm such an awful
mess."

"Please, don't apologize. I just wanted to tell you how sorry I am. If
there's anything I can do—"

"Just your being here is enough," she said, earnestly. "You don't know
how much it means, one of Tom's dearest friends, coming all this way."
The fact that she clearly thought TJ and I had been close made me feel
sneaky, and a little sad.

"Everyone, this is Garner Quinn," Caroline announced, "the famous
writer from up north Tom always went on so about." A smatter of *oohs*
and *ahhs* rose from the group. I tried to thaw my frozen smile, glad that
detectives Whitley and Tyree were nowhere in sight.

"Ford Childress." The silver-haired man extended a hand. "I'm
Caro's father." The intensity of his grip asserted his position as sire of this
dynasty. "Welcome to Edenfield. Have you met my wife, Faye?"

While father and daughter shared a tall, equine grace, Mrs. Childress was petite, raven-haired, and not a day over forty, with violet contact lenses swimming in her big, round eyes. Wife number two or three, no doubt. "So pleased to meet you," she said demurely.

"Oh, I'm sorry." Caroline pressed her lips together to keep from crying. "I should've introduced y'all at the—"

"Sit down now, Carrie," her stepmother said, "you're worn clean off your feet." Caroline telegraphed me a silent *help* as she was shuffled toward a sofa.

"How about a drink?" Ford Childress inquired in his deep, hearty voice.

"Yes, please," Caroline said. "Some seltzer. My mouth's like cotton."

I offered to get it. As anxious as I was to talk to TJ's widow, I could see it would be impossible to penetrate the family's strategically arranged flanks today.

4

"HOLY CHRISTMAS, THESE people are boring!" sighed the girl with the buzz-cut and pearls. "If TJ were here, he'd be going out of his mind." She turned to the bartender. "Dewar's on the rocks, with a twist. And my friend will have—"

"A Bloody Mary, and a glass of seltzer. You sound like you knew him quite well," I commented.

"I had a class with him. Fell madly in love. Got rejected. Started working for him. Fell out of love and into worshipful respect." The girl dabbed her nose with a Kleenex. "Oh, God. Here I go again."

The bartender slid over three glasses. She took a long gulp from hers. "I'm Sands McColl," she said. "And you—you're familiar."

"Garner Quinn." I studied her face, waiting for the lightbulb of recognition to go off, grateful when it didn't.

"You from New York?"

"Up that way, yes."

"I figured—New York, L.A., they're where it's at if you've got it going on. I give myself another six months down here, a year at the most." Sands tossed her shaved head. "Anyway, the second I saw you, I knew you didn't belong with this set." She took another sip of her scotch. "It's a crime, if you ask me."

"What?" I perked up, interested.

"Them here, tipping heads together, making their whispery little small talk, while a brilliant, talented man like TJ—" She stopped. Shrugged. Sniffed.

"You said you worked for him," I prompted. "What exactly did you do?"

"Donkey stuff at first," the girl replied. "Reading essays, grading tests. But he knew I wanted to be a writer, so eventually he started letting me help him on a more creative level, like with the projects he was working on, you know, professionally."

My heart was doing handsprings in my chest. "That must've been interesting."

"You can say that again." Sands drained her glass. "God, I can't believe he's gone."

Out of the corner of my eye I saw Detective Whitley making his way across the room. "Listen," I said, "I'm planning to be in Charlottesville for a few more days. Think we could get together? I'd like to talk some more."

"Give me a ring. I'm between jobs *and* apartments." Sands pulled out a card from her sedate little handbag. "But you can usually reach me here."

I slipped the card into my pocket and picked up the drinks. "Well, I'd better deliver this before they send out a search party," I said, managing to beat a hasty retreat from Leedon Whitley.

Caroline became upset when I told her I had to leave. "I don't see why you had to check into a hotel," she protested. "I assumed you'd be staying with me."

"There are a few things I need to take care of while I'm here. I don't want to bother you with my comings and goings."

"What bother? There's plenty of space. I just redecorated the guest room. Or you could use Tommy's office—that way you're completely on your own. It's got a shower, even a little kitchen. Tom just pulls out the daybed when he's working late—" Caroline's lips made a dry smacking sound like white gloves clapping. She looked almost frightened. "Say you'll stay, Garner, please."

I stood firm. "I can't, really. Why don't you sleep here tonight so you won't be alone?"

"Exactly what we've been saying." Faye Childress came over with a heaping plate of ham and biscuits. "I hate to think of her back in that empty house." She set the food down in front of her stepdaughter.

"It's my *home,*" Caroline said.

"Well, of course, darlin'," Faye sighed theatrically, "but this is, too."

"Do you have to leave right now?" Caroline asked.

"I'm afraid so." Actually, I'd been antsy since the moment I walked in. The girl with the shaved head had been right—TJ would've hated this send-off.

Caroline insisted on walking me to the door. "If it's okay with you," I said, "I'd like to stop by to see you tomorrow. There are some things—"

An elderly woman wearing a canary-yellow pantsuit hobbled over in a panic. "The caterers want to know, should they put out the dessert now."

"I don't care, Scottie," Caroline replied petulantly. "You'll have to ask Faye."

"Well, I would," the old lady muttered, "if I could find her."

I gave Caroline a last hug and stepped outside.

The air was warm and lightly fragrant. It triggered an early childhood memory, something I hadn't remembered for years and years—me, standing on tiptoe, reaching for a crystal atomizer on a glass tray, letting the silken tassel tickle my nose, squeezing the frayed rubber ball on the end, and smelling a warm, sweet puff of scent. Had it belonged to my mother? Or just one of my father's many ladyfriends?

"Hey." A sudden touch on the shoulder caused me to nearly jump out of my skin.

"Goddamn it, Whitley." I covered my embarrassment with outrage. "You trying to give me a heart attack?"

"Nope," the detective said. "Just your car keys." He dangled them, grinning. I made the grab. "Planning to be in Charlottesville long?" he asked.

"A few days."

"Maybe we could get together, catch some dinner." I wondered how old he was—twenty-eight? thirty?—it was hard to tell, between all the matinee-idol posturing and trumped-up self-confidence.

A hairline crack appeared in Whitley's facade. "What I mean is, you don't strike me as the type to give up on an idea so easy," he equivocated. "I thought, after all that nosing around you did today, you'd probably want to grill me some more about the case."

"Not really, Leedon," I said sweetly, opening the door to my car. Before sliding behind the wheel I added, "But if anything else occurs to me, I'll be sure to give you a call."

5

"HI, ANDY. IS Temple around?"

"Oh, Garn—yeah, sure." Andy sounded hoarse, as though his vocal cords had been stretched out from laughing too much. "Hold on a sec, I'll get her for you."

He put the phone down and said something. From the next room, a shrill voice protested, "No way, that's cheating!" I heard the scrape of chairs being moved.

"Hello?" Temple came on the line.

"Hello yourself, kiddo."

"Hi, Mom. Where are you?" She'd asked that question so often it had become automatic.

"Charlottesville, Virginia," I replied, jauntily. In yet another hermetically sealed, generically decorated, double-locked, sanitized-for-my-protection hotel room.

"What are you doing there?"

I looked around and thought, *Really*. "I had to go to a funeral." It seemed a bleak admission given all the raucous laughter coming from the other end. "Sounds like you're having a lot more fun."

"Uncle Mike and Uncle Joe are teaching me to play poker." The background voices were more distinct now. I pictured Temple walking into the next room with the phone tucked into the crook of one shoulder—not wanting to hurt my feelings, but longing to get back to the game.

"Watch them," I said, "they cheat." I pretended to be in a sudden rush. "Listen, Tem, I have to run. I'll call again tomorrow, okay?"

"We're leaving early to go to the beach."

"The next day, then." The full weight of my loneliness came hurtling, like an elevator down an empty shaft. "Tell everybody I said hi," I croaked. "I love you—"

"Me, too, Mom." Then the click, and nothing.

"What are you doing there?" she'd asked.

I glanced around the room, at the unpacked suitcase on the extra double bed; the television playing an "I Love Lucy" rerun soundlessly in the fake armoire; the discarded nylons snaking across the carpet like molted skins my kicked-off shoes had left behind; the lone face staring back from the mirror.

Why had I traveled all this way to attend the funeral of a man I didn't even like? For that matter, what made me think Sterling had been murdered when all the cold hard facts added up to suicide? And even if Gordon Spangler had pulled the trigger—which, I reminded myself, was a pretty big *if*—how did I expect to find a man who'd managed to stay hidden for over twenty years? The sensible thing would be to notify the authorities, tell them what little I knew, and get it off my conscience, out of my hands.

Before I could pick up the phone, I was blindsided by a sudden memory. *"What makes you think I won't call the feds?"* I'd asked TJ.

His reply had come with a confident smile. *"Because you owe me."*

One more day, Sterling, I muttered into the mirror, *and we're even. I'll talk to your wife. Then I'm heading home.* But the thought of my silent, empty house was as depressing as this silent, empty hotel room, so I turned up the volume on the television and pushed it out of my mind.

6

CHESWICK FOREST WAS an exclusive gated community just off Highway 250, a scant twenty miles from the hustle and bustle of downtown Charlottesville. A gold-embossed sign featured the silhouette of a scampering fox, along with a stern warning: "PRIVATE PROPERTY—PRIVATE PROPERTY—NO TRESPASSING OR SOLICITATION." I hit the brakes, passing through the stone arches slowly, expecting any minute to be flagged down by a uniformed guard. To my surprise, there wasn't one. Apparently, here in the genteel south, trespassers could be counted on to conform to the honor code.

The houses were all built on large, beautifully landscaped lots. Although some were grander than others, take away this one's gabled roof, or that one's columns, and they all boiled down to colonial. It didn't appear that this was the kind of place where an innovative architect would be invited to make his mark.

Very tallyho-and-all-that, as Detective Whitley would say.

The road meandered, following manicured scallops of emerald green fairway. As I cruised by, I sensed the golfers on each hole, glancing up from their putting and slicing, taking note in a cool, predatory way—as though the sight of my long hair flying through the open car window were the tail of a fox they might later choose to hunt. But that was pure fancy on my part; more likely they knew no bona-fide resident of Cheswick Forest would drive a thirty-year-old Volvo pitted with dings and rust spots.

According to the directions Caroline had given me on the phone, the main road forked at the Cheswick Forest Clubhouse. I spotted it on the hillcrest, an impressive brick edifice which resembled my savings bank back in Jersey, *sans* the drive-through window. I skirted the parking lot, trying to imagine TJ behind the wheel of one of these surreyed golf carts—sun-kissed and healthy, wearing crisp Jay Gatsby whites, on his way to enjoying the first martini of the day.

I could picture the martini part, but the rest seemed a stretch.

At the main entrance to the club, a man and woman in couple-coordinated golf attire lingered under the awning to watch me pass. Caroline had said to take a left here onto Steeplechase Drive, but after putting on my left blinker, I impulsively turned right. It was still early, I told myself. Might as well check out the neighborhood.

I made the next left, ending up on a narrow road called Huntington Lane. This seemed to be a more rural section of the compound. I had to crane my neck to catch glimpses of the houses, which were set back, and masked by tall privet hedges and trees.

After three winding country miles, Huntington abruptly dead-ended. A huge Neoclassic estate stood at the neck of the cul-de-sac. Despite the addition of a modern two-story garage, it maintained an air of historical authenticity, predating the other homes I'd seen in Cheswick Forest by at least a hundred years. The grounds were well maintained, but the house itself appeared to be empty.

Edging toward the front gate, I noticed something odd. What I'd assumed was a dead end, wasn't. A two-way ramp ran parallel to the eastern wall of the property. The wooded quietness thrummed with the heavy metal bass of distant traffic. *If this was a side entrance to the main highway, then it would be possible for someone to drive into Cheswick Forest without the risk of being seen by any of the watchful residents.*

I put the Volvo in park, and reached into my bag to grab the little point-and-shoot I always kept there. Leaving the car door wide open, I jogged over to the stone wall. Even without following it to the top, I could plainly see the cars zipping past, just beyond the trees. I snapped a few pictures, zooming in on the small sign that said "250 EAST." From behind me came the shrill screech of tires.

A beige Land Rover had pulled sideways behind my Volvo, effectively blocking it. A man of about forty stepped out, his ruddy tan and athletic build accentuated by a bright lavender Ralph Lauren polo shirt, khaki trousers, and Topsiders without socks.

"Can I help you?" he asked, with an unctuous smile.

7

"THEY'RE ALL LIKE that in Cheswick," Caroline said with a rueful little laugh. "A bunch of paranoid busybodies, that's what Tommy always said—too much time on their hands, too much money, and not enough brains to use either one properly."

I watched her pour two tall glasses of iced tea, unable to shake the image of the clench-jawed Aryan in the Land Rover from my mind. He'd insisted upon acting as my official escort, following close behind while I drove from the cul-de-sac to number 92 Steeplechase Drive. The Sterling home turned out to be a white brick cottage with climbing ivy, European-style shutters, and windowboxes of geraniums—charming, yet modest by neighborhood standards. I'd felt the man's cold stare on my back as I went up to ring the bell; he'd kept the engine idling until Caroline appeared at the door, and gave him the okay sign.

"It must've really bugged TJ," I commented, "living under a microscope like this."

Caroline's face turned wistful. "Actually, moving here was his idea. As much as he made fun of it, Tom secretly enjoyed Cheswick's snobbery—be a darlin' and grab that salad for me, will you? I thought we'd eat out in the sun room."

I picked up the bowl and followed her into a bright airy nook off the kitchen. The table had already been set for lunch. "I find myself coming in here a lot," Caroline said, setting down our glasses. "The dining room seems so big now—" Her voice trailed off.

"It's beautiful," I said honestly. "Very cheery." Swags of translucent white fabric floated like clouds over the French doors. A chandelier rained a whimsical cascade of stars overhead, and the chairs were upholstered in a bold animal print. Caroline had obviously taken care to soften the hard lines of stuffy respectability so evident in her family home at Edenfield.

She motioned me to a seat, asking, "Is it too sunny for you?"

"No, I'm fine." I took four of the dainty sandwiches passed to me, and filled my salad bowl with a small mountain of dressed greens. Caroline chose a single pale wedge of watercress. Now that she'd finally stopped fussing, she looked lost, as though unsure of what to do with her meager portion of food.

"So TJ picked out this house?" I prompted gently.

"Oh, yes." She rallied a little. "We looked into several of the new communities around Charlottesville—Daddy's in developing, you know. He offered to build us a huge place." Caroline shrugged indulgently. "But Tommy said he didn't want to live in any upscale, nouveau riche tract home. He wanted old Virginia money. So we came to Cheswick."

Suddenly it made sense to me—the clubbiness, the la-de-da neighbors, all this rampant elitism. How TJ would've relished infiltrating these closely guarded ranks! With Caroline's pedigree as a password, he'd been able to inveigle his way in; after that, it would've been business as usual. I pictured him at dinner parties, *good old Tom,* captivating the

Cheswickian upper crust with his easy charm while, in his brain, he sliced and diced them. Professionally, personally—it didn't matter. Sooner or later the people Sterling most avidly courted were used and discarded.

And let that be a lesson to you, Quinn, I thought.

"Legend has it that Cheswick Forest was originally designed by Thomas Jefferson," Caroline chattered on. "Though, in these parts, that means about as much as 'George Washington slept here' does up north. Tommy used to say that Yankees take their historic sites and build parking lots on them, while we Virginians turn ours into shrines—" She pressed her lips together. "I'm sorry."

"For what?"

"I keep going on and on about him, don't I?"

"It's good to talk," I told her. "You'll heal faster that way."

"I hope so." Her pretty mouth curled up doubtfully. "Because no matter how I try, I can't stop. And when no one's around to listen, it's Tom, Tom, Tom—roarin' through my head, like air trapped in a seashell." With one fingertip, she traced a line down the sweaty condensation of her tea glass. "Right before you came, I was rememberin' the first time I ever saw him."

"You met at a writers' conference?"

"Yes," Caroline said dreamily. "The spring of my junior year. I'd just turned twenty. He put it in a letter to me— *'So come and kiss me, sweet and twenty'*—that's Shakespeare, I think."

She traced another line on the glass. "I was attending an all-women's college here in Virginia. Very traditional, very . . . what I was used to. *The girls with the pearls.* That's what they used to call us"—she laughed as if this were the saddest thing she'd ever heard—*"the girls with the pearls . . .*

"My roommate Betsy dragged me to that conference. She was goin' to be a writer, and I—well, I didn't have a clue what I wanted to be. But I thought, what the heck? The first lecture I just about slept through. Then I walked into Tom's . . ." *And you sat down in the first row, crossed your long, magnificent legs, and lifted your slanty emerald baguette eyes up to the podium. And in the space of those fifteen seconds—one for every year of his marriage—TJ Sterling forgot all about his dull little wife Maureen, their three rabbity-faced daughters, and the new baby on the way.*

The version Caroline recounted while I ate my lunch was softer and more romantic, but not nearly as to-the-point. "I guess I'll never understand," she sighed when she'd finished, "how it all came unraveled the way it did."

"Unraveled?" I repeated, immediately picking up on the word. "You mean Tom unraveled?"

"Not Tom." The young woman shook her head. *"Things.* The lawsuits, all that trouble with his publisher."

"Caroline," I said quietly, "did TJ's . . . death . . . come as a surprise to you?"

"Well, of course." She nudged her plate away without having taken a bite. "I'm still in a state of shock."

"You had no idea he was that depressed?"

"No. Maybe if I had—" She began wringing her hands.

I reached across the table. "Stop. Look at me, Caroline. You can't hold yourself responsible for what happened."

Her eyes and nose had started to run, but somehow she still managed to look elegant. "I knew how much pressure he was under," she said softly, "and when the university didn't renew his contract—"

TJ had told me he was on sabbatical. "Why didn't they?"

"Something about it not being a tenure track position." Caroline dabbed her tears with the linen napkin. "I suppose that was the last straw."

"Strange," I said. "The last time I saw him, he didn't seem the least bit upset about not teaching anymore. In fact, I got the impression he was thrilled to have extra time for some new project he had in the works."

"I thought he'd been acting happier, too. But it looks like that's all it was," she sighed, "—acting."

"Did he discuss his new book with you?"

"Not really." Her lips tightened into a forced smile. "Tommy could be secretive that way. When we were first married, I read them all. Every time I finished one, he'd ask about a million questions, you know— what I thought, which part stuck out in my mind. It didn't seem to satisfy him, me just telling how good they were, though. I guess Tom expected a more intellectual type of critique." She twirled a strand of honey hair. "After that, he never talked much about his work."

I didn't think she'd find it reassuring to hear that his first wife had had the same complaint.

The afternoon sun fell in vertical lines through the windows, stippling Caroline's white cotton shirt. Outside, a lawn mower began to drone. I was trying to decide how best to proceed when she suddenly piped up, as though reading my mind. "If you'd like, we could go over to Tom's office," Caroline offered, "and I'll show you where it happened."

8

A GREEN MERCEDES station wagon was parked on a slant in front of the garage. We crossed the backyard, past a well-tended garden and an outdoor Jacuzzi. Everything appeared to be bursting with life.

"There it is, over there." Caroline pointed through the trees. I caught a glimpse of a whitewashed board-and-batten bungalow. "The slave quarters.

"That was another of Tom's little jokes—around here, it's chic to say you have slave quarters on your property." Caroline walked ahead, as tall and lanky as a boy in baggy trousers. Before reaching the porch, she paused to sweep a lock of hair off her forehead. "Whew, summer's here, for sure."

"Are you okay?" I asked, noticing how flushed she'd become. "Maybe this isn't such a good idea."

"I'm fine. Mind the steps now. I keep telling Tom to—" Caroline nervously jiggled her keys. Thinking she might need a moment to compose herself, I wandered over to the tiny flagstone patio. A barbeque grill and two lounge chairs had been set up next to a couple of empty terra-cotta planters. Less than fifty feet from the back of the cottage I could see a dilapidated shed, just wide enough to park a car, and beyond that, a dirt drive.

"Where does the road go?"

"What?" Caroline glanced over her shoulder. "Oh, that's just the rear way out of Cheswick." Just then the tumblers in the lock clicked. She pushed the door and it creaked open a few inches.

I could tell Caroline wanted me to go in first, but my feet suddenly felt like lead, as though they'd sooner mutiny than face another crime scene. "Maybe you'd better wait outside," I said hoarsely.

"I'm okay," she said as she stepped aside so I could cross the threshold.

The bungalow was neat as a pin, but its low ceiling and small windows made it seem cramped and claustrophobic. Ammonia disinfectant and vanilla potpourri battled for supremacy in the still air. Caroline turned on a lamp. "The police left the number of a professional cleaning company that handles . . . these sorts of situations." Her voice sounded breathless. "After they got through, Lettie and I came in and scrubbed the place down all over again.

"It's just this small kitchen area, and then the study—" I followed her, walking slowly, as though I were negotiating my way through a thick fog.

The afternoon sun didn't quite make it into this room. Caroline went to the desk and snapped on another lamp. "This is where I found him," she said.

The booze and crumpled paper I'd seen in the photographs had been carted away, and cleaning people armed with wire brushes had banished every last speck of blood and vomit. Still death lingered, like a bad hangover. "The shades were pulled down"—Caroline pointed at two small windows—"so at first I didn't realize—"

She wiped her forehead with the back of her hand. "I thought he'd passed out. In recent years, Tom had a problem . . . with his drinking."

I nodded, sympathetically. "Detective Whitley said you'd just returned from a trip with your parents?"

"Yes. My stepsister Vicki—that's Faye's daughter from her first marriage—was graduating from the University of Charleston. Tom and I had both planned on going, but at the last minute he said he had some important business to take care of here . . ." She moved away from the desk.

"When we spoke on the phone, I could tell something was wrong. He seemed . . . agitated. Not at all himself. So I decided to surprise him and come home a day early. I borrowed my sister's car and drove up Sunday morning. It was noon by the time I got to Cheswick. When he wasn't in the house, I assumed he'd be out here, working on the new book."

"*Could* he have been working on the book, before he died?"

"I don't know," Caroline said in a defeated tone. "I'm not even sure there *was* a book. It might've been just another made-up story in Tom's head." I had to admit she had a point. It would've been just like Sterling to cook up the Spangler sighting as a last-ditch effort to jumpstart his career. All he had to do was enlist the support of some key people— people like me—and he'd be back in the limelight again.

And yet, something didn't feel right. This room looked as though it should be roped off with velvet stanchions, like an exhibit in some museum. I scanned the titles on the bookshelves: a dozen different "Complete Works Of" collections—Hardy, Tolstoy, Dickens, Twain, Proust, James, Hemingway, Fitzgerald, Faulkner; the Pelican Shakespeare; several dictionaries—way too generic for a guy like Sterling. And where were his filing cabinets?

"Did Tom leave any notes? Any files or folders?" Caroline threw up her hands. I glanced at the computer sheathed in its gray cotton cover. "How about the documents on his hard drive?"

"The detectives checked it and went through the back-up disks. There was some old stuff—the last true crime he had published. A speech he gave to a local book club. Some lectures for his classes." Caroline swallowed several times, as if her throat were dry. "Why? Do you think it's impor—"

The color had drained from her face. Suddenly, she started sucking in the air like a caught fish. I reached her just before her knees buckled. "I'm sorry," she gasped. "I—"

"Take it easy." She was slender, but much taller and more athletically built than I. Somehow I managed to get her over to the daybed. "Put your head down," I said. "I'll call a doctor."

"No," Caroline murmured. "Maybe just some water."

"You're white as a ghost. This has been too much for you."

"It's not that." She took my hand and clung to it. "No one else knows yet—I didn't even get a chance to tell Tom." A hysterical sob escaped from her lips. "You see, I'm pregnant, Garner. I'm going to have a baby."

Shaken by the despair in her eyes, I uttered the only thing I could think of to say, "That's wonderful, Caroline. I'm happy for you. That's really, really great."

9

"HEY. WHILE YOU'RE sitting around with a phone stuck to your ear, I'm sixth row center, listening to Dave Matthews," the voice on the answering machine said. "Catch you there if you're lucky. If not, you know the drill."

I hung up. Sands McColl was shagging her shapely little butt off at some rock concert. My daughter and her newly blended family hadn't returned from the beach. Caroline Sterling seemed too fragile to carry the weight of my unfounded suspicions. *And I needed someone to talk to.* In a weak moment, I thought about calling Cilda in Jamaica. In an even weaker moment, I considered dialing the number of every hotel in Paris—but experience had taught me Dane Blackmoor wouldn't be easy to find.

So, instead, I leafed through my address book until I found the entry for J. Emmett Hogan, in MacLean, Virginia. I'd first met Special Agent Hogan in January of '88, during the course of researching my third book, *Dust to Dust*. At the time, he was one of a handful of criminal profilers in the FBI's Behavioral Science Investigative Support Unit in

Quantico. I had a couple of bestsellers to my credit, and didn't yet know what I didn't know. Together, we managed to end the career of a particularly despicable serial killer named Harold Beech. It had proved to be an intensely bonding experience for both of us.

If I was going to come clean to anyone about Sterling's claim of seeing Gordon Spangler, it might as well be to my old friend and cohort, Special Agent Emmett Hogan. *After all, I couldn't handle this on my own,* I reminded myself as I picked up the phone. *I had to bring someone else on board. Eventually.*

I SUGGESTED WE meet at the Old Ebbitt, Hogan's favorite haunt in downtown D.C. Despite the ninety-degree temperature, he arrived wearing his usual natty attire: linen sports jacket, cotton shirt, pink and yellow tie. His colleagues at the Bureau called him J. Emmett or—when they really wanted to needle him—J. Edgar, but I never did. He was always plain Hogan to me.

"Make it the usual," he told the waiter.

The usual was a bowl of soup and a beer. I knew this, just as I knew that the J in his name stood for Joseph—which was also the first name of his father, his father's five brothers, and every male child born into the Hogan family. Hogan's grandmother had believed that, by naming them after her patron saint, they'd all be assured of a happy death. *"As if there was such a thing,"* he'd muttered to me. In his line of work, he'd seen too many deaths that weren't.

"How's it going, Hogan?" I asked.

He looked down at his watch. "You got sixty minutes," he said with a surly growl. "—Make that fifty-nine and counting."

"What's the rush?"

"Who's the rush," Hogan corrected. "Sue's the rush. You know

Sue?—that short, blue-eyed blonde I've been happily married to for twenty-two years?" He wolfed down a roll without chewing. "We're celebrating our thirtieth anniversary next month."

"I thought you said—"

"The key word was *'happy.'* And, lemme tell you, this last decade's been a bitch—mainly because of having to associate with people like yourself who think nothing of tracking me down, all hours of the day and night, even Sundays, in the friggin' hot middle of June, when I'm supposed to be home packing the car for our first family vacation in seven years." Hogan popped another roll into his mouth. "Yep, this time Tuesday, I'll be shaking hands with Mickey Mouse."

"Stop swallowing your bread whole. It isn't healthy," I said.

"Yeah, well, nothing tastes good since I worked the Dahmer case."

The waiter returned with our order. "Speaking of old cases"—I began salting my turkey sandwich—"you remember Gordon Spangler?"

Hogan had tucked a napkin into his shirt collar and was busy spooning down his soup. "What about him?"

"Just wondering." I lapsed into one of my acquired aggressive guy behaviors, deliberately speaking with my mouth full. "Your profile indicate what he might be doing now? You know, jobs, interests, hobbies? Places he'd be drawn to?"

"Uh-huh." Hogan siphoned off the frothy head from his beer.

"Uh-huh, what?" I wanted to know.

"All of the above. Jobs, hobbies, places. What you said."

"Think I could take a look at it?"

Hogan put down his mug and took off his bib. "The Spangler profile?"

"Yes."

"No. But if you ask nice, I'll talk you through it."

I sighed. "Please."

Hogan glanced down at his watch. "Thirty-eight and a half—"

"Pretty please. Baby," I said, without the least inflection.

"You're a tough case, Quinn." He leaned back, crossed his arms over his chest, and proceeded to recite, "Gordon Frederick Spangler, Caucasian male, age—" It took him a moment to figure. "—sixty. Five feet ten. At the time of disappearance, one-sixty-five, brown and brown. Distinguishing marks—appendectomy scar. Wears glasses to correct an astigmatism." I knew the description by heart. Unfortunately, especially considering the ways in which looks could be cosmetically altered these days, it loosely fit the vitals of about one middle-aged man in three.

"Subject is well educated, with a degree in engineering from Roger Williams in Rhode Island. He may seek employment as an engineer, or in some related area—surveying, zoning, commercial real estate development. He worked for a time selling insurance, but without much success. Spangler's better with numbers than he is with people. He might have found a position as a bookkeeper, or in an accountant's office. His boss would regard him as competent, but inflexible and unimaginative. Lacking in interpersonal skills. This is one of the nameless, faceless drones who toil behind the scenes, but never really climb the ladder, or get ahead."

Hogan took a slow sip of his beer before continuing. "We also believe that he'd be actively associated with a church."

"Any particular denomination?"

"He was raised a Lutheran," Hogan said. "But it's possible he's switched to something more fundamental. Nothing too charismatic, though. No speaking in tongues, or emotional witnessing. He's much too controlled for that."

"Was his minister back in Jersey any help?"

"What a moron. He started out cooperative enough. Spangler had left a letter addressed to him—same bullshit, how he offed his family to save their souls. So the reverend's concerned that maybe old Gordo might take it upon himself to pay him the same favor, right? But after a few weeks go by, he figures he's in the clear, and all of a sudden he's mouthing the confidentiality line—how Spangler's spiritual tie to his once and future pastors is a protected relationship, *ya-bi-da, ya-bi-da.*

"Church bureaucrats," Hogan grumbled, "they're all the same. Don't have to tell you, huh, you grew up Catholic." He signaled the waiter for some coffee.

"Anyway, the preacher nearly had a conniption fit when he found out we mailed a wanted poster to every Lutheran church in the country that Spangler might've"—Hogan paused sarcastically—"*spiritually tied* himself to."

"No luck?"

"Nah. By then the trail was ice cold. Don't forget, he had a month's head start on us. Add to that the fact that the guy's our worst nightmare—a mild-mannered Mister Peepers. Nondescript. Colorless. No apparent bad habits. Keeps to himself. Stays out of trouble. He could be eating at the next table and you'd look right through him. Never notice he was there."

In spite of myself, I glanced around the room. Hogan saw me taking inventory, but he had enough good grace not to laugh. "Only had two passions that we know of. Board games and houses."

"Houses?"

"Nine of 'em, over a period of sixteen years. The Spangler shuffle. It starts with an underwhelming performance on the job and ends with a polite parting of the ways. A little severance pay, a nice recommendation, and the ineffectual twerp is shrugged off on some other unsuspecting company." Hogan went on, "So the Spanglers moved around a lot. And in each new location, Papa S would buy another home. Something out of his price range, grand and showy—at least on the outside, where everything had to be just so. Because this was always going to be the time it all worked out. The perfect house, in the perfect city, the perfect job."

I thought of Holly Hill, so tumbledown, cold and empty, the place where Gordon Spangler's big dreams took a left turn into nightmare. Then a disjointed image sprang to mind: the seemingly deserted Neo-classic estate at the end of Cheswick Forest cul-de-sac. What, I wondered, made me suddenly think of that?

"He also loved those World War II stratagems. *Third Reich* and the like," Hogan was saying. "These days, ole Gordo's probably hooked up to the Internet. You can get war games on CD-ROM now."

The waiter brought our decafs, and we joked about how we were both slowing down, getting old. But I could tell neither one of us really believed it.

10

"SEE?" I TEASED as Hogan poured cream into his cup. "Ten minutes to spare."

"So what's the sudden renewed interest in Spangler?"

One snowy night during the Beecher case, I'd made mention of my friendship with Lara. Now I regretted the confidence. "I've been spending a lot of time in Spring Lake," I said, trying to drink the scalding coffee straight down. "Fixing up my father's place. I guess it brought back memories, that's all."

"Don't insult me, Garner," J. Emmett Hogan said coldly.

Shit, I thought. "I'm not—"

"And spare me the wide-eyed innocent routine. It's bad enough my wife thinks I'm at Wal-Mart, buying a luggage rack for the car. If she knew I played beat the Beltway to come here and have soup with *you* . . . Jeez-louise, she's still got the divorce papers lying around the house from last time."

"I don't have a clue what you're talking about."

"No," Hogan said, not allowing me to look away. "You never do."

"I didn't even know Wal-Mart sold luggage racks."

"Give it up, Garner. Why Spangler all of a sudden?"

"Hypothetically?"

"Hypotheses are my life," the agent replied.

I frowned. "Say someone came to me, in confidence. And this person claimed to have seen Gordon Spangler."

"Where?"

"I don't know, exactly. The person wouldn't tell."

"Did you alert this person as to the moral, ethical, and legal ramifications of withholding such information?"

"I tried."

"Maybe you should try again."

"That's the problem," I said. "I can't."

"Why?"

"The person's presently . . . unreachable."

Hogan slammed his palms down on the table, sending up tiny whirlpools in the recesses of our coffee cups. "What the fuck have you gotten yourself into, Garner?"

"Nothing," I insisted. "I swear. It was probably just a hoax. I think he . . . she—this person—was trying to manipulate me."

"You must've thought there was something to it," Hogan said. "Or you wouldn't be here with me." I heard the underlying hurt in his voice.

When I touched his wrist to look down at his watch, he jumped. "Two more minutes, Hogan," I said softly.

"I thought, after what I heard about that last case of yours," he muttered, "with your kid almost ending up dead, that maybe you'd changed."

I felt my hair bristle from the roots, suddenly electric. "I did. I *have* . . . This has nothing to do with a book—"

"Then screw the hypotheses. Tell me the whole story."

"I told you all there is to know," I insisted. "Really."

"Who is he?" he pressed. "This *person?*"

"I can't say. At least not right now. It's complicated—" I reached into my wallet and pulled out a few bills.

"Don't insult me twice," Hogan said bitterly. I stayed perched on the edge of the chair, my shoulder bag on my lap. He laughed. "So where do you go from here?"

"Back home, I suppose," I said, vaguely.

"I'm going to be checking up on you," he warned. "They have phones in the Magic Kingdom, you know."

"I'm telling you, Hoge, it was probably just a bad tip."

He softened. "Yeah, well, over the years I've gotten more lousy tips than the counter boy at Burger King. But if there's so much as a shred of truth to this, don't screw around, Garner. The guy's already killed five people."

Let it be just five, I prayed, thinking of TJ, sprawled across his desk, facedown in a pool of brain matter and booze.

"And they were his own flesh-and-blood," Hogan was reminding me. "You have to figure—he could do that, he could do anything. Do any*body.*"

"Hey, aren't you the one who called Spangler a spent sparkler?" I asked lightly.

"Sure. The quote, unquote 'average Joe' who commits a sudden, explosive act of violence against his family usually never acts out again," he admitted. "If you asked my professional opinion, I'd tell you Spangler's probably living in the suburb of a small city, working at some respectable but humdrum job. He's married to a woman his age or slightly older, someone he met at church, with no children of her own, or other family to speak of. Acquaintances and co-workers regard him as a boring but harmless little man. Which is probably exactly what he is." I caught the ambivalence in Hogan's tone.

"Probably?"

"As long as he's able to avoid the type of situation that originally triggered him, he'll walk the line. But Spangler needs to feel in control. He doesn't respond well to pressure. Logical as he may appear to be, once he feels threatened, his reasoning disintegrates into shades of black and white. It's a *me versus them* mindset. Or, in this case, kill or be killed."

Our waiter came over with the check which Hogan paid in cash, explaining affably, "Sue goes over the receipts with a magnifying glass and finetooth comb."

To my surprise, when I rose to leave, Hogan didn't budge. "You go ahead." Loosening his tie, he leaned back in his chair. "I'm gonna have one more for the road. I'll tell her Wal-Mart was out of luggage racks." He nodded toward the door. "Go on. I make it a point never to walk out of a bar with a beautiful woman I'm not married to."

I leaned over and planted a kiss next to his ear. "Thanks."

Hogan straightened his tie and began to sing Cole Porter. *"Everytime we say good-bye, I die a little—"*

"See you around, Hogan."

"Garner," he called me back. "D'ja hear I'm retiring come Christmas?"

I stopped in my tracks.

"Yep. Finally got tired of the B.S." A bittersweet smile crossed Hogan's face. "Remember, back in the eighties when it was just a few of us, working Behavioral Science down there in the basement? Man oh man we took some flak!—'that profiling mumbo-jumbo,' they used to call it.

"Not anymore, though." His eyes burned into mine. "We're hot stuff these days. In the movies, on TV, and all those true-crime bestsellers. Everybody wants to take a profiler to lunch, ha. Only recently, the funny thing is, I've been thinking maybe they had it right at the beginning. Maybe it is all just mumbo-jumbo."

I realized once again, without rhyme or reason, J. Emmett Hogan and I had ended up at the same place at the same time. "Don't be so hard on yourself," I said. "We do what we can."

"And still the odds run just about fifty-fifty. And still guys like Gordon Spangler are out there, on the loose," Hogan said. "That's why I don't want you to go off, half-cocked, without taking note of this little disclaimer. At least one person has believed all along I was wrong to conclude that Gordon Spangler poses no imminent danger. For twenty years now, this lady's insisted that Spangler's been stalking her family."

Hogan shrugged. "Used to be, I wrote her off as loony, but now"— his mouth sagged into a weary line—"I don't know. I don't know 'bout nothin' no more."

He scrawled something on a napkin, then handed it to me. "Give a call, see what you think. If nothing else, it might help put this hypothetical Spangler sighting of yours into a whole new perspective." I read the name he'd written—*Ellen Wilcox Kresky*—and looked at him, questioningly.

"Spangler's sister-in-law. She lives in Wilmington, Delaware," Hogan told me. "Kresky and her mother are your friend Lara's only surviving relatives."

11

ELLEN KRESKY SEEMED confused by my call, but agreed to meet as long as I didn't mind driving to St. Francis Hospital. When I said that I didn't want to bother her at work, she laughed wearily. Kresky told me she didn't work in the hospital, she just stayed there, watching her mother fight the last stand in a losing battle with pancreatic cancer. We fixed a time for later that evening, and I hung up wondering why the hell I should drive another couple of hours just to bother some poor, paranoid woman in the middle of a deathwatch vigil.

Before getting back in the car, I used my phone card to dial Andy's number in New York. If Temple answered, I told myself I'd take it as a sign I was meant to head home without stopping at the hospital in Wilmington.

On the third ring, a chipper voice I barely recognized as my ex-husband's announced that Candace, Andy, and Temple weren't at home, and would I please leave a message after the beep? I slammed down the receiver, causing the woman on the payphone next to me to hunker protectively over her handbag.

Then I remembered that I had a room on hold at the hotel in

Charlottesville. "You had two messages, Miss Quinn," the woman at the front desk told me, "both from a Detective Whitley. Do you need that number?"

I thanked her and said no.

"QUINN?" ELLEN KRESKY repeated in a puzzled voice. "Not *Flynn?* I thought you were that lady from the hospice, the one my brother-in-law talked to."

Now it was my turn to be confused. "Your brother-in-law?"

"Howard. My late husband's brother." Tiny stitches appeared on the ridge between her nose and eyebrows. "Why?" she asked, suddenly suspicious. "Who'd you think I meant?"

A couple of feet away, an emaciated woman leadered with tubes struggled from breath to breath. The plastic name tag on the end of the bed read, *WILCOX, Pearl.*

This was Lara's maternal grandmother.

"I'm sorry," I told Ellen Kresky, "I should've never come at a time like this. But when you seemed to recognize my name, I thought—"

She took a step toward me, her eyes narrowing. "You do look familiar. Have we met before?"

"I'm a writer," I said. "And I was a friend of your niece, Lara."

Kresky's hand flew to her mouth. Glancing over at her mother, still motionless in the bed, she gestured toward the door.

I apologized again in the hall, but Ellen Kresky cut me off. "Has there been any news?" she asked. "News about *him?*"

"No. Unfortunately not." Her face sagged into pouchy folds. The unforgiving lights tacked on another decade. "I'm sorry," I repeated.

"I just thought maybe . . ." Kresky dug into the pocket of her denim skirt and pulled out a travel-pack of tissues. "Every night I pray to God. I say, dear Lord, let somebody see him today. Please, just let him get caught, so Mom can go in peace."

I wanted to tell her about Sterling, to give her that small comfort, but all I could manage was a weak "I'm sure it'll happen someday."

A nurse passed by and stopped. "How's Mama doing tonight, Ellie?"

"Not so good, Lynette." But the woman's kindness had made her smile, and all of a sudden, I caught a glimpse of family resemblance—a tiny flicker of Lara in Ellen Kresky's blue-gray eyes, and in the sweet uptilt of her mouth. Seeing it dislodged a feeling of such profound loss, I had to choke back a sob.

"It'll happen all right," Kresky said when we were alone again. "I just hoped it would be sooner rather than later. Before he manages to get every last one of us."

"What do you mean?"

She looked both ways down the corridor. The lights had already been lowered to that level of perpetual twilight which, in hospitals, passes for nighttime. Now that the nurse was gone, there wasn't another soul in sight.

"He's out there, is all," Lara's aunt said quietly. "Nearly half my life, I've felt him, lurking behind me, like a shadow.

"My husband Ken and I were only young when it happened. Kenneth Junior had just been born. Estelle and him were Kenny's godparents, for heaven's sake. We thought we really *knew* him." Ellen let out a painful little laugh, her eyes no longer looking at me, but at a print hanging on the wall opposite us—a watercolor of a boy gathering seashells on a beach.

"After the murders, Ken had all the locks changed and"—she paused— "I never told anyone this . . . but from that day on, he never once fell asleep with the lights off. Poor man was ashamed to let me know at first. After I went up to bed, he'd just stay downstairs with the TV going and the lights glaring. It took me a while to figure. Finally I said, 'Come on up, Ken, I got the reading lamp on.' And that's how we kept it until the day he died."

"I'm sorry," I murmured, not knowing what else to say.

"Ken had a heart attack last year." Ellen seemed compelled to go on. "Just went out to mow the lawn. An hour later, I found him, his face all"—she clenched her fists—"constricted—as if the fear had hardened it like a mask. I can't say for sure what the last thing he saw was, but I know for certain what he *thought* he saw. It was Gordon Spangler who killed my husband, sure as I'm standing here."

With a sinking feeling I recalled what Hogan had said: Ellen and Pearl were Lara's only surviving relatives. "And your son?" I asked gently.

"Kenny died in a hit-and-run." Ellen stared at the picture. "Five and a half years after the murders." She stuffed the tissues back into her pocket. "Well, I better go check on Ma." I watched her shuffle down the corridor. For a long while, I just stood there in front of the picture of the boy on the beach, trying to process Ellen Kresky's words. Then I walked slowly back toward her mother's room.

Ellen was sitting on the edge of the high hospital bed, holding Pearl's wasted hand. " 'Yea, though I walk through the valley of the shadow of death, I will fear no evil,' " she recited fervently, " 'for thou are with me'—"

Mrs. Wilcox began to thrash around in a state of severe agitation, yanking on the tubes protruding from her thin arms and nostrils, flapping her jaws in a pitiful attempt to speak. "Sppaa," she cried, eyes wide open in terror, "Nnnnsppaa . . ."

In that moment, I understood. I understood the living terror of Pearl Wilcox, of Ken and Ellen Kresky, old Chief McGlynn in Spring Lake, and all those others who'd known Gordon Spangler and died afraid. As long as he remained out there, they'd be haunted by him.

"It's okay, Ma, go to sleep," Ellen comforted the woman. "You're safe, Mom. No one'll hurt you. I'm here . . ."

ALTHOUGH IT WAS after nine, a shimmer still clung to the air, rendering the darkness fickle and impermanent, as though night were unsure of coming or going. I headed for the visitors' parking lot, walking quickly, keys in hand, aware of the lonely sound my heels made against the macadam, and the way the ebony void sidled up to the mercury vapor lamps. Most of the cars that had been parked here a couple of hours ago were now gone. My Volvo waited forlornly at the end of a row of empty spaces.

An image of Mrs. Wilcox—gaunt and wild-eyed—sprang to mind. She was trying to tell something to her daughter. *Sppaa.* What did that mean? I glanced under the car and checked the backseat. By the time I slid behind the wheel, I was feeling sheepish and ashamed of myself.

It occured to me that I had no clue where I was headed. I could make it home in just a few hours. It would be heaven, I thought, to sleep in my own bed.

Sppaa . . .

I kept hearing the old woman's cry, over and over again, like the melody of some annoying jingle that somehow gets stuck in your head. I rolled down the window and put the radio on, hoping that the cool air and loud music would clear out the cobwebs, and stop me from thinking too much.

When I came to the fork in the road, I took the highway that led back to Virginia.

I STOPPED AT a rest area for a greasy hamburger and coffee, then bought a half-pound bag of M&M's to keep me occupied for the rest of the drive. By the time I reached Charlottesville I felt logy and sick to my stomach.

Booths had been set up all over the atrium of the hotel. A pasteboard sign announced "The Fifth Annual Downtown Job Fair" starting tomorrow morning at nine. Two stubble-headed Marines were helping to hang a banner for a pert little blonde from a fried chicken franchise.

"You have a message," the man at the reservation desk told me, "from Detective Leedon—"

"—Whitley," I finished for him. "I picked that up this afternoon."

"This one came in at eight-thirty P.M., ma'am."

Three calls in one day. For the first time it occurred to me that maybe Whitley had something on his mind besides asking me out to dinner. I took the message slip and the keys, and wove around the empty career opportunity booths (*"There's a SPOT for YOU at FLAIR CLEANERS!"*) toward the elevator.

My room was hot and smelled like old polyester. I put the air conditioner on low, took a shower, and fell into bed without spending the requisite half hour with the blow-dryer. Tomorrow I wouldn't be able to get a comb through my most prominent feature—my awful, wonderful hair. This man I loved, Dane Blackmoor, said it could make me look like snarling Medusa or a pre-Raphaelite Ophelia, depending on my level of crankiness on any given day.

When I was under stress, I often had nightmares about cutting my hair off, but I didn't this night. Instead I dreamt of running through the woods of Cheswick Forest. The soles of my saddle shoes weren't giving me enough traction, and I kept sliding, muddying my uniform. It seemed logical, the way things often do in dreams, that I should be fourteen again, and in Virginia, not my hometown of Spring Lake.

Suddenly, I found myself in a circular clearing, ringed by broccoli-spear trees. Lara Spangler was there, sitting crosslegged. In front of her were six black candles. I saw the cut on her index finger when she waved.

"Got a light?" she called.

"No," I said.

Lara smiled. "You could ask my father."

The trees melted, revealing a golf course. TJ and some man with a blurry face (Gordon Spangler?) stood on the green, talking to a pert little blonde. In lieu of golf bags, they were carrying Austrian pistols.

Fear turned on, blinding and quick; it was like screwing in a hundred-watt bulb with the switch already up.

"Ask him," Lara urged. The fear was a part of the dream now—a palpable, lurking presence.

"I can't," I cried, backing away.

"Yes, you can," Lara tried to tell me, "you're Garner Quinn. A perfect number three"—only the words got lost after her lips shaped them until all that was left was a shuddering sound. *Spppaa . . . spppaa . . .*

I forced myself to come awake.

The numbers of the clock read five-ten. Long experience with nightmares had taught me there was no use trying to go back to sleep. My usual remedy was to get out of bed and start writing. But I wasn't a writer anymore; I had to find another way to conquer my fears.

13

IT TOOK SEVEN rings before someone picked up the phone. "What?" Sands McColl croaked.

"Did I wake you?"

"Hope so." She cleared her throat. "Otherwise I'm talking in my sleep."

"This is Garner Quinn." When she didn't respond, I added, "I spoke with you at TJ Sterling's funeral."

"Oh, right." Sands sounded as if she were slowly waking. "You're the one with the hair."

I didn't tell her that, in my mind, she was the one *without* the hair. "I was wondering if you were free today for lunch."

I heard her yawn. "What's today?"

"Monday."

"Doesn't ring a bell. Which is good, considering this hangover."

"It's eleven now," I said, anticipating her next question. "Pick a time and place."

"How about around two-ish, in the Corner? There's a place on Elliewood called the Biltmore Grill." I told her I'd find it.

Upon hanging up, I immediately dialed Andy's. Temple was on her way to a fitting for the wedding, but she promised to call back tonight. Or tomorrow. *Gotta jet. Love you.*

Undaunted, I tried another number. I was in one of those moods; I wanted to talk to someone. Detective Whitley wasn't in yet, the young woman who answered the line told me. Would I care to leave a message? I said no, I'd call back later.

THE BILTMORE GRILL boasted a large outdoor patio, complete with paddle fans and a trellised ceiling climbing with wisteria. A waitress wearing a polo shirt and khaki shorts led me to a table for two. I took a seat on the bench against the wall so I could face the entrance. At the next table, three nice-looking young men in their early twenties were swapping ideas for the ideal *Politically Incorrect* panel lineup.

"Elizabeth Dole, Pamela Sue Anderson," one suggested, "um, that crippled guy—whatsisface, the nuclear physicist?"

"Stephen Hawking?"

"Right. Lizzie, Pam, Steve Hawking, and Howard Stern."

"How about LaToya Jackson, Tammy Faye Bakker, Martha Stewart, and O.J. Simpson?"

The boy sitting closest to me cracked up. "Outstanding! It could be a theme show, you know—women you'd like to see get wrastled around . . ." He glanced in my direction as though hoping I might chime in with an opinion. I kept my lip buttoned, pulled out an area map, and spread it out on the table.

What little I knew of Sands McColl indicated that "two-ish" might signify a small, elastic eternity. Might as well familiarize myself with the layout of the university, I told myself. A few locations caught my eye right away—the Rotunda; the Lawn; Wilson Hall, which housed the

English department—places TJ Sterling would've regularly frequented. I circled each of them with a red marker.

If TJ had spotted Gordon Spangler somewhere on campus, I knew the odds of my being able to track him down were poor to nil. According to the chatty information on the back of my map, some eighteen thousand students attended UVA. But the spring semester had ended weeks ago. By mid-June, the place was a comparative ghost town, pared down to its summer bones.

This hip, young environment seemed all wrong to me, anyway. Spangler had eluded capture because he possessed the ability to blend into the background; but a man in his sixties, no matter how drab and unremarkable, would stick out like a sore thumb in a sea of fresh-faced undergraduates. Unless . . .

Unless he had hidden himself among the ranks of those who toiled in menial positions, workers rarely noted, even when seen: custodians, clerks, cooks and dishwashers, the faceless crews mowing the lawn and tending flowers. I looked down at the map. There were too many administrative and maintenance buildings to count.

"Don't worry. When I first came here, it took me forever to get my bearings." Sands McColl plopped down in the empty chair. "But once you do, it's a cinch." She was wearing a clingy little sweater that stopped just above her midriff, a tulip-shaped print skirt, backless muslin shoes with three-inch platform heels, pearls, and two nose rings. She was, as I'd remembered, still virtually bald.

Plunging right in, I asked, "You're not originally from Charlottesville?"

"Me? Jeez, no. I hail from way out in the sticks. My parents were native New Yorkers, kind of recycled hippies who moved up to Maine, you know, to raise pigs and kids? One pig and four kids, as it turned out. My brother, Sky. My sisters, Autumn and Three. And me. The pig and I were the only ones who didn't legally change our names. Sky switched his to Michael. Three is now Emily. And Autumn is Tara—which, to me, is like, hey, why even bother?"

The boys at the next table swapped glances, visibly torn between lusting and laughing at the girl. Sands turned to them with a demure smile. If they were finished with it, she asked, might we have the rest of their bread? They passed her the straw basket, watching as she dipped her finger into the little white ceramic pot and sucked butter off it. "Garner," she said, "is kind of unusual, too. Where'd you get that from?"

"It was my grandmother's."

"Very nice. I'm always collecting names for characters." Sands peeled the crust off a piece of bread and ate the middle. "For when I write the great American novel."

"You plan to be a novelist?"

"A novelist, a poet, a screenwriter maybe." She cocked her shaved head, thoughtfully. "I just plan to be *somebody.*"

The waitress asked if we were ready. I ordered a burger. Sands studied the menu, finally deciding on the shrimp crostini and a glass of wine. "How come you didn't tell me you were famous?" she asked when we were alone.

The question caught me off guard. "I guess it didn't come up."

"I knew you looked familiar," she said, "like maybe you were an actress, or one of those models from the early eighties who took up wildlife photography or something. But then a friend of mine said you wrote that Tom Cruise movie—"

"The book," I corrected her. "I write true crime."

"And that's how you knew TJ?"

"Yes."

"He was great, wasn't he?" Tears welled up in Sands's eyes. "Excuse me," she said to the boys at the next table, "could I borrow that extra napkin? Thanks." She turned back to me. "Oh, God, my mascara's running. I look like a raccoon, don't I?"

"No," I said. As far as I knew, raccoons didn't wear nose rings.

Sands waved both hands helplessly in the air. "I just can't believe he did it."

"Had he been depressed?"

"Uh-uh," she sniffed, dabbing her cheeks. "Not that I could see."

"You didn't notice anything different about his behavior at all?"

She thought a moment. "Tee'j was such an upbeat kind of guy. Always jazzed about one thing or another. Especially when it came to his writing. But there was this sadness in his eyes . . . and, of course, his drinking was *way* over the top. I think that's what made him so attractive. Like you just knew he needed someone to save him."

"And that was you?" I kept my tone casual.

"Nah." Sands busied herself pleating the borrowed napkin. "At least not in the grand operatic sense. What I did was more the mundane, day-to-day type of saving—a little research, lots of typing, running errands."

The waitress came with our food. I bit into my burger. "What was TJ working on before he died?"

Sands's soft brown eyes hardened suddenly. "Why do you want to know?"

"The last time I saw him, he seemed really excited about some new project."

"And what?" With her arms folded across her chest, the girl looked positively formidable. "You thought, like, maybe you could *finish* it for him?"

"Of course not. I just was curious—"

"Because TJ was real-real protective of his stuff," she said.

"Well, you don't have to worry about me," I replied jovially. "I'm out of the book business." The good-looking guys were getting ready to leave. McColl smiled up at them. I was losing her. "Listen, Sands." I leaned forward, with urgency. "What if I said I don't think TJ killed himself?"

"But the police—"

"Sometimes they're wrong."

"Oh, wow," she gasped. "You mean like a *cover-up?*" This girl had obviously seen one too many Oliver Stone flicks.

"Well, no, not necessarily." I took a shot. "Does the name Gordon Spangler mean anything to you?"

"Uh-uh." Sands wrinkled her nose, then sat up straight in her seat. "Why? Is he the one who—"

"I don't know. I'm only suggesting that there's a chance—a *slight* chance—that TJ's death might somehow be connected to the last book he was writing. I tried to find the manuscript in his office but—"

"Back up a minute." Sands held up a hand. "You went to TJ's office?"

"Yes. With his wife, the day after the funeral."

"*Caroline* took you?" All at once, the tension drained from her face. She started to laugh. "Oh, you mean—you're talking about the *slave* quarters? That place out in back of their house?" I nodded. "That wasn't really his office."

Sands searched my face as though trying to come to a decision. "See, TJ said it was a drag, working at home. Caroline meant well, but she always expected things to look a certain way, *be* a certain way, you know, so"—she took a deep breath—"he leased another space in town."

Excitement, like a tiny winged bird, flapped against my chest, then nested deep in my bowels. Instinctively I knew that this was it—the moment it would all turn around; the place where my initial leap of faith would land. "TJ had an office Caroline never knew about?"

Sands twisted her pearl necklace and smiled sheepishly.

"And you didn't tell the police?"

"I would've," she became defensive, "if they'd said anything about murder. But this Detective Wheatley I talked to—"

"Whitley."

"The one who looks like Denzel Washington? He told me TJ committed suicide."

"You withheld evidence, Sands."

"Maybe." Defiance flickered in her brown eyes. "But I kept putting myself in Caroline's place. I mean, wouldn't it be bad enough, finding your husband shot in the head like that, without having to deal with this whole secret life he had going behind your back? It just seemed way harsh to me."

After a moment of silence, McColl sighed. "Are you going to tell her?"

"I'm not sure yet."

This seemed to satisfy the girl. She said, "I suppose you'd like to see the place."

1 4

SANDS DIRECTED ME to a two-story building on a quiet, tree-lined street only a few blocks from the university. "You can pull in the drive," she said. "The upstairs tenants won't be back until next semester." I parked the car and got out to take a closer look at what had once been TJ Sterling's secret hideaway.

It resembled a free-standing condominium unit, with the sort of clean, minimalist lines that would attract students fleeing from the frantic jumble of dormitory life. "This way." Sands pointed toward the rear of the property. "TJ had the whole ground floor."

A tall, unpainted fence blocked the yard off from the driveway. McColl reached over the gate and unfastened the latch. "The key's in the Weber grill," she said, lifting the round metal cover to show me.

"TJ didn't carry one?"

"Said he couldn't chance it. Caroline kept pretty close tabs on his things." I thought of J. Emmett Hogan's wife, poring over the monthly invoices.

"Who else had a key?"

"Just Tee'j and me. Oh pooh, this heat's got the wood all swollen." She twisted the lock on the sliding door. "Um, and the landlady. But she's on vacation in Europe this summer."

"Where's yours?"

"At home." Sands met my eyes with a serene smile. "I wasn't exactly expecting to come here today." She yanked the handle, sliding the door open on its tracks. "After you."

I stepped inside, blinking in the sudden darkness.

"The switch is back here somewhere." I heard Sands poking about under the heavy drapes. "Got it."

The room jolted into artificial brightness. "Yes," I said, almost to myself.

I knew I'd come to the right place. The furniture was one part Salvation Army, two parts Ikea. A varicolored rag rug served as a mat near the doors, and burgundy velour drapes hung from wooden rods over the sliders. Otherwise, everything else was either black or beige. The leather sectional had been unlinked, smaller pieces scattered around a main hull like flotation devices that could be used as lifeboats. Track lighting ran in strips overhead. Sterling's hardcover first editions lined the shelves of a trellis bookcase. More books spilled out of stackable plastic crates and cardboard boxes. I even spotted a couple of mine.

"It's sweltering in here." Sands crossed into the narrow front hall. "I'll turn on the air." Instead of following her, I did a slow pass around the room, running my fingers over the shelf tops and the backs of chairs, as though they might have secrets written on them, in invisible ink, or braille.

Against a back wall, an assemble-it-yourself storage unit looked like some weird postmodern sculpture. Featured prominently were a few chilling items from the writer's private weapon collection—a Colt detective special mounted in a shadow box, next to the cover art from a sleazy true crime . . . an ornate machete with a carved handle . . . some rope, of the kind Ed Finch had used to strangle his victims. Behind these, two Schwinn bicycle frames, *sans* tires, hung from grappling hooks. A pair of fox stoles had been draped over the handlebars, their sleek, delicate paws dangling like ornamental tassels. I noted that Sterling had customized his dartboard with a photo of John Grisham. There was also a dressmaker's dummy in a Wonderbra, and two black lawn jockeys holding hockey sticks.

How loaded was TJ, I wondered, *when he arranged this little sideshow? Or was it the work of his gal Friday, with the tasteful pearls and the rings in her nose?* I continued my informal search of the room. In the corner a metal card table held an old Olivetti typewriter and a portable radio. TJ's desk was a wood-veneer-on-metal affair, the kind that reverberated like a drum when you opened the drawers. Yellow Post-its carrying elliptic notes were stuck everywhere— *S: COFFEE & p. towels . . . p/u dry-cleaning . . . A.R.—b of c?*

I stepped over a loosely spiraled mile of telephone cord to get a closer look, feeling strangely saddened by the smudged glass tumbler with its shriveled lemon twist, and the framed photograph of four pale, blond little girls decked out in Christmas finery. The chair was swiveled away from the desk and toward the sliding doors, as though TJ had gotten up just a moment ago, to head home. To his wife.

"The rent's paid through September," Sands said, ducking back into the room. "I thought that would give me enough time to figure out what to do with his stuff."

I started opening up drawers, disappointed when the first two proved empty. "Not that there's all that much, really. The place was partially furnished when he got it." A nervous edge crept into the girl's voice. "Still, by rights, everything else belongs to Caroline—though probably all she'd want would be the books, don't you think?" When I didn't answer, she went on, "I considered mailing them to her, like anonymously. Or pretending one of the secretaries found them boxed up at his old office in Wilson Hall."

The third drawer was a hodgepodge of newspaper clippings and invoices. It would take several hours to go through them properly. Without much hope, I opened the last drawer. Inside was a manuscript crisscrossed with rubber bands. "That's it," Sands said. "That's the last thing he was working on."

My knees suddenly felt weak. I sank down into TJ's chair with the manuscript on my lap. "Are you sure?"

She sat on the corner of the desk next to me. "Absolutely."

I scrolled off the elastic. The boldface print appeared to jump off the title page—

CONJUGATING DESIRE
by TJ Sterling

What kind of title was that? I wondered, and then, halfway through the opening paragraph, it hit me. "This is a novel," I said.

"It's about this guy who's failed," Sands explained, "in his career, and in his personal relationships. So he takes a job teaching at this all-girls college—"

I shook my head. "There has to be something else."

But where? I looked around the room, overwhelmed by all the cubbyholes and boxes. What I was searching for might be no bigger than a slip of paper stuck in any one of a hundred books. I tossed the manuscript on the desk.

"Sorry," Sands said, "that's the only project I know about." She frowned. "You think what you're looking for could be in the story, like maybe fictionalized?"

I had to admit it was a possibility. "Was there any mention of a man who'd killed his family?"

"No," the girl sighed. "Nothing like that."

"What about someone who changed his identity and moved to a new place?"

"Well, the protagonist *does* leave his job as a successful soap opera writer to teach English down south," she offered, trying to be helpful.

I gave the metal desk a swift kick. The drawer rumbled like thunder. And then the slim leather pocket organizer—the same one TJ had been carrying at our dinner together—slid into view.

"I suppose there could've been another book," Sands was saying. "It's not like I was privy to his inner thoughts. In fact, the only reason he let me work on *Desire* was because I sort of gave him the idea for the story—or if not the idea, at least, I brought it to his attention, you know, that the situation would make a really good—" I'd already started to leaf through the pages of the calendar. "Oh, you found TJ's little black book." McColl grinned. "He kept it here, on account of Caroline."

"I can't understand his writing."

"Yeah, really," Sands said. "Tom used all these code names, like he was a spy or something."

I flipped backward. The last entry appeared to be for Friday, June 11th. The day before Sterling died. I read the cryptic notation: *Luth. C of F—3 PM.* Sands continued talking, something about the bills that would be coming in, and did I think she should call the phone company to have his service disconnected?

"The more I get into this," she fretted, "the more complicated it seems. I almost wish I'd been up front with Caroline from the beginning."

I thought of Sterling's young widow—alone, frightened, and pregnant. "It's not your fault," I assured the girl. "TJ was the one who should've been up front with her."

"I guess he kinda left me holding the bag." Sands's eyes turned shrewd, the way they had at the restaurant when the subject of TJ's latest project first came up. "Like for instance, with the novel—Tommy always said how he wanted us to collaborate on a screenplay version. I even have a couple of letters where he mentioned it, you know, in writing. What do you think'll happen with that now?"

"I don't know," I said. "You'll have to take it up with the family."

"Oh," Sands sighed as if the thought didn't please her; but in the next second, she was back to her old self. "Hey, wanna see the rest of the apartment?"

"Sure. Lead on, McColl." I waited until she'd turned her back before slipping TJ's datebook into my shoulder bag.

15

SANDS WAS SUBLETTING a fifth-floor walk-up on Jefferson Park Avenue. I waited in the car while she ran inside to get Sterling's key.

As much as I'd been disarmed by her ardent willingness to cooperate, the minute the young woman was gone, I began to have doubts. Had she really kept TJ's secret out of concern for Caroline's feelings? Or did Sands McColl have a darker reason for staying silent?

By her own account, Sterling's death had left her "between jobs." At Edenfield she'd also mentioned that she was "between apartments." Living rent-free for a few months would certainly relieve any financial pressure the girl might be feeling—not to mention that TJ's hideaway came equipped with a wide-screen TV, stereo system, and a microwave—features not found in too many fifth-floor walk-ups—luxury items which, in a pinch, could be sold for a quick buck.

And then there was Sterling's manuscript. From the handwritten cross-outs and margin notes, I could tell it was an early draft. *An early draft of a novel by an author known only for nonfiction, who just happened to be dead. A work that the writer's widow didn't even know existed.* What might that mean in the hands of an ambitious young woman whose main ambition in life is to be somebody? A person who claims to have letters from the dead writer substantiating a collaborative relationship? A girl with a little flair, and a lot of what my agent Max would call *chutzpah?*

I watched Sands McColl running down the front walk toward the car. She'd ditched her muslin platforms, and now had bare feet to go with her bare tummy and bald head. It would take a lot of brass to chop off all your hair, I decided.

"Sorry," she apologized, leaning in through the passenger window to hand me the key. "The stupid phone rang—" Her brown eyes turned serious. "Have you made up your mind whether or not you're going to tell Caroline about the apartment?"

"I'll notify the police first." I started the engine. "They can take it from there."

"Am I going to get into trouble over this?" she asked in a small voice.

I don't know yet, I thought.

I slouched down in the seat and shrugged. "Not from what you've told me so far." Glancing sideways, I double-checked to make sure my shoulder bag was where I'd left it, on the passenger-side floor mat. I could see the rectangular outline of TJ's journal against the leather. "I'll be in touch." I waved.

A worried Sands McColl waved back as I pulled away from the curb.

16

THE ALBEMARLE COUNTY offices were located in one of the new red brick colonials that had been built to blend with the old red brick colonials so plentiful in this part of Virginia. I sat in the parking lot with the windows rolled down and the air-conditioner going, poring over TJ's little black book.

Sterling's entry for May 20th made my stomach take a nosedive—*GQ—Fromag. (X 109 to Rumson Rd.) 8PM.*

I remembered TJ's face under the white lights of the parking lot, the tremulous lilt in his voice when he called seeing Spangler a gift from God, a second chance to set things right. *It's changed my life,* he'd said. And now that life was over.

I found the postscript next to my name to be equally disturbing. *ALL SYSTEMS GO,* Sterling had written, using cheerful upper-case letters.

Other entries proved more difficult to decipher. In his own haphazard, secretive fashion, TJ had peppered the journal with abbreviations and a veritable alphabet soup of initials. Telephone numbers appeared next to code names like Gidget, Little Ms. Muffet, Shaft, and the Big

Cheez. He also kept a running tally of what I assumed to be business expenses. *"LMM —+ $4000"* appeared on the first and third Thursdays of each month.

Several notations appeared to be for places—*Shangri-La . . . B. Bird . . . Brasil . . . Larkspur . . .* These were sometimes circled, underlined, or set off in wavy boxes. I reminded myself to pick up an area entertainment guide so I could mix and match the local bars and restaurants against Sterling's creative shorthand.

The reference to *Luth. C of F* which appeared in his final entry turned up again in both April and May. What it meant, however, didn't become clear until I back-paged to the end of March. There, on the 28th of the month, TJ had underlined the words *Lutheran Circle of Faith*. A tingle of excitement ran down my spine.

Gordon Spangler had been raised a Lutheran. J. Emmett Hogan's prediction rang through my head—"Whatever he's doing," he'd said, "we believe he'd be actively associated with a church."

I tucked the small leather journal into my bag. Outside, a fluffy continent of clouds lumbered by, temporarily blocking the sun. I rolled up the windows, got out of the car, and locked the doors. It didn't seem wise to stay out here by myself any longer.

AN ATTRACTIVE YOUNG black woman in uniform sat behind a Plexiglas window in the lobby. I asked to see Detective Whitley. She put down her pen and scrutinized me, as if the nature of my request merited special consideration.

"You have an appointment?"

"No. Could you just tell him Garner Quinn's here?"

She ran a hand through her henna-red hair and punched a button on the phone. "A Garver Quint is here to see you." I would've set her straight, but apparently Whitley already had. "I only repeat the way I'm told," Officer Red-henna muttered, disconnecting him.

"You can go on back," she announced with a put-upon sigh. I wondered if she hated Whitley, or whether they were lovers. From what I knew of the detective, I wouldn't have been surprised, either way.

I found him sitting at a desk, a few feet from his partner, the laconic Bill Tyree. They were both on the phone, although I had a strong feeling that Leedon might've dialed up the weather service, just to make me wait.

"Uh-huh." With the receiver crooked on his shoulder, he pointed to a chair. "Yeah. That's cool." I sat down. Crossed my legs and smoothed the folds of my dress. Felt Tyree's stare from across the aisle, and followed it up my thigh.

In my line of work, there's a maxim: *visibility equals vulnerability.* One of the cardinal rules—never wear a skirt to a prison, a police precinct, or any predominantly male habitat. It seemed swearing off true crime had made me sloppy. I reminded myself that, if there was even a slight chance of encountering Gordon Spangler, I'd have to stay sharp and focused. Or I might end up like TJ.

"Um-hm," Whitley said into the phone. I uncrossed my legs, plopped my bag on my lap, and stared brazenly at Tyree.

"Later, man." Whitley slammed down the receiver.

"So, is it going to rain?" I asked.

"Say what?"

"Forget it."

I raised my voice enough so that the other detectives could hear. "Did you know that TJ Sterling kept an office in town?"

The movie-star smile vanished from Whitley's face. His eyes shifted to Tyree, and then back to me. "Let's get a cup of coffee," he said.

"I'm not thirsty."

"I am." He took hold of my arm, guiding me past the water coolers and down a hallway, stopping at the door of an empty interview room.

"Have a seat," he said, "I'll be right back." Again I had the sense that this was a guy who got off on exerting even the smallest measure of control.

Well, knock yourself out, Leedon, I thought wryly.

Moments later Whitley reappeared carrying two plastic foam containers of coffee. Hooking the door shut with his foot, he straddled a chair and slid a cup over to me.

"Did you know," I repeated, "that Sterling had an office in town?"

"Yes," he replied. "I did."

My mouth dropped open. "But how—?"

"*How* did I find out?" Leedon rounded his words with grand, elocutionary style. "Or *how* was it I didn't tell you?"

"How come," I said through gritted teeth, "you didn't put it in your report?"

"It wasn't pertinent." The detective blew into his cup. "See, the thing you need to remember is that even with all the development going on these last few years, this is essentially still a small town."

"Are you suggesting it was common knowledge in Charlottesville that Sterling had a downtown pied-à-terre?"

"A peed on what?" he needled me. "Oh, you mean the love shack?"

"Yeah," I said. "Right."

"Sure, people knew. That's what got him fired. Some of the stuffier members of the faculty took exception to Professor Sterling's manner of private tutoring. What's the matter, does that shock you, Miss Quinn? I bet it just irks you to pieces when you're not the first to find something out."

I rose, haughtily. "I've been sitting in the parking lot for the past half hour trying to decide who I should talk to first, you or Caroline. Apparently, I made the wrong call."

"Whoa." The detective stumbled to his feet. "Chill a minute—" But I was already on my way out of there.

"Wait." He grabbed my arm. "I was there, okay—does that make you happy? I knew about Sterling's place from the start." When he saw he had my attention, Whitley lowered his voice. "Now shut the door and come back inside, Garner. Please."

With a testy little sigh, I sat. "Wasn't any fancy police work involved," Whitley said. "Like I told you, your man Sterling was a lush, pure and simple. He'd teach his classes, then mosey over to one of the local drinking establishments where he'd hold court until closing time. Getting the pink slip didn't change things much. It just gave him an opportunity to start boozing earlier, so by last call he'd be real piss face, fall-in-the-gutter inebriated."

"Did he cause any trouble?"

"The local cops more or less gave him the kid-glove treatment." He shrugged. "Sterling was considered a celebrity of sorts. Plus, his father-in-law has a lot of pull in local politics. It was definitely a case of big fish, little pond."

In a small pond, a larger-than-life man like TJ Sterling would be bound to whip up a few waves. But what about someone nondescript and ordinary— *'a mild-mannered Mister Peepers'*? Would such an unobtrusive presence cause even the slightest ripple in this town? I wondered.

Whitley took a sip of coffee. "Anyway, one night this past May, I happened to be walking into a bar downtown, just as Sterling comes stumbling out. Now I could see the man was in no condition to drive, so I said, hey, Mr. Sterling, can I buy you a cup of coffee? No, he says, but I surely would appreciate a ride home. And I'm thinking, *shi-iit,* now I'm gonna hafta hustle my black ass way the hell out to horse country."

He shook his head, with a bitter laugh. "Only Sterling tells me he's gonna stay at this place he's got here in town. So, fine. We get in my car, and I'm driving him, and the whole way he's taking hits out of a pocket flask. By the time we get there, I'm his best friend—yep, me and ole Tee'j, we tight."

"Did he know you were a cop?"

"No, that came somewhat later, after he showed off the bachelor pad and his various awards." Whitley leaned across the table. "How many framed eight-by-tens you got in your house? Garner Quinn shaking hands with a lotta famous celebrities?"

"I don't like having my picture taken."

The detective's eyes glittered. "No kidding? Well, your pal TJ had *his* snapped with just about everybody. Lou Holtz. Ted Kennedy. Frank Serpico, even. Oh, and lest I forget, the late Arthur Ashe. He was especially pleased to show me that one, seeing how I *am* black and all."

"It must've been a real memorable night for you," I commented dryly. "Then what happened?"

"Well, he signed a couple of books—'*To Detective Leedon Whitley*.' Yeah, that put a spring in his step all right. We should talk, he says. Then I told him about this idea I had, this cop story, and he said, yeah, he'd like to hear it sometime . . ."

Something in the detective's voice—a sudden, youthful earnestness—made me glance up. "Never did get round to it, though," he said, avoiding my eyes. "Next time I saw him he was doing the dead man's float in a pool of puke, the wife's hysterical, and her daddy's throwing his weight around all over the place."

"Did Childress know about the apartment?"

"He said no when I took him aside and told him. But it's hard to tell." Whitley grinned. "Blue-blooded WASPs like him don't go around wearing their emotions on their sleeves. He did ask if we could keep the information from his daughter, though."

"What did you tell him?"

"I said as long as it didn't turn out to be a criminal matter, we'd try our best to be discreet." He added, "And it wasn't, so we were."

A middle-aged detective with jowls like the Cowardly Lion poked his head into the room. "Your mama's on the phone, Denzel," he told Whitley, with a wicked cackle.

"You sure it's *my* mama, Haney?" Leedon called after him, " 'cause after last night, I sure was expectin' a call from yours—"

When the cackling faded, Whitley asked if I might excuse him for a minute. I said yes, grateful to be left in this drab and comfortless room— alone, with my thoughts.

I'D BEEN ON the verge of spilling the whole story—I swear—the very verge. Common sense dictated it. The situation had obviously escalated past the point where I could handle all the angles. But, then, from the arrogant core of my being came a whisper: *nobody handles angles better than you . . .*

I reminded myself that I was no longer a true-crime writer. That my ego mustn't stand in the way of tracking Spangler down in the most expeditious manner possible. And, apart from my old FBI friend, Hogan, Leedon Whitley seemed to be my best bet. He was smart. He knew the area. What's more, I had a feeling he could be counted on in a crunch.

I'd wanted to tell him. I'd planned to tell him. Yet something had stopped me. Sitting in the empty interview room, I replayed our conversation through my head. At what point had the warning bell gone off? Was it when he admitted he'd known about TJ's hideaway all along? Or was it when he spoke of actually being there, only weeks before Sterling turned up dead?

No. Those things might have set off a distant pealing, but the clanging hadn't started in earnest until the detective's face turned all wishy-hopey, talking about the idea he had for a cop story. It was my second encounter with veiled ambition in one day, and along with it had come the unsettling feeling that there might be more to TJ's death than I'd ever imagined.

"Sorry about that." Whitley breezed through the door.

"No problem. Just one more thing," I said, already adjusting the straps of my shoulder bag. "A friend of Sterling's took me through the apartment earlier—"

"Does this friend happen to have a shaved head and a coupla nose rings?" Before I could respond, Whitley said, "Don't worry. We know all about Sands McColl."

"I'm more concerned about what's going to happen to TJ's personal belongings. He had a few valuable books there, not to mention the first draft of a new novel."

"Childress is supposed to work that out with the landlady once she gets back from vacation."

I summoned a pensive look to my face, trusting that Whitley would pick up on it. He did. "What?"

"Nothing," I sighed. "It's just that Sands didn't seem to know how many keys were floating around. I couldn't help thinking, in that situation, I'd want to make sure all Sterling's stuff was protected. You never know—something falls into the wrong hands, it might prove embarrassing later on."

It was obvious that Whitley hadn't considered this. "I'll speak to Childress. Tell him to have the locks changed."

"Or you could mention you'd been talking to me," I suggested, "and that I offered to stay on a few more days, you know, to help sift through

TJ's papers and put aside the stuff that could be hurtful to Caroline and the family."

Whitley stared. I worried I'd pushed this too far. Then he broke into one of his dazzling smiles, "And if I mention such a thing to Mr.C, does it mean you might not turn down my next invitation to dinner?"

"You never know," I said, flashing a dazzler right back at him.

17

DURING THE TIME I'd been inside, a small gray army of clouds had infiltrated the sky, turncoating the air until it was thick and muggy. This sudden rise in humidity, combined with the events of the day, left me feeling like a limp dishrag. Figuring there was nothing else I could do for now, I went back to the hotel, ordered room service, and settled in to wait. It wasn't until after eight o'clock that I remembered to check my answering machine at home.

Temple had left me a message earlier that afternoon.

"We have to go to a fund-raiser for Candace's hospital tonight," she said. "So unless you get this like right away, I probably won't get a chance to talk to you until tomorrow . . ." Pause. The sound of a sigh. "Are you still in Virginia? Or are you back home, and just out?"

Another pause. "Well, call me soon, okay?—I miss you." She perked up enough to say, "Love you, Mom," but I heard an emotional ripple-and-crack in her voice. "Take care of yourself, okay?"

Soft, shuffling noises. A little click.

The first thought that ran through my head was, *See, Andy? Na-na-*

na-na-na—she still loves me best! But a second after my heart swelled, it shattered into pieces. My daughter needed me, and I was off chasing shadows again. It seemed the more I tried to change things, the more they stayed the same.

After a series of hang-ups, J. Emmett Hogan's voice snapped me out of self-pity. "I'm here in Disneyworld, Quinn—where the hell are you?" *Tap. Tap. Tap.* "Pick up, Garner, if you're there." *Tap. Tap. Tap.* "I swear to God, if you're off playing lady bounty hunter—" He throttled the mouthpiece with an exhaled breath.

"We're at the Yacht Club. So call me." Hogan repeated, "Call me or I'll hunt you down. I mean it, Garner. Remember what they say—" and, with that spontaneous wackiness I found so loveable, he began singing in a low, whispery voice, *"It's a small world after all . . ."*

Then he hung up.

THE NEXT MORNING, I slept through the alarm. It was almost nine when I finally stumbled out of bed. Drawing aside the drapes, I was dismayed to see rain-gutted roofs and a sky blanketed in twisty sheets of drizzle.

I took a long, hot shower, donned a white shirt and khakis—neutral, and yet very Charlottesville—and bunched my hair into a fat braid. In the lobby I stopped to pick up a guidebook before pushing through the doors that led to the downtown mall.

The shops were already beginning to open. I walked through the gentle rain, keeping an eye out for a place to have breakfast—somewhere with a private table, in a quiet corner, so I could dawdle over coffee, while comparing the notes in TJ's journal with the listing of bars and restaurants.

.   .   .

IT HAD SOUNDED like a good plan, but the task of slogging through hundreds of Charlottesville hotspots and matching them up with the numbers in Sterling's black book alternately daunted and bored me. Yet, however far my attention wandered, it always seemed to end up in the same place—at the entries where TJ had scrawled "Luth. C of F."

Lutheran Circle of Faith.

Feeling suddenly too wired to eat, I paid for my coffee and left. The drizzle felt like a warm, wet kiss on my face. I wandered through a few stores on the mall, hoping to find some quirky little souvenir for Temple, but I just couldn't rouse myself out of my preoccupied funk. Then a shop window filled with toys and novelties caught my eye. The sign over the door said TRIVIAL PURSUITS.

I poked my head inside, peering past a kiosk bursting with fanciful puppets—velvet peapods and silk butterflies, whales, bats, and aliens. A heavyset woman stood within a peninsula of glass display cases reading the morning paper. She had long, straight, graying hair and wore an Indian print tunic over flowing palazzo pants. When I came closer I saw that one of her elaborately mismatched earrings featured a dangling array of little penises.

"Excuse me," I said. "Do you carry board games?"

"Back wall," she replied, licking her finger to turn a page.

I persisted, "I'm particularly interested in World War II strata-gems—"

Disapproval and disinterest appeared equally distributed on the woman's face. "Back wall," she repeated.

I wandered over to the shelves of alphabetized games and counted up to sixty before approaching the woman again. This time she didn't even look up. "Excuse me again. Would you happen to know of any groups or clubs that meet locally to play these sorts of games?"

"No."

"How about regular customers who come in specifically to buy them?"

"What about them?"

"Do you put their names on a mailing list, anything like that?"

"No." The woman's eyes drifted back to her open paper. I felt like shaking her.

"What about inventory records," I said sweetly. "You must keep track of the items you sell so they can be restocked, right?"

"I don't know anything about that," she replied with an impatient sigh. "You'll have to ask the owner. I'm only here four hours three times a week."

"When will the owner be in?"

"He's at a trade show," said the woman. "Won't be back till Saturday." She tilted her head sending all the little enamel penises jangling. "Anything else I can help you with?"

INSTEAD OF RETURNING to my room, I headed toward the parking garage, and my little red Volvo. The listing in the phone book had said West Albemarle. It took less than twenty minutes to get there, following 250 past Cheswick Forest. After about three miles I spotted a small sign for the Lutheran Circle of Faith with an arrow pointing left, but the turnoff was so abrupt I missed it and had to double back.

This can't be right, I thought as I pulled through the gate. It seemed to be another private community, complete with resort condominiums, a golf course, and manicured grounds. I drove by a cluster of brand-new buildings—a medical center, a restaurant, a gift shop, a post office, a

1 8 4

general store. I kept going. The road curved next to a playground, flanked by a picturesque pond. Another arrow pointed toward the Circle of Faith.

Sterling's *Luth. C of F* turned out to be a large, barnlike structure, reminiscent of a colonial meetinghouse. Adjacent were two one-story buildings with flat roofs. I circled around the perimeter of the parking lot, wondering what possible connection there could be between TJ and this place. Sterling wasn't a religious man. Even when he'd called seeing Spangler "a gift from God," he'd sounded more like a man who'd just won the lottery than someone in the throes of a spiritual awakening. Moreover, the pastor at TJ's funeral had been an Anglican, not a Lutheran as was the minister who performed the final rites for the Spangler family.

I made another slow loop. About a dozen cars were parked in the spaces next to the meetinghouse, and a blue van with a Circle of Faith logo painted on its door stood at the curb. I craned my neck, trying to peer into the rows of windows. *Be patient,* I told myself. Today was Tuesday. Sterling had made his visits here on Wednesdays and Fridays. I might only have one chance at this. It was important that I do it right.

18

IT TOOK ME a few tries, but I finally found the exit ramp that led to the big old estate at the end of the cul-de-sac in Cheswick Forest. This time, instead of parking by the front gate, I edged the Volvo onto the narrow patch of grass near the eastern wall of the property and turned off the engine.

A sudden air pocket of fear burbled in my chest, leaving me breathless. As much as it ticked me off to admit it, I was afraid of being discovered by one of the roving neighborhood Gestapo. For all I knew, repeat offense trespassers might be bungee-corded to the back of a four-wheel-drive vehicle and dragged up and down the charming streets of Cheswick until their cheeky hides wore off.

I crept quietly up to the front lawn. There were no cars in the driveway. As before, the place appeared to be deserted. For the first time I noticed a number on the gate—79—with the almost imperceptible outline of a mail drop underneath it. Tugging on the lid, I reached inside and felt around. My fingers brushed against something slick— the back page of a Gardeners Eden catalogue, which had apparently been acci-

dently torn off. The label read: MRS ROBERT TITLE OR CUR-
RENT RESIDENT.

Before I could slip it back into the mailbox, I heard a noise. The front
door to the house swung open and a shapely young black woman in a
bright pink tee shirt and stonewashed jeans stepped onto the porch. I
tried to duck behind the bushes, but it was too late: she was looking
directly at me.

With one (relatively) smooth motion I stuffed the catalogue page into
my pants pocket and waved. "Hi."

The woman started down the steps, cupping her hand over her eyes.
"Who's there?"

"I'm Susan Flynn, the lifestyle columnist for *Albemarle Today*?" I
barrelled through the introduction in the belief that lies, like obstacle
courses, are best begun with a running start. "I have a two o'clock
meeting with the Titles, um, about the article we're doing on the house."

The young woman frowned. "I'm afraid there must be some mistake," she said, speaking with the faintest hint of a Jamaican accent. "Mr.
and Mrs. Title are not at home."

"They're not?"

"No, they've been on holiday for the past month. Won't be back until
Sunday. I'm just here to water the plants and feed the fish."

The word *fish* zapped me with the unexpected juice of an electric
shock. The Titles kept fish. So had Gordon Spangler.

"Are you sure it was two o'clock today?" the young woman asked,
opening the gate.

"Well, yes, I think—" In an inspired moment, I pulled TJ's datebook
from my bag and began leafing through it. "Omigosh, I don't believe it.
Shoot, this is soooo embarrassing." Grimacing, I clutched the open
calendar to my chest. "Our appointment was for *next* week. I feel like
such a doofus."

"Oh, well." The girl smiled. "No harm done, eh?" She reached into the mailbox and fished around. "That's strange. I thought maybe . . ." She trailed off, shaking her head.

"You know, while I'm here, maybe you can help me," I said. "See, part of my job is assigning a photographer for each feature, and I find it helps if I match them up, you know, personality-wise, to the subjects they'll be shooting. Like Mr. and Mrs. Title, for instance. Now I've only spoken with them over the phone, but I get the feeling they're, what, in their sixties?"

"Oh no, I think maybe not that old," the young woman said. "At least not her."

"What about him?"

She thought for a minute. "He might be sixty. It's hard to tell. He keeps himself nice. Very stylish, very dapper for such a small man."

"Small?"

The girl marked off the air under her chin, giggling. "I could eat soup off his head. Maybe the photo man can pose them with Mrs. Title sitting down," she suggested, "then it might not be so noticeable."

"Good idea," I said. "Well, sorry to have bothered you."

"No problem." As I walked away, she called, "What did you say your name was?"

"Oh, please"—I turned—"don't tell them I was here. They'll think I'm a scatterbrain."

The cul-de-sac had turned out to be a dead end after all. While it was possible that Gordon Spangler had altered his appearance, what he couldn't do was make himself a foot shorter. It seemed doubtful that he'd achieved the kind of financial success to land him in a place like Cheswick Forest anyway. I put the Volvo into drive and did a U-ie on the ramp, thinking about board games, big houses, and the Lutheran Circle of Faith.

·   ·   ·

BACK IN MY hotel room, I picked up the phone and dialed.

"Circle of Faith," a woman answered.

"I'm wonderin' if you could help me?" I said, taking my voice up half an octave, and feathering it with breath. "We're just new in the area? And I was hopin' you could tell me a little bit about your church."

"Well, dear, I'm afraid you've called the wrong number. Circle of Faith is a social organization. Adult education and community outreach programs, that sort of thing. We also have a nursery, and a grammar school, grades one to six on the premises. But if it's a church you're looking for," she said, "I can give you the number for Saint Luke's, in town."

"Why, thank you." I jotted it down just in case.

Impulsively, I opened TJ's datebook and punched in the number for the person he'd nicknamed the Big Cheez.

"Mr. Childress's office," sang a perky voice.

Somehow I managed to stammer, "Is this *Dr.* Childress, um, the pediatrician?"

"No, ma'am, this *Mr.* Childress, president of the Albemarle Planning and Development Corporation."

I MUST'VE FALLEN asleep watching television. The soft peal of the phone woke me. Except for the light from the screen, the room was dark. "This is a first," Leedon Whitley said. "I was beginning to think you were routing all my calls directly to the front desk."

"I slipped up this time," I croaked.

"Be nice. I did your dirty work and talked to Childress."

So how's the Big Cheez doing? I thought. "And?"

"Well, to paraphrase, he said he thought it was damn white of you, offering to clean up his son-in-law's mess for him. Offered you complete use of the apartment for however long it takes. By the way, you need a key?"

"No, I have McColl's," I said.

"Now, about the finder's fee for these plush new accommodations of yours—say dinner, Friday night?"

"I need another favor."

I heard Whitley sigh. "Why doesn't that surprise me?"

"Can you ask Madame medical examiner if it's possible that Sterling passed out *before* the bullet went through his head?"

There was a long silence on the other line. "You don't give up, do you?" Whitley muttered.

I laughed, and softly hung up the receiver.

19

THE NEXT MORNING I checked out of the hotel, threw my overnighter and suitbag into the trunk, and headed over to the late TJ Sterling's home away from home.

Yesterday's rain had scrubbed fresh the air. I drove with the windows down, trying to imagine what this sleepy street would be like in September, when the students came roaring back from vacation, invading the multiple-family dwellings and apartment buildings, lining the curbs with their Volkswagens and Jeep Wranglers, putting speakers next to open windows so they could blast music into the street. Today the road was empty and quiet, just a crescent-shaped afterthought to the main campus beat.

I pulled into the driveway, hefting my luggage toward the back fence. The latch on the wooden gate gave easily. I shut it behind me and went over to the Weber grill. Sterling's key was still there. For the moment I decided to leave it there, as a litmus test of Sands McColl's honesty. I used my own copy to unlock the sliding doors.

Once again, the darkness of the interior took me unawares.

TJ's hideaway, that was how I'd begun to think of the place. The very
fact that the entrance was located at the rear of the building seemed
significant. Sands had explained that the front door opened onto a
common stairway leading to the other units, which was why TJ preferred using the back. But I knew the real reason for the heavy drapes at
the windows, the code names in his datebook, and the hidden key in the
grill: it had all to do with intrigue, with secrecy.

I found the switch and triggered the strips of track lighting. My first
order of business was to check the answering machine in the bedroom.
The message light was off. Making a note of the telephone number, I
went back into the office to compare it to the one on the old rotary
model on TJ's desk. I'd promised to call Temple as soon as I got settled;
but before I could pick up the receiver, my attention wandered over to
the typewriter on the card table, and suddenly, it hit me. How could I
have not noticed before? *TJ's manuscript had been typed on a Macintosh.* I
knew because I used one myself. But there wasn't a Mac here. There
wasn't any kind of computer at all. No printer, either. Just the old
Olivetti, covered in a layer of dust.

Leedon Whitley said that the place had been searched after Sterling's
death. It was possible, I supposed, that the investigators removed the
Macintosh from the premises in order to have the contents analyzed. Or
perhaps, the thought crept into my head, someone got here *before* the
police arrived, and took the computer away for a private reason of his—
or her—own.

When I called Whitley I was told the detective wouldn't be in until
late afternoon. I left a message saying I needed to talk to him, ASAP.

20

A LINE OF bright yellow school buses waited at the curb in front of the Circle of Faith. I inched past, pulling the Volvo into the lot behind the meetinghouse. At that moment the doors to one of the barrack-style buildings flew open. A stream of children filed out, orderly at first, then seeming to spontaneously combust when they hit the fresh air. This barrage of war whoops and battling bookbags went straight to my heart. I half expected to see Temple come rushing toward me, eight years old again, and full of beans. But, of course, I'd seldom been around to witness these sorts of sunburst moments back then, when she was eight.

"Slow down, you two," chastised a pretty schoolteacher. "Timmy—where's the fire?" She tried to sound stern, but from her smile I could tell she was still young enough to remember what it felt like to have all that combustible energy exploding inside.

I turned toward the Circle of Faith, trying to summon some inner spark of my own, feeling suddenly much older than my thirty-seven years, and cold. Stone cold.

The sign on the bulletin board said:

VISITORS WELCOME!
Need Assistance?
Ask Ruth—Room 115, Mon-Fri 9AM-5PM
or 5-10 PM—Mr. Larson, B-6
Please See Calendar for Scheduling

A neatly printed oak-tag chart listed the meetings and events for the month of June. Under it, another notice asked that all groups remember to

Please Leave Rooms The Same Way You Find Them
(stack chairs, used cups in trash, etc.)
DON'T FORGET TO SHUT OFF THE LIGHTS!

I pushed through a pair of double doors that smelled as if they'd been freshly painted. The pebbled linoleum in the hallway, although worn flat brown in places, was spotlessly clean. Posters and religious banners lined the walls on both sides. Under a tissue-paper rainbow ("What's *your* promise to God?") a dozen first-grade essays spilled from the pot of gold—the boys' handwriting all lopsided and smudgy, the girls', spidery delicate.

I walked past a pin-up gallery of social issues stressing the importance of inoculating my baby . . . cleaning up the environment . . . striving for world peace. But the graphics and artwork were upbeat and colorful, and I saw no hint of the dark, judgmental doctrine that Gordon Spangler had professed in his letter confessing the murders.

A shingle saying "Office of the Director" hung over Room 115. Through the open door I saw a well-dressed woman of about fifty stapling a stack of papers at the front desk.

"Hello," I said.

"Well, hi there," she replied breezily. "Give me just a minute, will you, dear?" The woman jotted a few words on a pad, then smiled. "If I don't remember to write down these things when they occur to me, they fly right out of my head."

"I can relate." I nodded toward a brass plaque with *Mrs. Ruth Bass* engraved in serifed letters. "The sign said to ask Ruth for assistance, so I guess I'm in the right place."

"You sure are." She gestured toward a chair. "Now, what can I help you with, dear?"

For the last twenty-four hours, I'd been considering that very question. The safest course would be to tread lightly on the narrow balance between the whole truth and a lie—what the prosecuting attorney at TJ's trial had called one of my "soft, fuzzy lapses in honesty." Sitting across from this sweet, smiling woman, I felt torn between my conscience and my better judgment.

"My name is Garner Quinn," I began, "and I'm a—"

Not a flicker of recognition had passed over her face.

I abruptly changed course. "—Well, to be honest, I'm, uh . . . in a bit of a quandary."

I folded my hands and looked down at my lap. "You see, a close friend of mine passed away last week."

"Oh, I'm so sorry," Mrs. Bass said.

I acknowledged her sympathy with a wan smile. "Suddenly I find myself dealing with a lot of . . . unfinished business."

Mrs. Bass nodded. "Of course, dear. We have a grief and bereavement support group that meets here every Thursday night, that's for families, friends, loved ones." She began shuffling through a stack of papers on her desk. "And on the first Monday of the month, there's a very informative seminar." She looked up, almost hopefully. "Did your friend happen to have cancer?"

"No, I'm afraid he killed himself."

"Oh, my. Well, I'm sure the Thursday group—"

"Actually, that's not the reason I'm here," I said, hastily. "After going through my friend's papers, I discovered he'd been coming to the Circle of Faith for several months. His name was TJ Sterling . . . Tom. Thomas Sterling."

Again, no response. I passed her a newspaper clipping with Sterling's picture. "He'd put on weight since this was taken," I explained, "and he probably wouldn't have been wearing glasses—"

"I'm sorry, dear," Mrs. Bass said, after studying the photograph. "I'm afraid he doesn't look familiar. But then, so many people come in and out every day. Most of the groups aren't even affiliated with the Circle of Faith, they only make use of our facilities."

"In his journal he marked off Wednesdays and Fridays at three," I said hopefully.

Ruth checked the monthly calendar on her desk. "Let's see," she said, "we have Overeaters Anonymous at three-thirty. Seniors Bible Study runs from two to four. And then, there's Circle Aftercare for the children with working parents, that's three to five. Oh, and we did have the moms-to-be aerobics class, but that was changed to noon on Tuesdays and Thursdays."

"Doesn't sound like any of those," I said. "What about for April and May?"

The woman's effervescence had started to go flat. "Well, I suppose." Ruth Bass shrugged, reluctantly swiveling her chair toward the filing cabinets. "The schedules *do* change, from month to month."

She pulled out a folder and shimmied back to the desk. "Let's see. It looks like, besides Aftercare, the only activities on Wednesdays at three were a do-it-yourself tax seminar—that ran from January to mid-April, and then the AA meeting which met in B-10, down in the basement every Wednesday at three until just last month, when they switched over to Mondays at six."

For a second I was speechless. Seeing my expression, Ruth Bass suggested gently, "Perhaps your friend had a drinking problem, dear."

Could it be possible? Had TJ come to this place—not as a journalist on the trail of the monster Spangler—but as an alcoholic, attempting to wrestle with a different sort of demon? Ruth Bass was talking on and on, something about anonymity and the need for closure. "What I'm saying, dear"—she leaned over and patted me on the shoulder—"is that sometimes, as much as we search, we don't get the answers we're looking for. Not in this life, anyway."

I saw that she meant these words as an exit line. Already her attention was drifting back to the stack of papers waiting to be stapled on the desk; and yet somehow I couldn't give up just yet. "But I promised Tom's family I would settle his affairs," I said, fervently.

"I'm not sure I understand"—although her voice was still kind, tiny apostrophes of vexation had appeared over Mrs. Bass's eyebrows—"what it is that you hoped to accomplish by coming here, Miss—?"

"Quinn." It was, I knew, the moment of truth.

Either that, or the time to lie.

"Actually, I'm trying to find a man." The words came blurting out. "Someone my friend saw here, or met here . . . I don't know exactly. I don't know his name, either. But I can give you a general description of what he looks like."

"As I said, Miss Quinn," she sighed, "we have no direct affiliation with the twelve-step organizations that meet here."

"I believe this person may be actively involved in the Lutheran church. He'd be sixty now. Medium height and build. Trim for his age.

He has brown eyes, probably wears glasses." I spoke rapidly, trying to stave off the woman's growing disapproval. "Very ordinary in appearance, except for being a little formal in his dress. The kind of man who wouldn't stand out in a crowd. Sort of a Mister Peepers type—"

"There's no one here like that," Ruth Bass said with a firmness that surprised me.

"He's extremely neat, almost fastidious," I persisted desperately, "and if he had an accent, it would probably be more midwestern than southern."

"I'm afraid I can't help you." Mrs. Bass stood. "And I must say, I find it difficult to understand what any of this has to do with your friend who killed himself." She had me there.

I said, "Please—is there anyone else I could speak to?" I glanced toward the closed door behind her, with the jaunty little sign hanging from the knob: "GONE FISHIN'," it said. "Perhaps the director—?"

"Dr. Kohler is out this afternoon," Ruth Bass replied.

"I could come back tomorrow." I wrote down my name and the address and phone number for TJ's apartment.

"I'll find out what his schedule is"—she took it from me grudgingly—"and get back to you."

"Thank you for your time."

I walked down the poster-bright corridor. About twelve heavyset people were seated in a circle in one of the open classrooms. The only man in the group was in his early twenties, at least a hundred pounds overweight, and black. Farther down the hall, the big paper rainbow once again snagged my attention.

In answer to the question "What's *your* promise to God?" one little girl had written, "I promise not to tell lies. Not even little ones."

I replayed the conversation with Mrs. Bass in my head, telling myself that whatever license I'd taken in the editing and creative presentation of the facts, when it came right down to it, I'd mostly told the truth. *Isn't that like being a little pregnant, Miss Quinn?* The mocking words of the attorney who'd grilled me that day on the stand rang in my ears. Poised under the colored arc of tissue paper I made my own promise to God.

If You help me find Gordon Spangler, I promise not to tell lies, either. Not even little ones.

I pushed through the double doors, and started down the steps, the leather soles of my shoes echoing dully in the narrow stairwell. A man was coming up from the basement. When he looked up at me, I stopped dead in my tracks.

He was at least sixty, with a bland, colorless face, thinning hair, and glasses. In spite of the heat, he wore a gray sports jacket over blue polyester trousers.

My knees nearly buckled. I gripped the banister to keep from falling.

The man looked away the instant that he saw me, continuing to climb slowly toward the first floor. I forced myself to keep moving, matching each descending step to his own, until we were a hair's breadth away from brushing each other's sleeves. A hit of pure fear zapped me with the force of a stun gun. I went barreling out the front door, my shoulder bag flapping in one-two rhythm against my side.

Before I got into the Volvo, I glanced back at the building. It took me a moment to spot him. He was up on the first floor now, glaring down at me from one of the Circle of Faith's spotlessly clean windows.

I CALLED CAROLINE from a crowded bar on University Avenue.

"Garner," she cried. "I thought you'd gone back north without saying good-bye."

"No," I said, feeling guilty. "I'm over at a friend's place in town for a couple of days."

"Will I see you again before you leave?"

"That's why I'm calling," I told her. "Are you free tonight?"

"Oh, I'm sorry." She sounded disappointed. "I already made plans. Everyone's been so sweet, you know, tryin' to take my mind off things."

"That's great," I said. "What about tomorrow?"

"Daddy and Faye talked me into staying at Edenfield through the weekend. Why don't you come over for dinner?"

"I don't want to intrude." I hesitated, adding, "I was hoping to speak to you privately."

"Come early. I'll be out in the stables all afternoon. You can't get much more private than that, if you don't mind putting up with the smell."

I told her I'd be there around four, then I hung up and ordered another drink.

WEDNESDAY, JUNE 23

HE'D WOKEN UP this morning with the familiar knot of worry already in the pit of his stomach. The invincible feeling of a few days ago had come and gone—as ill-founded and premature as always. It seemed no matter what he did, the same troubles plagued him.

At the office, he'd kept to himself, even more than usual. Finding out he'd been once again bypassed for promotion was one thing. Worse than that was the dreadful sense of déjà vu. It was like Knoxville all over again. And Grand Rapids and Cincinnati and . . . They were trying to humiliate him, to get him to quit.

But he wouldn't this time. Couldn't. Even taking into account the night job, he fell well short of the amount they needed for the down payment on the house. Nancy was already paying twice his share, and recently she'd begun to complain about having to sink so much of her savings into what she considered an extravagant investment.

But when he thought about it, that was what he admired most about her—the safe, conservative manner in which she chose to live her life. Such a simple thing as going shopping for groceries together was a pleasure. Nancy religiously clipped coupons and filed them alphabetically. She didn't think twice about stopping at two or three different stores in order to save a few cents. Only the premium brands had been good enough for his first wife. She used to sit at the kitchen table, watching him put everything away, wrinkling up her nose in distaste when he brought home the generic tissue instead of Kleenex.

Even Nancy's looks suited him—her well-coiffed hair, lacquered and sprayed so that not even a strand was out of place, the sharp angularity of her body. If he were to describe her, the words which came first to mind would be clean. Clean and dry.

Only occasionally did the sight of a woman harken back darker feelings. It had happened to him today. And really, when he thought back on it now, the girl had looked nothing like Lara—only perhaps around the right age, with the same bold look in her eyes.

He decided he'd wait until the secretary left for the day and then call Nancy. Using the phone for personal matters was frowned upon, but he needed to tell her he missed her, try to smooth things out.

He couldn't afford to lose her. Especially now.

21

BY THE TIME I got back to TJ's place it was nearly dark. I used the tiny flashlight on my keychain to unlock the sliding door, silently cursing myself for not having kept a lamp burning inside.

Everything appeared to be exactly how I'd left it—the garment bag looped over the crown molding of the closet, the nonperishables still in the grocery bag on the counter. I stepped out of my shoes and tossed my shoulder bag on TJ's desk. On the wall next to the desk I found another light switch. I flipped it and a seam of white light zippered down the center of the curtains. Parting them, I peered outside.

A hazy white glow fell from the outdoor floods, glazing the dome of the Weber grill, the cement slab of the porch, and a small patch of grass. Beyond that, the bushes and trees were just black cutouts against an inky darkness. I pulled on the door to make sure it was locked, leaving moist palmprints on the brass handles. Sweat seemed to be pouring off me.

On the way to the bedroom, I turned up the air conditioning. There was a message from Temple on the answering machine—they'd gone to stay at Candace's sister's house in Greenwich, and guess what?

Candace had two teenaged nephews! She sounded happier than she had in days. I played the tape over a few times while I changed out of my clothes.

It wasn't until I was in my oversized tee shirt and comfortably seated at TJ's desk that I allowed myself to relive that moment, coming down the stairs, at the Circle of Faith. I remembered the cool, bumpy feel of the banister, the sound of my heels slapping against the treads, mingling with the muffled footfalls from the basement. That first glimpse of the man had been from a distorted perspective. Comically foreshortened, on the lower landing, he was nothing more than a dome of thinning hair, gray shoulders, the polished tips of shoes. He could've been anyone.

Then he glanced up, and I saw his face.

I removed the plain manila mailer containing all my notes on the Spangler case from my shoulder bag. The article I wanted was right on top—not an original like the one Chief McGlynn had carried around every day for over twenty years, but a photocopy of the same headline ("5 SLAIN IN HOUSE OF HORROR"), and the photograph of that inscrutable, unremarkable man who steadfastly refused to look at the camera.

I walked over to a mirror and held the picture up to it. *What would you look like in twenty-three years?* I wondered.

I thought of my father. At sixty he'd been at the height of his game, both physically and mentally. But Dudley had started out with a lucky hand, which couldn't be said of Gordon Spangler. Even in this photograph, taken when he was only in his thirties, Spangler looked as though life had already sapped him of the energy it would take to laugh or cry, to toss a ball to his kids or make love to his wife. He looked old, worn beyond his years. Add to that the stress of having to hide his true identity for over two decades, and what would you have? What—or who?

Mentally, I added lines, relaxing the jaw line and letting it sag into soft folds. Acting as my own sketch artist, I grayed . . . thinned . . . hollowed . . . receded. Then I superimposed this image onto my already fading memory of the man on the stairwell. I shut my eyes, picturing his face. Opened them quickly and looked at the picture again.

It was him, I thought. *It had to be.*

The phone rang, startling me so that the article dropped out of my hand and fluttered to the floor. I scrambled over to TJ's desk, getting tangled in the long cord of the old rotary. "Yes?"

"You all right?" asked Leedon Whitley. "You sound spooked."

My gaze drifted toward the picture of Gordon Spangler on the floor. "I'm fine," I said. "What's up?"

"Just thought you might want to know that the M.E. says it's possible Sterling passed out that night. In fact, from the state of his liver, he'd probably been having blackouts for quite some time. However, she's been operating on the assumption that he came to long enough to pull the trigger—which I have a feeling isn't an assumption you hold in common."

"Yeah, well."

"*Yeah, well?*" he mimicked me.

But I was already ahead of him. "Do you know what happened to TJ's Macintosh?"

"Do I . . .?" Whitley's frustration palpitated over the phone. "Sure, I told you. We removed it from the scene and had the hard drive checked out."

"Not that Mac," I said. "The one he kept in the apartment."

"There wasn't a computer there," the detective replied. "Just some old typewriter." I kept silent. "What?"

"The manuscript I found here was written on a Mac."

"So?"

"Well, according to Sands McColl, Sterling rented this place because he was having trouble working at home—"

"When are you gonna get it, Quinn?" Whitley said with a patronizing sigh. *"Writing* wasn't the business Sterling was getting down to in that pad." Again I said nothing. "You still there?"

"Yes. Thanks, Leedon."

"That's it? Just thanks?" When I didn't reply, he asked again, "You sick, or just comin' down with a rare case of politeness?"

"I'm tired," I said. "I'll call you tomorrow."

"Hold on," Whitley protested. "While you're being human, what about our dinner?"

"I'm meeting Caroline Sterling tomorrow," I told him. "How about Friday at one of those places on the mall?"

"Well, okay." He pretended to waver. "But dress nice. I got a reputation to uphold."

PUSHING THE PIECES of the sectional together, I snuggled up with TJ's manuscript.

It took me forever to get through the first chapter. In comparison to his nonfiction work, which was written in a clean, straightforward style, this prose seemed overripe and labored. My attention kept wandering, until finally I broke down and began scanning pages, searching for veiled references to Gordon Spangler.

There were none.

But if I learned nothing new about Spangler, the book told me more about TJ Sterling than I'd ever wanted to know. Sterling obviously identified deeply with his protagonist, a middle-aged writer named Teddy Cummings who—having never been able to live up to the promise of his first brilliant novel—has sunk to writing storylines for a steamy New York soap opera.

After scores of empty sexual encounters and a failed marriage, Teddy (*"a man galvanized by anger and hamstrung by his own ingrained sense of inadequacy"*) takes a job at a conservative women's college, to teach the classics and complete his half-finished novel. By day, TJ's hero lectures on great pieces of romantic literature. His tutorials, however, are more sordid than lofty.

I couldn't help wondering how much of the racy stuff was auto-biographical, and how much just wishful thinking on Sterling's part. I'd long considered him a veritable poster boy for arrested development—a graying adolescent who talked the talk, but ultimately preferred the company of men to women. The female characters, particularly when speed-read, meshed together, distinguished only in the way their body parts were metaphorically related to various kinds of fruit: an Afro-American student had breasts that swelled like firm mangos under her sweater; the nipples of a slender dance major were the color of champage grapes; another's privates he called "moist and bitable, like a peach."

Halfway through the book, Teddy meets and falls head-over-heels for the virginal Helene—whose cool, untouchable beauty and unbelievably long legs immediately harkened an image of Caroline to my mind. Not long afterward, my attention began wandering again. Teddy's unrequited love for his young student seemed naive and silly, his italicized sexual fantasies just a couple of pornographic steps up from a Harlequin romance.

I fell asleep, with all the lights on.

22

WHILE HIS SECRETARY might never have heard of Garner Quinn, the director of services for the Lutheran Circle of Faith knew exactly who I was. "I saw that interview they did on *60 Minutes*," Dr. Kohler said, shaking my hand. "The way you handled Ed Bradley when he put you on the spot about your father—well, I have to say, I give you a lot of credit for not losing your cool."

He ushered me past Mrs. Bass's empty desk. I wondered if she was out to lunch or simply avoiding me. "Unfortunately, the only recreational reading I'm wont to do these days is when I sneak the occasional Tom Clancy," he said as I followed him into his office. Photographs lined the wall, offset by childish drawings, plaster of Paris palm prints, and needle-point slogans—

"Bless This Mess"

"I ♥ FISHING"

"Of All the Things I've Lost, the Thing I Miss Most Is My Mind."

"This place," he said, sitting behind his cluttered desk with a smile, "tends to eat up all my spare time."

"I realize that," I said, taking the seat across from him. "And I appreciate your seeing me on such short notice."

"My pleasure." Dr. Kohler's hospitality seemed genuine. "Although I have to say, according to what Ruth's already told me, I doubt I'll be able to be of much service."

"I'm afraid I wasn't completely up front with Mrs. Bass yesterday," I admitted.

"Ms. Quinn," Reverend Kohler began, "if this has to do with some sort of investigation into the death of your friend Mr. Sterling, let me assure you again that we have no record—"

"It's not that. May I?" I gestured toward the open door.

"Of course," said the reverend.

After it was shut, I asked, "Does the name Gordon Spangler mean anything to you?"

Kohler's brows knit, and I saw that he was sweating, although whether from nerves, or the poor ventilation in the room, I couldn't really tell. "It sounds vaguely familiar," he said, "but I can't—"

"In 1970, he killed his entire family—his wife, mother, and three children. He left a written confession, then disappeared, never to be seen again."

"That's right," Kohler said. "Happened somewhere up north, didn't it?"

"Spring Lake, New Jersey," I said. "My hometown."

"Awful." Beads of sweat had started to form on his upper lip. "Just terrible . . ."

"A few weeks before he died, Sterling told me he'd seen Gordon Spangler. I know from his datebook that Tom had been coming here on a regular basis during the last few months of his life. And since Spangler was a devout Lutheran—"

"You . . ." He sounded incredulous. "You think Mr. Sterling saw the man here?"

I took the newspaper article from my bag and handed it to him. "Before the murders, Spangler burned all the pictures of himself he could find. This is the only photograph we have left. It was probably taken close to thirty years ago."

Kohler stared at the picture for a moment, then he opened his top desk drawer and put on some reading glasses. "No," he said, clearing his throat, and again, "No. This is not someone I recognize."

"Are you sure, Dr. Kohler? Try to picture how he might look after all this time."

The reverend shook his head. I'd seen the same cold look of disavowal in Mrs. Bass's eyes only a day before. "I'm afraid I can't help you." When I met his gaze, he glanced away. "Sorry," he said, sliding the photocopy back to me.

"That's strange," I said, "because on my way out yesterday, I saw a man who was a dead ringer for him."

Frederick Kohler reddened. "As Ruth may have told you, people come in and out of this building every day. Whoever you saw may have resembled this man Spangler. Or perhaps—no offense—you simply *thought* he did, because you so desperately wanted him to. Either way, I can assure you we harbor no fugitives here at the Circle of Faith. We simply provide a safe haven for those in need of support, or a little encouragement. And it is out of respect for them that I must ask you to drop this line of inquiry. Please, Miss Quinn. Drop it before someone gets hurt."

The interview was clearly over.

Dr. Kohler insisted upon walking me to my car, and although his conversation was genial, it seemed obvious I would not be allowed to linger in the building a moment longer than necessary. "I wish you Godspeed," he said, watching as I pulled away.

I drove past the school, turning right onto the main road. The minute I was sure Kohler could no longer see me, I began hammering the steering wheel. "Damn!" I pounded my fists. "Dammit to hell—"

A little boy darted into the road, chasing a basketball. Jamming on the brakes, I swerved to a stop.

"Timmy!" The pretty teacher I'd noticed yesterday near the buses scooped the boy into her arms. I edged the Volvo to the side of the road and put it into park.

"Is he hurt?" I called, getting out of the car.

"No, thank heavens." The young woman's relief settled into anger. "How many times do I have to tell you, Timothy? You could've been killed!"

Several children had ventured toward the playground's edge. "Shoo!" the teacher told them. "Five more minutes and play period's over." Timmy and his friends ran back toward the jungle gym and slides.

"That boy's making me gray," she sighed, "before my time."

Actually, her hair was strawberry blond, and with her long flowered dress and red Mary Jane shoes, she looked to be all of twenty. "What about you?" she politely inquired. "You must've had quite a shock."

I patted my heart. "Nothing a nitroglycerine tablet couldn't cure."

"I'm Lisa Briggs." She offered her hand. "I teach third grade over at Faith Elementary."

"Garner Quinn." Before she could place the name, I added, "I feel so responsible. I just came from a meeting with Dr. Kohler over at the center, and I was driving along, trying to remember the name of a man he'd introduced me to, and I wasn't paying enough attention to the road."

"Please," Lisa Briggs said, "it wasn't your fault. Timmy ran out without looking." She glanced toward the children—a second more and I would lose her.

"Maybe you can help me with this name. It's right on the tip of my tongue—an older man, about sixty? Sort of ordinary looking, but very neatly dressed?"

Her pretty face lit up. "Oh, you must mean Mr. Larson."

I snapped my fingers. "That's it." The name from the bulletin board—*Mr. Larson, B-6.*

"He's a bit of an odd duck," the young teacher said thoughtfully.

"In what way?"

"Keeps to himself a lot. He's new in the area. I think he's a widower or something." She suddenly seemed embarrassed. "I don't know. He's probably just shy."

"Probably," I said. "You wouldn't happen to know his first name?"

Lisa Briggs rested a finger on her lips. "Owen, I think." Then she nodded. "Yes, that's it—Owen Larson."

23

CAROLINE'S MERCEDES WAGON was parked in front of the stables next to a brand-new silver Honda Accord with vanity plates reading "VRC 21." I found Caroline inside, sweaty and soap-streaked from scrubbing down a chestnut mare. Clearly, she was in her element. "Garner," she cried, "forgive me, I'm a mess!"

In fact, she looked wonderful with her faded blue jeans and man's shirt rolled up to the elbows, her long, honey hair caught up in a baseball cap. "I won't be riding for the next few months, but they sure can't keep me out of here."

"Your stepmother says you should stop working yourself to the bone," I relayed, "and come back to the house for something to eat."

"Faye just wants me to get fat. She can't wait to see me tottering around in some dowdy maternity dress, big as ole Lady Love." Caroline patted the horse's flank, and it did a tap-shoe sidestep. I jumped back. "Why, Garner Quinn, don't tell me you're afraid of a little pony? And here I thought you were so brave."

"That's all a clever front," I said. "Inside I'm pretty much a quivering coward."

"Well, you don't have to worry about Lady here—she listens to my every command."

I sat down on a bale of hay, watching her brush the mare. "You look a hundred percent better than the last time I saw you," I said. "No more fainting spells, I hope."

"No." Caroline stopped, mid-stroke. "I wanted to thank you for that."

"Are you kidding? I never should've let you go in there in the first place."

"I'm talking about . . . your reaction when I told you about the baby." She went back to grooming the horse. "How happy you seemed—it was the first time since Tommy's death that I felt a tiny glimmer of hope that there might be happiness in my future after all."

"Of course there will."

She pushed away a tendril of damp hair off her forehead with the crook of her elbow. "Until I talked to you I felt so alone and scared. But then, after you left I realized, my God—you brought up your daughter all by yourself, too."

"Yeah, well, I'm not exactly a hallmark of successful single parenting." Softening, I added, "You'll do fine, Caroline. I know you will."

"It means a lot to hear you say so." She led Lady Love into a stall. "Did I tell you I'm going to have an amnio? My OB-GYN assures me it really isn't necessary, seeing I'm only in my twenties. But I think it'd be nice to know whether it's a boy or a girl. It makes the baby more real somehow. I could talk to her. Or him. Maybe that way I won't feel so damn lonesome."

Caroline plopped down on a bale of hay next to me. "Enough self-pity." She took the hat off and shook out her hair. "So what was it you wanted to talk to me about?"

I hesitated. "Are you sure you're up to this?"

"Absolutely."

Here goes, I thought. "Well, I've been doing some investigating," I said, "into Tom's death. And I've come to the conclusion that maybe things aren't what they seem."

Her face darkened. "You're scaring me, Garner, acting so serious. What are you trying to say?"

I stood, unable to look her in the eye. "I think TJ may have been murdered."

"But . . . I don't understand," Caroline sputtered. "The police . . . and the coroner—" A soft whinny came from the stall, as though Lady Love were trying to comfort her mistress. "I saw him, Garner. Laying in all that blood with the pistol in his hand."

"It's possible that someone arranged it to look like a suicide."

"But that's crazy." The young woman seemed dazed. "Who—?"

I knelt beside her. "Remember how you told me you read all of Tom's books?" Caroline nodded, dumbly. "Do you remember who Gordon Spangler is?"

She rubbed her temple. "That man who killed his wife and children?"

"Killed them and disappeared." I took her hands in mine; they were trembling. "Listen to me, Caroline. A few weeks before he died, TJ told me he'd seen Spangler."

"He . . . ?—Where?"

"He wouldn't say. But he hinted he'd been on his trail for some time."

"If that were true"—Caroline appeared to be trying to make sense of all this— "why didn't Tom turn him into the authorities?"

"He wanted to get a book deal in place first. He asked me to pull some strings at my publisher's."

Caroline's shoulders drooped. "That sounds just like Tommy," she said softly.

"Are you all right?"

She got to her feet. "I need some fresh air," she said.

In the riding ring adjacent to the stables, a dark-haired girl was putting a frisky dapple-gray pony through its paces. She glanced in our direction and Caroline waved. "That's my stepsister, Vicki," she said, with unmistakable fondness.

For a long while we just stood there watching the girl ride. Finally Caroline spoke again. "I just can't seem to get my mind around it. How could it have happened?"

"Say Spangler realized he was being tracked. He might've turned the tables on TJ." I leaned up against the fence. "Spangler's sixty now, about five-ten, trim. Thinning hair, glasses. Do you recall seeing anyone like that in the neighborhood?"

"I don't think so. You know how Cheswick is, Garner. People keep an eye out for folks who don't belong."

"Any strange phone calls before you went to Charleston?" I persisted.

"No," Caroline sighed. "What about the police? Don't they have any leads?" When I didn't reply, she noticed immediately. *"Garner?"*

"I haven't said anything to them yet."

She faced me squarely. "Tell me you're not serious."

"Up until now," I said, "I was afraid the whole Spangler thing might be some kind of hoax Tom cooked up."

"What changed your mind?"

I rested my elbows on the fence rail. "I think I've finally figured out where their paths may have crossed." Omitting any reference to TJ's datebook, I told her about my visit to the Circle of Faith, and my brief encounter with the man who called himself Owen Larson.

Caroline hugged her arms. "You're givin' me chill bumps. You mean to tell me you were standing only a few inches away? And he looked right at you? My God, Garner—what if he recognized you?" With a jolt, I realized I hadn't considered that possibility. I'd felt secure, knowing how little I resembled the girl who rang the Spanglers' doorbell, once upon a time, all those years ago. Now I thought about those millions of books with my picture on the back cover.

"Don't worry about me," I assured Caroline, recklessly.

"Don't worry?" she echoed, an edge of hysteria creeping into her voice. "According to you, this man murdered my husband—"

The dark-haired girl had dismounted and was walking toward us, reins in hand. "Hey," she called. Even from a distance I could make out the concern on her face.

"Hey, yourself." Caroline smiled weakly. When they were close enough, she reached over to pat the muzzle of the horse. "Vicki, this is Tom's friend, Garner Quinn. Garner, meet my sister, Victoria Ryan."

Although Vicki had inherited her mother's build and coloring, she'd clearly rejected Faye's sense of style. Devoid of makeup, with her long straight hair pulled back, Victoria Ryan seemed intent on making herself look as plain as possible. "Nice to meet you," she said, her grave eyes never leaving Caroline.

"How's my baby?" The young widow stroked the horse's neck. "How's my Smoke?"

"He's fine," Vicki said. "Not so much as a limp."

"He twisted his ankle a few days ago." Caroline cooed, "Didn't you? And you miss your Caro, don't you, Smokey? You miss me coming over every day to ride."

Vicki turned to me. "I hear you're going to be joining us for dinner."

"I'm looking forward to it."

"That makes one of us. Well, I'd better go clean up, or Faye'll throw one of her hissy fits at the table." She exchanged a look with Caroline. "Wouldn't want to scare the company."

We watched her walk the horse back to the stable. "Poor darlin'." Caroline shook her head. "Ever since . . . it happened . . . she's been stickin' to me like a shadow."

"Funny," I said. "I don't remember meeting her at the funeral."

"She couldn't come. Tommy's death hit her so hard she took to bed."

If this reaction sounded extreme to me, it didn't appear to faze Caroline. "She and TJ were close?"

"Of course they got along," she said lightly. "But mainly I think Vicki just felt devastated on account of me. I know stepkids are supposed to hate each other, but it was never that way with us. From the very beginning we each completely tapped into what the other one was thinking."

"I once had a friend like that." I looked out over the fence, toward the riding ring and the fields beyond. The sun had begun a westerly slant. Its searing brilliance drilled into the hinges of my mandibles with a buzzing sound, causing my jaw to drop, and my eyes to tear.

I turned my head. "When I was fourteen, my eighth-grade English teacher Sister Judith decided I should be a writer. She signed me up to apprentice at the local community theater—said it would give me a greater appreciation of the English language." I shrugged. "Personally, I would've preferred a month of detention." The genuineness of Caroline's smile encouraged me to go on.

"They were rehearsing for a production of *Romeo and Juliet*. I remember coming into the dark auditorium. Sort of freezing in the middle of the aisle, waiting for my eyes to adjust." By now I was feeling almost feverish, unable to stop the words from tumbling out. "There was this girl up on stage.

"She wasn't much older than I was, but no more like me than a butterfly is to a gnat. She had a husky voice, and blue eyes that every now and then caught fire, you know, like flint throwing off sparks? And the way she said her lines—as if each word was being ripped out of some deep, secret place within herself . . ."

Another of those glass bubble memories sprang to mind: a lean, wavy-haired Romeo lowering himself from the balcony, as Juliet in a tattered muslin rehearsal skirt gasps,

> *O God! I have an ill-divining soul.*
> *Methinks I see thee, now thou art below,*
> *As one dead in the bottom of a tomb . . .*

I held onto the top rail of the fence, stretching out my arms. "After that scene, Lady Capulet is supposed to enter, only the actress had apparently come down with the flu. The director starts yelling, where the hell's the new apprentice? And before I know it, the stage manager's shoving a script in my hand, and I'm trying to tell him—I can't do this, I don't know how—but he just pushes me onto the stage. Then I hear somebody shout, that's your cue, kid, and the whole cast's staring at me, so I take a big step forward . . ." I grimaced. ". . . tripped over a chair, and fell flat on my face."

Caroline's sympathetic sigh ruffled the settling twilight.

"For a minute I actually considered just staying on the floor. Playing dead until they all got tired of laughing and went home. But suddenly the girl playing Juliet was pulling me to my feet, whispering not to worry. I remember her saying something like, 'Once you get used to it, you'll see being up here is a whole lot easier than being out there'—and our eyes kind of locked, and it was as though I knew—knew exactly what she meant by *out there*."

A shiver went down my spine. "I also knew that we were going to be friends."

To my surprise, I experienced a giddy rush of relief. It was the way I used to feel walking out of St. Catharine's after confession, as a child. I leaned over the fence, staring straight ahead. "I don't know why I told you all that."

"I'm glad you did," Caroline said. "It sounds like your friend was really special. What was her name?"

"Lara." I turned to her. "Lara Spangler."

A look of astonishment crossed Caroline's face, then, very thoughtfully, she nodded. We stood for another long while, just watching the sunset. "You want to bring him in yourself, don't you?" she asked finally.

"Yes," I admitted, "but I won't try to. I just need a little more time." As I uttered the words, I couldn't help thinking of TJ. *Three more weeks, GQ,* he'd predicted, *and you'll be reading about me in the papers.*

"Three more days," I said to Caroline, "and I promise I'll bring in the rest of the troops."

24

DINNER IN THE Childresses' lovely formal dining room turned out to be alternately strained and subdued. Faye Childress, resplendent in tangerine silk and freshwater pearls, presided over the meal like a talk-show host whose main responsibility was to ask questions and keep things moving. Caroline and her stepsister, Victoria, consistently derailed Faye's bright chatter with one-word responses. She, in turn, made a big show of not noticing.

Ford Childress joined us womenfolk halfway through the chicken gumbo. At first he seemed startled to see me, but when Caroline explained that I was staying in Charlottesville a few extra days to attend to some personal business, he relaxed. "Hope that means you'll be a frequent visitor." He smiled, signaling the maid for more soup. "—Course, if you aren't careful, the girls here are liable to put you to work out in the stables."

"I've already tried," Caroline said merrily, "only it turns out she's scared of horses. She just about fainted when Lady Love swished her tail." Vicki laughed.

"A slight exaggeration," I scoffed.

"Well, once the baby's born, I expect you to bring your daughter down for a nice long visit," Caroline suggested, "and I'll teach you both how to ride."

"Temple can ride. I'll sit on the sidelines and soak up the gorgeous scenery."

"That's the spirit," Childress seconded. "I keep reminding the girls how blessed we are—living smack in the middle of God's country." He waved his butter knife in my direction. "You ever consider relocating, come talk to me, Garner. I'll set you up first class."

It was just the segue I needed to turn the conversation toward the Albemarle Planning and Development Corporation. "I understand your company's been instrumental in growing this whole area," I commented. "I'd love to see some of your properties sometime."

"Well, give a holler, and I'd be happy to give you the nickel tour."

"Ford has some darling houses going up over at Ashford Hills," Faye said.

"She wouldn't be interested in those," he replied impatiently. "A custom estate, some investment property—that's more what you had in mind, isn't it, Garner?"

"Sounds good to me."

"What I always say is"—Childress sliced into the thick, juicy steak he'd just been served—"real estate is the only *real* estate you can leave your children. Right, sugars?"

"Right, Daddy," the girls chimed in.

At that moment I pictured TJ sitting in the empty chair at the foot of the table—drunk and morose, lifting those sly, judgmental eyes of his as he raised his glass in a toast. "Up the Cheez!" he'd say.

And I knew that Caroline's father must have hated him.

. . .

AFTER DINNER, CHILDRESS invited me into the library, ostensibly to see the plans for a new country club he was building. "How's that . . . er, project of yours going?" he asked when we were alone.

"I've sorted through most of TJ's papers. Anything that might upset Caroline I put in a separate file." Childress held up a bottle of brandy, and I shook my head. "You might want to take a look through his novel yourself. It's got commercial potential—middle-aged professor falls in lust with young student, that sort of thing." I watched his face carefully for a reaction that didn't come. "Whether or not it should be published is your call."

Childress poured himself a snifterful. "Beyond this book," he said with maddening cool, "there's nothing—"

"Embarrassing?" I filled in the blank for him. "Not from what I've seen so far. A couple of things puzzle me, though. TJ wrote his book on a Macintosh, but there doesn't appear to be one in the apartment now."

"Perhaps the police confiscated it."

"Detective Whitley says no."

Childress sat in the wing chair across from me. "I'm sure it's possible that one of Tom's devoted protégés may have taken it"—his lips curled in distaste—"as a memento. It's really of very little concern."

"I hope you're right," I said. "Because if there was something damaging on that hard drive, it would be a shame to see it fall into the wrong hands."

Ford's tongue darted nervously over his lower lip, the first sign that his emotions weren't completely in check. "I hadn't considered that," he admitted, his gaze suddenly narrowing. "You said 'a couple of things.' What else?"

"It may be none of my business, but in going through his bills and receipts, I couldn't help noticing how extravagant TJ's lifestyle was." I forged ahead. "I'd assumed, between the divorce and the lawsuits, he must've been in a financial bind, yet somehow he managed to make child support and mortgage payments, pay rent on an apartment, and singlehandedly keep half of the bars in town afloat. Do you have any idea where he got that kind of money?"

"I'm afraid I do," Childress said quietly, staring down at the brandy glass in his hand. "When Caroline told me they were struggling, I pulled some strings to get Tom into the UVA English department. I also created a position for him at AP&D. The title, I believe, was Executive Director of Real Estate Marketing and Club Membership for the Ashford Hills Estates—possibly the most highly paid no-show job ever on record. Although that in itself wasn't enough to disengage my son-in-law's sharp tongue. He enjoyed poking fun, playing practical jokes on the sales consultant we have out there. Said they were nothing more than tract houses. A middle-class *Shangri-La*." He mimicked TJ's sarcastic tone.

A Shangri-La owned by a Big Cheez.

"In spite of his little digs, he managed to pick up his handsome checks every other Thursday. And I kept sending them." Ford Childress fastened his hazel eyes on me and held them there. "You see, Miss Quinn, I love my family very much."

"And we love you, too." Vicki's voice echoed behind me. I had no idea how long she'd been listening to our conversation.

THE METAL HASP tapped against the fence, blown by the soft evening breeze. It seemed, not only had I forgotten to leave on a light, I'd also neglected to close the latch. I shut the gate and made my way to the sliding glass doors.

As soon as I turned on the light, I knew something was wrong.

There were no ransacked drawers, empty shelves, or open closets—

no dramatic signs of forced entry at all—yet instinctively I sensed an intruder's presence. TJ's chair had been pushed neatly under his desk. The manila envelope I'd left on the blotter suddenly faced the opposite way, its flap undone. A peek inside revealed that a good portion of the background material on Gordon Spangler had been removed.

TJ's manuscript was where it should've been, on the sectional, but upon taking a closer look, I saw that the stained, dog-eared pages now appeared pristine and perfect. I set my palm down on the title sheet and was met with the familiar warmth that lingers on freshly printed paper. My heart began pounding a mile a minute.

I made another quick scan of the room. Slung over their handlebars, the fox pelts bore witness with their vacant, glass-eyed stares. On the dartboard, John Grisham seemed in need of a good laugh and a shave. I took a hockey stick from the outstretched hand of a lawn jockey and set off to search the rest of the house.

A tiny red light blinked on the answering machine in the bedroom. I pushed the button.

"Hi Garner, it's me, Sands. Sorry I've been so hard to reach . . . I have this thing going with a friend. I'm staying at his place tonight, um, that's Thursday. But try me tomorrow, okay? And, oh, by the way—I can't believe TJ's Mac is missing. I could've sworn it was there the day I took you, but if it wasn't, then I really don't know . . . So anyway, call me if you want." I rewound the tape and went back into the office.

A minute later, the hockey stick still in my hand, I was out on the patio. The floods iced the cement porch, turning it into a flat white rink. All I needed were skates and a mouthguard. I walked over to the Weber kettle, reminding myself that the silent, hulking shadows at the end of the yard were only trees. To my relief, I found TJ's key glinting slyly inside the grill. I picked it up and stuffed it into my pocket. My little experiment in honesty no longer seemed like such a good idea.

THERE WERE A dozen Larsons in the telephone book, but only one with the first initial O. The address was listed as 415 Rio Ridge Road, Charlottesville. According to my map, that meant the man who called himself Owen Larson lived within walking distance of the university; the odds that TJ had seen him around campus were suddenly increasing.

Once again the humidity had dropped overnight. The disk jockey on the radio assured me that I could expect a clear, sunny day with temperatures in the seventies. Despite the fact that I'd barely slept a wink, I felt energetic and raring to go. I'd left a message on Sands McColl's answering machine, asking her to meet me at the Biltmore Grill on the Corner at 11 P.M., figuring that would leave plenty of time for my dinner with Whitley.

415 proved to be a number in Rio Ridge Gardens, a rambling brick apartment complex advertising "ONE, TWO, THREE BEDROOM RENTALS, with utilities." From the front they looked all the same, but driving along I noted some personal touches. On the rear balconies, some industrious tenants were growing tomato plants and flowers; on others,

Power Ranger and Aladdin beach blankets had been slung over the railings to dry. Apparently, this place didn't cater primarily to students.

I found the 400 building and pulled into one of the numbered parking slots. Although it was only a little after nine, space 415 was empty. I left the Volvo unlocked and made a beeline for the closest YOU-ARE-HERE floorplan map. Larson's apartment was located on the second floor. I stepped back, squinting into the sun, trying to see his balcony.

"Looking for Mr. Larson?" a voice inquired. The screen door on the patio next to me slid open, and a woman of about seventy stepped outside, wearing a red and blue sailer romper and white patent leather mules.

"Ma'am?"

"I saw you staring above," she said. "Thought maybe you'd come to see Mr. Larson."

"Actually, I have." I smiled. "But I guess I must've missed him."

"Oh, my yes." The woman had hair the color of peach taffy, and when she shook her head, not a strand moved. "He leaves at eight-fifteen on the dot every morning. You can set your watch by him."

"Do you happen to know where he works?"

"Some kind of office, I expect." The woman sat down on a waffle-weave chaise lounge. Her legs had veins as thick as soda straws. "Couldn't tell you where, though. At night I think he manages some sort of church group over in West Albemarle."

"Does he ever come home for lunch?"

"Not a once."

She leaned against the slant-back lounger, her peach hair frilling stiffly like a wide-brimmed hat. "Between the two jobs, he's hardly around a'tall except to sleep. I think he might have a lady friend, too." The old woman shrugged. "Not that it's any of my business."

"Has Mr. Larson lived here long?"

"I guess it's going on a year now. Ever since he moved down from wherever he was living, out there in the midwest." She sat up straight. "You the daughter?"

"Pardon?" I stammered.

"He told Mr. Parker next door he was married once," the woman explained. "I thought maybe you were his daughter."

"No, just an acquaintance." Then I ventured, "He told Mr. Parker he had a daughter?"

It was one question too many. "I don't know that he did." The woman crossed her knobby legs with great decorum. "All I know is, Mr. Larson makes a good neighbor. Always a polite hello. Takes out the trash. Keeps his nose out of other people's affairs. Which is more," she added huffily, "than some folks I could mention."

As I walked to my car, I couldn't help thinking that, up until December 15, 1970, most of Gordon Spangler's neighbors in Spring Lake would've described him in precisely the same manner. On the outside chance of catching her off guard, I turned back to the woman. "By the way," I called, "what kind of car does Mr. Larson drive?"

"A 1986 Caprice," the old lady replied promptly. "Maroon, with a cloth interior."

FOR A LONG while I cruised around the neighborhood, on a quixotic search for maroon Caprices. It wasn't until a couple of hours later when my stomach started growling that I reluctantly tossed in the towel. I needed help and I needed food—and while not necessarily in that order, I needed them both fast.

After a quick stop for pizza, I headed back to TJ's, where I tried Hogan at his hotel in Orlando. The front desk picked up on the fourth ring. I hesitated, debating whether to leave my name. If Hogan's wife found a message from Garner Quinn, I was afraid it might be the end of their happy family vacation. Not to mention their thirty-year marriage.

"Could you ask Mr. Hogan to call Harriet Beech," I said, counting that this name would have hidden meaning—*Harold* Beech was the serial killer we tracked down together. "Tell him it's urgent," I added, before rattling off the number for Sterling's apartment.

I spent the rest of the day packing TJ's belongings into cartons. It took me over an hour to dismantle the storage display unit. The fox stoles, the machete and rope, and the shadow box with the gun all fit in one box. Behind the John Grisham dartboard, I found a shoebox with several thousand beautifully embossed business cards for the Ashford Hills Estates personalized for *Thomas J. Sterling, Executive Director of Real Estate Marketing and Club Membership.* I tucked a few into the front flap of TJ's journal and tossed the rest into the trash.

Nowhere was there even the vaguest reference to Gordon Spangler or Owen Larson.

"YES, I'LL GET her," said the small voice. Once again the phone dropped before I could protest. I'd already spoken to a succession of Cilda's great nieces and nephews. Given the poor quality of the connection, and the little time I had to spare, it made sense to just hang up; but already the child was shouting, *"Auntie Cilda! Auntie Cilda!"*, and so I waited, hoping that maybe one of the older Fieldses might answer the call.

A full minute passed. Finally I heard the sound of footsteps and more phone jostling. "Yes, 'ello?"

My heart leapt at the garrulous tone. "It's me, Cilda."

From the other end came the jangling cacophony of a dozen Jamaican children talking all at once— *" 'ho is it, Auntie, please tell, 'ho is it?"*

"It's Ga'ner Quinn," the old woman hissed, "now go away."

"How're you doing down there?" I asked.

" 'ow you t'ink, wit' a bunch of children 'ho don't 'ave no respect?"

"Come on, they sound adorable."

"Not talking about the young ones," she grumbled, "h'I'm talking about the *h'old* ones. Especially them that's got too big for 'er britches." This, I suspected, was a not-so-subtle dig at her daughter Mercedes— the only person who'd ever been known to go head-to-head with Cilda Fields.

"Well, tell everybody I said hi."

"What's wrong wit' you?"

"Nothing," I replied breezily. "Temple's having a good time at Andy's. Apparently the wedding-of-the-century's still on—"

"No," Cilda cut me dead. "What's wrong wit' *you*?"

I'm scared, I wanted to sob. *I feel like I'm in the middle of one of those nightmares I used to have as a kid—the kind where everything's fine, and then— wham! this incredible sense of dread wraps around your throat and knots there until you can't talk, can't scream, can't breathe, and the most ordinary things become dark and menacing, and shadows are alive, and everyone has the same face, but no one is who they appear to be. And I want to call out for you, Cilda, the way I always did, but you're so far away. And anyhow, I'm not really dreaming. I'm not even asleep.* "I'm just tired," I said.

"Ga'ner Quinn," clucked Cilda Fields, "what 'ave you gotten your-self into?"

"Probably nothing," I replied, wanting to change the subject. "Did I tell you I'm having dinner with a man who looks like Denzel Washing-ton?"

Cilda was not impressed. "And what kind of criminal is 'e?"

"He's one of the good guys," I said. To which I added a silent, *I hope.*

ON FRIDAY NIGHTS the downtown mall transformed into a fluid open-air carnival. The five o'clock end of the work week meant that people who'd been cooped indoors all week long could finally step into the last garish dazzle of sun, don Ray-Bans and wraparound Arnettes, and let down their hair. Or at the very least loosen their ties. Street entertainers and musicians competed for their attention. Shops set out enticing displays, and every restaurant suddenly had its own small outdoor café.

I weaved my way through the crowd, stopping to watch a group of tiny gymnasts in purple velvet leotards who were cartwheeling and back-flipping to an orchestrated rendition of "The Wind Beneath My Wings." As adorable as they were, I found myself distracted by the other onlookers—attentive moms and dads, adoring grandparents, middle-aged loners, and businessmen in their shirts and ties. So many faces, most of them nondescript and ordinary. Suddenly I was seized by an irrational fear.

He might be here. Right now. This minute. Spangler-Larson. He could be watching.

The circle of people spun to a crazy blur. I started to feel hemmed in, claustrophobic. Pushing through the spectators, I melted anonymously into the moving throng. Moments later a group of bizarrely outfitted teenagers skateboarded past, relishing the negative attention their tattoos and Crayola-colored hair had engendered among the Ralph Lauren set. One boy, razor-thin, with heavily moussed Statue of Liberty spikes, brushed against my sleeve.

"Sorry," he apologized. Close up, he had a bad case of acne. His black tee shirt said, "OH YEAH?" He stared for a moment, then his scabby face broke into a smile. "I know you— you're the one who wrote about that ghost rapist guy. Man, that book was the *bomb*."

"It sure was," said a voice behind me. "You think maybe I could have your autograph?" Leedon Whitley flashed his pearly whites, adding to the boy, "Pick up the skateboard, son, or I'll have to write you out a summons."

The kid picked up his board. "Nice meeting you anyway," he mumbled.

"Another member of your fan club?" Whitley watched as the spike-haired boy jogged off toward his friends.

"No, just my personal stylist."

"Well, I like the dress he picked out," the detective said, openly checking me out. We fell into step together. "You're early. Where'd you park?"

"Back near the Omni."

The detective checked his watch. "We got a while. Might as well enjoy the show."

We walked by a young violinist playing earnest Stravinski, her open instrument case a wishing well for dollar bills and spare change. By the time we reached the next block, the sound of strings was eclipsed by African drums. A large crowd had gathered in front of these musicians—

three barefoot men in traditional African garb, and a little boy in a Bulls tee shirt and Nikes.

"Dance with me," Whitley said.

"No thanks."

The detective raised his voice over the pounding drums. "Why not? Is it because I'm *black?*" Around us, eavesdroppers—both black and white—waited for my response. Whitley laughed. "Or just 'cause I'm so much younger and better lookin' than you?"

"I'm not a very good dancer, that's all."

"Versus, say someone like me, who has natural rhythm?"

"Listen." I poked a finger into his chest. "I'm getting tired of this angry young black man routine. Why don't you drop it?"

"Maybe I will, soon as you stop playing hardass lady writer." We resumed walking, locked in a prickly silence, until Whitley broke out laughing. As much as I tried not to, pretty soon I was laughing, too.

HAMILTON'S, THE PLACE Whitley had chosen for dinner, seemed quite the happening place. A smart-looking couple ahead of us was turned away for not having reservations. Whitley started to argue with the hostess when she led us to an outside table, but I put an end to it by insisting I preferred the fresh air, anyway. In truth, a part of me believed that if we sat on the mall long enough, the fugitive calling himself Owen Larson would pass by in his pale gray jacket and tie. I stared into the horde of people milling through the silvery dusk.

"What hairpin turns you taking in that busy mind of yours, Garner Quinn?" asked Leedon Whitley.

"Just enjoying the view."

"I bet. Is it any better than the one over at the late great Mister Sterling's?"

"Yes. Lots."

Whitley stretched his legs out on the cobblestones, the casual gesture undercut by the persistent tapping of his foot. "Damn freakhouse if you ask me," he said. "What's with the racist lawn statuary, and them moth-eaten fox coats? The more I think about it, coulda been PETA that done ole TJ in. PETA, or maybe the N double A CP." Detective Whitley seemed to have perfect recall of Sterling's apartment.

"Pardon?" I asked, flippantly. "I thought the man committed suicide."

A pretty waitress came over and asked us what we'd like to drink. I ordered a glass of the house white; Whitley asked for a kir. "What a coincidence," I remarked. "That was one of TJ's favorite drinks."

"Oh yeah? Well, I saw the coroner's report," Whitley shot back, his foot jiggling, "and from the looks of it, Sterling never met a drink he didn't like."

"You're probably right," I admitted, turning my attention back to the passersby.

Whitley breached the awkward silence. "So everything's copacetic at the lovenest?"

"You keep insinuating that Sterling was involved in extramarital activities."

"He got canned from UVA, didn't he?"

"His wife said that was because he didn't have a tenure track position."

Whitley gave me a patronizing smile. "Uh-huh, well, maybe instead of his wife, you should ask the man's faithful personal assistant."

"Maybe I'll do that," I said. "I'm meeting her in the Corner later on tonight."

This seemed to irk him. "You sure do make the rounds. Guess I should be grateful you managed to squeeze me into your busy schedule." The waitress brought our aperitifs and the menus. "I've heard everything's pretty good here," Whitley said, and when I glanced up, I caught him looking achingly earnest and very, very young. I realized suddenly he wanted to impress me.

I said, "It all sounds wonderful." Under his overly padded jacket, his shoulders relaxed.

We ordered mixed greens with goat cheese, and penne and shrimp in a red pepper sauce. I told him about my dinner with Caroline, offering some pointed observations of Ford, Faye, and the horsey life at Edenfield. I figured it would be safe ground for two outsiders like us to cover—the young Afro-American male and the perpetual observer—one who'd never belong to the club, and one born into it as a wallflower; both fated to never fit in.

The food turned out to be better than good; it was exceptional. We continued to chat about the Childresses while we ate. "Caroline and her stepsister—there's a pair for you." Whitley shook his head. "Miss Vicki puts me in mind of that old movie *The Bad Seed*."

"She does seem to have a dark side."

"Think she was getting it on with old TJ behind her sister's back?"

"You've got a one-track mind."

"Yeah, well, you ask me," Whitley said, "something's rotten in the state of Stepford."

"I'll admit Ford doesn't seem excessively broken up by his son-in-law's passing," I commented. "TJ'd been collecting a substantial weekly paycheck from the family business, which he used in part to fund his secret life."

"Ouch. So in addition to PETA and the coloreds"—the detective spoke with his mouth full—"Big Daddy also had a motive for wanting Sterling out of the picture."

"*If* he was murdered," I reminded the detective, "which, of course, he wasn't."

He stared at me for a moment, then resumed eating. "Yeah, I keep forgetting."

Tempted as I was to put an end to this childish game of *Clue* we'd found ourselves playing, once again a niggling inner voice stopped me from telling Whitley about Gordon Spangler. After this morning's fruitless stakeout, I'd promised myself not to do or say anything else that might jeopardize an already unstable situation—at least until I'd had a chance to discuss it with J. Emmett Hogan. Hogan had experience in these matters. He knew Spangler, and I knew Hogan. I trusted him.

But looking at him now, I realized I was beginning to trust Leedon Whitley, too.

"I've got a yen for key lime pie," he said, pushing away an empty plate. His quick eyes caught me. "—What?"

"Pardon?"

"You looked like you were gonna say something."

I smiled. "Tell her to bring two spoons," I said.

DURING DESSERT, I steered the conversation in a more personal direction. "Have you lived in Charlottesville all your life, Leedon?"

"Don't let this southern gentility fool you," he scoffed. "I'm from Cleveland."

"You're kidding."

"Born, bred, and raised by a grandma"—the detective dug hungrily into the pie—"who put enough of the fear of God into me so I learned to act like a gentleman and be respectful to my elders. Umm . . . you *got* to try some of this."

Whitley went on talking. "Course to me it was just another con. I found out if I looked and talked a certain way, I could pull the wool over Grandma's eyes. And if I could fool her"—he flashed his movie star smile—"believe me, everybody else was cake."

"Gee," I said wryly, "and here I thought you were more than just a pretty face."

"That came later," he said. "Back in Cleveland, everybody loved young Leedon. That wily little punk had the world on a string. Played a good game of B-ball. Pulled decent grades. Even managed to get himself a scholarship at Oberlin. Was gonna be an *ac-tuh,* like Paul-freakin-Robeson."

I took a bite of key lime. "What happened?"

"Halfway through the spring semester, I got kicked out for stealing an English exam. It was a blow to my inflated ego, getting caught like that." He started tapping his foot again. "After all, I'd been doing it for years. You want to finish this last little bit?"

I shook my head and watched him scarf it down, my stomach churning. But really, I chided myself, what did stealing exams as a kid have to do with a missing Macintosh anyway?

"After that," Whitley was saying, "I did a brief stint in the Marine Corps. Pissed my pants every day for the first three months I was so scared, but it ended up turning me around. When I got out, I came down here. By that time, my mother had remarried. My stepdad was a cop. One of the good guys." He leaned back in his chair. "He passed away last year. But he helped me get started on the force. And me and Mom, well, we ended up pretty close."

"So that detective wasn't kidding when he said your mama was on the line?"

Whitley laughed. "They like to tease because they're jealous. See, I'm the local babe magnet." He leaned forward. "You got a boyfriend, Garner Quinn?"

At some point his foot had stopped jiggling and mine had started. "Not really. There was someone but"—I looked down at my hands, completely mortified by my sudden urge to tell the truth—"the last time I saw him he told me it could never work between us."

"How come?"

"He said I didn't know when to leave well enough alone."

Whitley's smile went from ear to ear. "*Shi-iit,*" he crowed. "He sure got you pegged."

ON THE WAY back to my car we stopped by the windows of an indoor skating rink. As the skaters glided by, Whitley casually said, "How 'bout sometime I tell you the idea I got for this cop story?"

My spine stiffened. It might've been the carelessness in his tone, or maybe, backlit by the icy brightness of the skating rink, I saw a sudden glint of that handsome, wily boy who knew how to fool his elders. "Better not cast your pearls to other writers, Leedon," I replied. "Most of them are born scavengers. They just love picking up material wherever they can find it." *Like off of somebody else's hard drive,* I thought to myself.

"Sorry I brought it up," he said frostily.

"Tell you what," I said, softening. "Once you have something on paper, show it to me. I'll see what I can do." I felt a surge of guilt when I saw the grateful expression on Whitley's face. My offer had come with strings attached. I was determined to find out, once and for all, if the young detective had anything to do with the disappearance of TJ Sterling's computer.

27

IT WAS TEN-FIFTY when I reached the Biltmore Grill. I used the phone near the restrooms to check TJ's answering machine. The only message was from Hogan, who sounded tense. "Miss Beech, this is Mr. Bundy calling. What the hell are you doing still in Virginia?" A pause. "Okay, well, I'm leaving Fantasyland in the morning. I'll try you again from the road."

Sands McColl hadn't canceled, so I ordered a drink and sat down at a table on the patio. When she didn't show by eleven-thirty I called her apartment. Not even the machine picked up. I tried TJ's again. Nothing. By midnight it was obvious I'd been stood up. The glass of wine I'd had with dinner, plus the two I'd nursed here, made me feel sleepy. I paid the check and walked to the parking garage where I'd left the car.

The Volvo had a flat tire.

"Can't change it," the attendant told me. "I got a slipped disc."

"Could I leave it? I'll have someone come by and fix it in the morning."

"Sure," he said genially. "It'll cost you, though."

Sterling's place was only a couple of miles away—a stone's throw, really, if only I'd had on the right shoes. *The walk will do you good,* I told myself, mincing away uncertainly in my high heels.

ONCE ACROSS THE street, the all-hours buzz of the Corner gave way to an unsettling quiet. Thomas Jefferson's Rotunda looked like some magnificent mausoleum for long-dead kings. I began following an uneven band of road-level pavement. The campus lawn swelled above me like steadily rising cake, its curtain of heavy foliage obliterating the buildings and streetlights. I realized, belatedly, that this was probably one of those paths that students would be told to avoid, walking by themselves, late at night.

Walking faster now, I passed under a railroad track trellis, my ridiculously high heels clattering in the still air. It's difficult to say when I became aware of the footsteps. For a while they were nothing more than a percussive tattoo, counterpointing my tempo— speeding up when I hurried, slowing down when I stopped. Real fear didn't grip me until the steps settled into their own rhythm. Whoever it was seemed intent on closing the gap between us. I could feel him gaining on me, bearing down.

The path inclined sharply upward. A huge heroic statue reared out from the clearing on my right—George Rogers Clark on horseback, surrounded by Indians. On the crest of the curving hill I saw a traffic light, and the liquid shape of cars darting through the darkness like pellets of shiny mercury. Instinct told me that the person moving through the shadows had no intention of letting me get to safety. He was only a few yards away, so close I could hear the hot, tumultuous gusts of his breath.

I began to run. Halfway up the hill, my high heel got stuck in a crack of the pavement, wrenching my ankle. The pain was so intense, it shot thousands of tiny stars into the sky behind George Rogers Clark. The hooves of his rearing bronze horse glinted over my head ready to slash me into bits, and grind what was left into the sparkly mica sidewalk. Only a few feet, the darkness behind panted and strained. My only hope was the street.

I scrambled to my feet and stumbled out onto the blacktop.

The approaching headlights were water. They splish-splashed over my silk dress, bathing my entire body in a split-second of false serenity. Then I felt the impact of the car hitting, and I rolled, in exaggerated slo-mo, off the dark hood and hit bottom.

SATURDAY, JUNE 26

IF HE LET her, she would ruin everything. All those years—the formative years, he'd come to think of them, because it had been like starting over from the beginning. Carefully, so carefully, he'd taken one small step after another. That string of menial jobs in the noisy kitchens of truck stops and diners. The first telephone listing in his new name. And, of course, the social security card and the driver's license—both truly developmental milestones.

Each different city had added another layer to the dermis of his identity until, after that first decade, he could actually look in the mirror and see more of the person he was now than the man he once had been.

And tonight, on the verge of settling into a comfortable middle age, the measly consolation prize he'd worked, and slaved, for—the reward he so richly deserved as compensation for the slings and arrows, the personal slights he'd endured—tonight she threatened to take it all away.

He'd acted rashly, but that wouldn't happen again. The way he would succeed was the way he'd always succeeded. He must slough off this feeling of panic and despair and snap back into action. If he regarded the situation with a gamer's eye, he might still win it all.

Strategy and tactics, they were the key. A bold move was called for—perhaps the hedgehog, the old defensive-offensive.

What bothered him, though, was that these dire circumstances would force him to act quickly. In the next twenty-four hours it must be done. Until then, he'd just wait.

Wait patiently. And watch.

28

FOR THE HUNDREDTH time I woke with a start, forcing my conscious self to climb out from the treacherous backslide of sleep. *You're in the hospital,* I told myself, parroting the words of the kind paramedic who'd brought me. *You had an accident.*

CAN YOU TELL me your name, miss? Do you know where you are?

I'm Garner Quinn and I'm in Virginia, I answered in a singsong, and the kind paramedic looked alarmed when I laughed.

A white-haired woman in a blue smock came over with a clipboard, but I wasn't going to answer her questions until I had a chance to ask a few of my own. "What kind of accident?"

The paramedic crouched to face level. "Some kids we talked to said they saw you run into the street. A car hit you, then left the scene." He patted the edge of the stretcher. "You're lucky to be alive."

I didn't feel so lucky. "A hit-and-run," I repeated dully.

"Yes."

Ellen Kresky's son Kenny had been killed in a hit-and-run.

"What kind of car was it?"

The lady in the smock was getting impatient, but the kind paramedic put her off with an understanding wink. "A policeman will be in to talk to you about that later, Miss Quinn," he said, "after the doctors check you out."

"It was, uhmm . . ." My attempt to sit up was cut short by pain. ". . . A maroon Caprice, wasn't it? Was it a maroon Caprice?"

The paramedic looked surprised. "A dark sedan was all they said. Lay back now, miss. You need to stay quiet until they take a look at those ribs." Then he asked curiously, "Why'd you go running into the road, anyway?"

"Somebody was chasing me," I said. But my breath was coming in wheezes by then, and I don't know whether he even heard.

I HAD ANOTHER ten-second dream. A little boy was gathering seashells by the ocean. When he turned I could see that he looked a lot like Lara's little brother, Gordy.

For the hundred and first time, I startled myself awake.

My head throbbed, and it felt as though my ribs had been surgically removed and replaced by a sharp-edged metal cage. I looked around the darkened room. My black silk dress hung limply from a hook on the wall, like a shadow that had lost its shape after being caught. I knew he was out there somewhere, patiently waiting—just another silent, sterile, soulless presence in this silent, sterile, soulless place. Despite my fear, I could feel my eyelids lowering.

This time it was the soft padded footsteps of the nurse that made me jump. "Wha—what time is it?"

She checked her watch, efficiently. "Three-thirty-six."

"In the morning?"

"Yes. Why don't you try to get some rest?"

"Will you stay with me?"

The nurse sighed. "For a minute." I nodded gratefully, knowing that in the space of a minute I could pack any number of deep, dark dream-filled sleeps.

MY NIGHT TERRORS evaporated in the first light of dawn. By mid-morning I'd already begun to wonder whether the footsteps that had sent me rushing into oncoming traffic were real; or if too much wine, added to my anxiety about Spangler, had fermented into paranoia. After all, I told myself, he couldn't be after me. How would he even know where I was?

You left TJ's address and number with Ruth at the Circle of Faith, whispered a small voice inside my head. To banish it, I snapped into action, only to find that even a simple task like dialing the phone took some doing, given the soreness of my ribs and battered body.

Temple's faraway hello made me want to cry. "Hey, kiddo," I said.

"Mom." She sounded relieved, then worried. "What's the matter?"

"Just feeling my age, that's all," I replied, knowing she wouldn't buy the answer. We'd had so many of these long-distance conversations, we were attuned to the smallest nuance in each other's voices that might signify trouble.

"Where are you?" she asked.

"Still in Virginia, unfortunately."

Temple was crestfallen. "For how long?"

"I'm not sure, Tem." Now it was my turn to read between my daughter's lines. "Why?"

"I was kind of hoping we could spend a few days together . . . before Dad's wedding."

My heart throbbed against the splintery wreck of my rib cage. "Well, gee, sweetie," I said. "Do you think he'd be okay with that?"

"I already asked." What began as a sigh ended in a strangulated sob. "I really miss you, Mom."

"I miss you too, baby," I whispered softly. "Put your father on, okay? We'll work something out."

"Promise?"

"You bet."

"Great." Temple started sobbing in earnest. "I love you."

"Me, too."

I heard the muffled sounds of the receiver being handed off, then Andy's hello. Temmy's overtired, he said. They'd been really keeping her on the go. And since he and Candace were swamped with last-minute preparations, maybe a little down time with me would be a good thing for all of us. I considered his choice of words—*down time*—and figured there was probably a subtext here.

"I have a few things to iron out on my end," I told him. *Like some cracked ribs, a slight concussion, a fugitive murderer on the run.* Luckily, Andy had never been in tune with the subtleties of my voice; to him, I probably sounded swell.

"It should take another day or so. Meantime, I'll book a little getaway for Temple and me. Think you can bring her to the airport, say, the day after tomorrow?"

Andy sighed, wrestling with the impatience that for years had been the only emotion he showed. In the ensuing silence, I could almost hear him griping—*Dammit, Garner, don't you think I have better things to do? Why can't you come get her yourself?*—until the new, improved Andy Matera got himself together.

"I suppose so," he said. "Just call my secretary with the details."

THE NOVELTY OF this hospital stay had completely worn off. I spent the next couple of hours rattling the cage of every passing nurse and doctor I could find, demanding to be released. While the painfully slow process of being signed out got under way, I continued to treat my hospital room as a makeshift office.

Sands McColl appeared to have fallen into a black hole.

I left a message on Caroline Sterling's answering machine at Cheswick Forest saying I was leaving town in the morning and that I'd call in a few days; then, still suffering from a hangover of last night's paranoia, I added, "Do me a favor and stay at your parents' until you hear from me. I haven't talked to the authorities yet. So just sit tight."

Finally, on a gamble, I tried J. Emmett Hogan at his office, but only got his voice mail. It took me several minutes to summon up enough nerve to dial him at home. "Yeah?" he answered brusquely.

"Hi."

"Where the hell are you?"

"University Hospital in Charlottesville."

"Jesus," he groaned. "What happened?"

"I had a little accident, but that's not important now." I hurried on. "Listen, Hoge, you know TJ Sterling, right?—the writer who was found shot to death last week?"

"I've heard of him," came the cautionary reply.

"I think he was murdered by Gordon Spangler."

I heard Hogan sucking in a long breath. *"Sterling* was your source?"

"Uh-huh."

"He did a book on the murders, didn't he?"

"Yes," I said, closing my eyes in an attempt to ease my splitting headache. "A month ago, he asked me to dinner. Said he'd seen Spangler, that he had him under surveillance. I begged him to call you, but he convinced me to give him a little more time."

I let Hogan swear for a while before continuing. "Anyway, at some point Spangler must've realized he was being trailed, and he decided Sterling had to go."

"How did it happen?"

"He just waited for the right opportunity. Sterling had a stupid habit of hiding his key outside. It would've been simple for Spangler to find it and get into the office."

I went on, building my case. "TJ had been on a drinking jag for months. All Spangler needed to do was lurk in the shadows until the poor sucker passed out. Oh, and you'll enjoy this. Sterling kept a loaded Austrian Steyr in his desk drawer."

Hogan groaned, "Jesus. For Spangler it would've been like riding a bike . . ."

I suddenly felt beat. "Help me, Hogan," I said. "There's a man named Owen Larson. He has a night job with a Lutheran organization down here called the Circle of Faith. He fits Spangler's general description, but—"

Leedon Whitley walked into my room carrying a bouquet of daisies.

"Well, what do you know," I said with false cheeriness, "looks like I have a visitor."

"Damn you, Garner," J. Emmett Hogan protested, "don't you dare hang up—"

"I'll call you back later. In the meantime, maybe you could check around? Thanks a million." Hogan's voice was just a small tinny roar in the earpiece. I tried to hang up the phone, but the receiver fell out of my hand and dropped off the bed. Whitley stooped over and replaced it on the cradle.

"That was my contractor back in Jersey," I explained. "I'm in the middle of some intense renovations."

"If you say so," he said.

"How'd you know I was here?"

"Like I told you"—the detective walked over to the windowsill and picked up an empty vase—"all of Charlottesville is my oyster."

"Don't bother with the flowers," I said. "I'm bailing out momentarily."

"That's cool." Whitley shrugged. "But it don't look like you'll be driving anytime soon."

"I can call a taxi."

"You could." He grinned. "Or if you promise to put that slinky black dress back on again, I might even let you hitch a ride with me."

IT WAS AFTER three o'clock when the nurse helped me out of the wheelchair and left me standing with Whitley's cellophane cone of daisies on the sidewalk in front of the hospital. A few minutes later the detective pulled up in a black Chevy Caprice.

The intake of breath pierced my ribs like an arrow. I hobbled to the passenger side.

"You okay?" the detective asked. "Your face just went gray."

"I'm just a little shaky," I said, lowering myself into the seat with difficulty.

Whitley reached across my lap to shut the door, then straightened up and pressed the auto lock. Four sets of doorlocks snapped shut at once. "Want me to get the seat belt for you?" he asked solicitously.

"No." When I shook my head, everything hurt. "I can do it." As we pulled away from the curb, I stared out over the long, dark hood, and once again I felt the impact . . . the slow-motion roll . . . the slap of the macadam. It was possible, I realized. Whitley could've followed me to the Corner. But why would he want to hurt me?

Again my mind went back to Sterling's Macintosh.

The pain in my ribs made it impossible to turn, so I sneaked a sideways glance and saw Leedon Whitley, lazily palming the steering wheel, humming a tune, his face a blank. "You know, I've changed my mind," I said suddenly. "I don't feel like going back to TJ's, after all. Why don't you just drop me off at the Omni?"

Whitley frowned. "What about your stuff?"

"I'll pick it up tomorrow."

"That's dumb. We can swing by now, and I'll run in and get your bags."

"No," I told him, too loudly. "I need a hot bath and some room service. Take me to the hotel. Please."

He shook his head and muttered, "No wonder why that boyfriend you had ran off on you. Probably was either that, or end up wringin' your pretty neck."

I CHAIN-LOCKED THE door to my room and dragged a chair over in front of it. The scalding hot water in the tub first repelled, and then seduced, my aching body. I felt as though I'd been hit by a truck—or at the very least, I thought wryly, a dark Chevrolet. Half an hour later, wrapped in a terry cloth guest robe, I drifted into sleep.

I had a dream that Lara and I were jumping rope on the flat green surface of my father's tennis court. Temple was there, too, turning the rope with me. Suddenly, Caroline's stepsister, Vicki, broke into our game.

She pushed Lara aside and started skipping so fast, we had to struggle to keep up with her. The crack of the rope against the court made my head ache—

The next thing I knew, it was dark outside and the clock read 9 P.M. I put on my black dress and high-heeled shoes. Down in the lobby, I bought a bottle of mineral water and some Advil. Then I had the girl at the reception desk call a taxi.

30

THE DRIVER STARED straight ahead with an air of mute annoyance while I folded my bruised and battered body into the backseat of his cab. I gave him the address and, without a word, he slipped the gear out of park and lurched away into the night. The face-front picture on the license affixed to the dashboard showed a weary man with bloodshot eyes and skin like pocked saddle leather. His name was Wilson P. Rose, and although probably only my age, life had long ago stitched permanent lines of anger onto his face. We passed the trip in silence.

The minute the car pulled up to Sterling's dark apartment building, I experienced a rush of sudden panic. "Could you pull in the drive, please?" I asked. Mr. Rose grudgingly followed my request, but kept the engine idling. "How much do I owe you?"

"Eight-seventy-five."

I gave him a ten and a five, and told him to keep the change. It seemed to take me forever to get out the door. As I was limping away, he shouted, "Sure you all right goin' in? You want, I could check it out first."

His unexpected kindness caught me by surprise. I turned. "Thanks," I called back, wincing from the sudden sideways motion, "but I'm okay."

Under the dome light, Rose's face reorganized itself into angry pleats. It occurred to me he'd taken offense, but before I had a chance to smooth things over, the taxi veered into reverse and careened down the quiet street. When the red smear of its brake lights vanished I resumed walking at a snail's pace toward the back of the building.

You're really quite the picture, aren't you, I laughed to myself, *in your rumpled dress and wobble-heeled pumps?* Only yesterday, this sleek black frock had seemed the height of understated sophistication. Twenty-four hours later, I looked and felt like a mid-priced call girl after an extended booking—smudged, bedraggled, and sore in places that shouldn't be spoken of in polite company.

Pushing through the gate, I was pleased to see that at least I'd remembered to leave the patio light on. On a whim, I checked the Weber kettle just to make sure Sterling's key hadn't magically reappeared. It hadn't. I unlocked the glass door and slid it open.

The figure disengaged from the shadows as soon as I stepped inside, catching me before I could reach for the switch. In one split-freeze-frame-millisecond, I saw the patio light glinting off a pistol, heard the click, and then the gun firing.

I fell backward.

It took another moment to realize that I hadn't been hit, but that was a moment too long. Spangler charged at me. I groped around in the darkness, somehow miraculously connecting with the hockey stick I'd kept propped up against the wall since the night of the break-in. I brought the stick down hard on his arm, knocking the gun to the floor.

A spray of hysterical laughter exploded in my throat and stuck there; it tasted like bile. *Just get to the door,* I told myself, *run away and then throw up.* White light poured through the partially open slider and spilled on the floor like milk. My legs were numb and shaking so hard I had to hang on to the curtains to stay upright. Pain spliced through my rib cage.

Three more steps, I urged, *two*—

Then his elbow hooked around my neck and yanked hard from behind.

You bastard! I screamed—or maybe I just thought it—because by then the crushing blow to my windpipe had left me speechless. Lifting me right out of my shoes, Spangler dragged me back toward TJ's desk. I kicked and squirmed, fighting for air. The darkness turned peacock blue, shooting stars that were jabs of the purest, most exquisite kind of pain. I flailed my arms, wildly. My fingers must've brushed against his face, because I remember thinking, *Strange, his skin is black and woolly,* then— *oh, he's wearing a ski mask;* and somehow that seemed the cruellest part of all, that Gordon Spangler would remain faceless to the very end of my life.

We collided with the desk and everything on it went flying. With his free hand he fumbled around, feeling for something on the blotter. I heard a thudding sound, some heavy object falling, and then a faint buzzing, which meshed with the ringing in my ears of a faraway chorus—'Hallelujah, hallelujah' . . .

His grip loosened, ever so slightly. The sudden rush of air was like a fist rammed down my throat. I choked and sputtered, but somehow found the strength to push myself away. Without shoes, I could move faster. I'd almost reached the card table when I felt the long telephone cord loop around my neck and lasso me back. The coated wire was eating its way into my skin, causing the peacock night to run all around me in slow, inky blobs.

I heard *pop, pop, pop,* such tiny, delicate little noises—probably the bones in my neck breaking—and then I remembered Lara, and the moonstone necklace, and I understood that I was only a couple of breaths away from dying the same kind of death.

He had jammed me against the desk, using both hands to tighten the phone-cord noose. Beneath us the cheap metal desk rolled like thunder. His head was just a black knob with two eyeholes. As he leaned forward I sank my teeth into his arm, biting right through the sleeve of his sweatshirt. He grunted in pain.

Desperately groping for anything I could find on the desktop, I grabbed a sharpened pencil—and drove it as hard as I could into his shoulder. A cry rattled around in his throat. He let go of me so quickly, that when I fell the floor hit my ribs with the force of a two-by-four. After the room stopped turning, I struggled to my feet.

He was already gone.

I removed the cord from around my neck, pulling myself along its snaking path until I found the phone. My hands trembled as though palsied, and yet somehow the number came. I heard Hogan's gruff hello.

"Gordon Spangler just tried to kill me," I sobbed hoarsely. "Come quick, Hogan. You've got to catch him."

PART THREE

"WHY!" SAID HUXTER, SUDDENLY,

"THAT'S NOT A MAN AT ALL. IT'S JUST

EMPTY CLOTHES."

H . G . W E L L S
THE INVISIBLE MAN

1

MONDAY, JUNE 28

AT 8:15 A.M., two FBI agents intercepted Owen Larson as he
emerged from his apartment in the Rio Ridge Gardens on his way to go
to work. The twelve-person stake-out team which surrounded the
complex included members of local law enforcement—among them,
detectives William Tyree and Leedon Whitley; as well as interested
observers, namely, special agent J. Emmett Hogan from the FBI's Investigative Support Unit and me.

For most of that previous night, Hogan and I had sat in a parked
car, drinking coffee, seldom talking. Although every muscle in my
body hurt, I refused Hogan's pleas to go back to the hotel, choos-
ing instead to palm down Advils as if they were going out of style.
When the news finally came over the squawk box that Larson had
been taken into custody, Hogan turned to me and said, "Garner
Quinn, you've just captured Gordon Spangler. What're you going to
do now?"

"I guess I'm going to Disneyworld," I replied, feeling dazed and
uncertain.

"Mention my name," he suggested wryly. "They'll give you a set of good ears."

BACK AT THE hotel, I took a long, hot shower, and mentally ticked off the names of people I needed to call: Temple, to tell her I loved her; my travel agent, so she could book two flights to Orlando; Andy's secretary; my agent, Max (*no, Max, this doesn't mean I'm coming out of retirement*); Caroline—and heck, while I was at it, Maureen; then Ellen Kresky, who'd be the most relieved of all . . .

Hogan's call came as I was towel-drying my hair. "Garner," he said, and the ensuing quietude made my heart stop.

"He escaped?"

"No. We let him go," Hogan sighed. "He wasn't our man, Garner. He wasn't Spangler."

I'D HAD ONE small part of it right.

Owen Larson *was* living under an assumed name, but his real one wasn't Gordon Spangler, it was Roger Lang. For almost fifty-five years, Mr. Lang had lived a life of relative obscurity in a small suburb of Minneapolis, teaching mathematics at the senior high and Sunday school at Grace Lutheran. He'd been married for nearly thirty years to his college sweetheart. The couple had a teenaged daughter—from all accounts a lovely child—named Irene.

Then one day Lang's seemingly devoted wife contracted one of his students to kill him, and everything changed.

In a tragic twist, the car bomb meant to splatter Roger all over his driveway ended up killing young Irene. Mr. Lang found himself excruciatingly alone, and smack dab in the public eye. Reeling with grief and shock, he endured the humiliation of a highly publicized trial where he learned—among other things—that his wife had been unfaithful to him for years. Hounded by the press, with his life still in ruins, Lang sold his house and moved to Virginia. There he changed his name to Owen Larson, eventually settling in Charlottesville. He got a job at a local library, and to pass the long nights, began doing odd jobs at the Lutheran Circle of Faith. Ultimately, this led to a salaried custodial position. Lang confided his story to the Circle's director, who felt protective of the shy little fellow and promised to respect his hard-won anonymity.

In recent months, he'd started to court a widow who attended a bereavement group at the Circle. His co-workers said he'd seemed guardedly happy for the first time in years.

One newspaper reported that Lang-Larson might sue me for harassment and libel. Secretly, I hoped that he would. A nice hefty settlement seemed the very least that I owed the poor man.

2

DISNEYWORLD NO LONGER seemed like such a good idea. Instead, my agent kindly offered me the use of his private beach house in Captiva.

In fact, the words *kind* and *generous* best describe the outpouring of support from friends and business acquaintances during those first few awful days after Owen Larson's arrest. Amazing how far a major public disgrace can go in endearing you to people—it was as if Garner Quinn, the screw-up, was somehow more lovable than Garner Quinn, the success. At one point an irreverent thought popped into my head, *Oh, if only Dudley were alive to see me now . . .*

I MET MY daughter in Fort Myers, Florida. Despite the crushing temperature, she convinced me to put the top down on our rented green Mustang, so the sun could beat mercilessly on us all the way from the airport to Sanibel Island. By the time we reached Max's secluded haven on the tip of Captiva, Temple was flushed and giddy, while I felt bone-bleached and dried up—in danger of being blown away by the hot wind like a small pile of dust.

I didn't let on, though. If nothing else, I was good at pretending.

Temple never mentioned Larson or Gordon Spangler, although I felt certain she must've seen the embarrassing headlines before she left New York. We spent the coolest hours of every morning gathering seashells in galvanized tin buckets. Later we stacked them into careful piles, like fanciful, one-of-a-kind Christmas gifts we planned to give some imaginary friends. Temple fashioned jewelry out of the smallest, most perfect shells. She put one on a silver chain and wore it every day.

On the beach, slathered with sunblock and literally stunned by the heat, I hid under my wide-brimmed hat and dark sunglasses, reverting to old childhood games. I pretended I was a terminally ill woman; a Mafia princess; a spy. Temple bobbed in the surf, her stylish, close-cropped hair still such a surprise to me that sometimes, in a sudden panic, I'd lose her among the other swimmers before realizing, *Oh, thank God, there she is—that gorgeous young woman belongs to me . . .*

Despite my insistence on frequent applications of lotion, my daughter's skin quickly grew brown, except for two pink patches high on her cheekbones where some of my Irish had seeped through her father's dominant Mediterranean coloring. In her aqua maillot with the delicate shell pendant, she looked too thin, and, I thought, a little sad, but I didn't say so. *Kind* and *generous*—these were the watchwords.

During the scorching afternoon hours we napped or played gin rummy, then we took a ridiculously long time to dress for dinner. Each night I'd drive to a different fancy restaurant, with Temple straddling the console, begging please, please could she steer. Mostly, we kept to ourselves. My daughter appeared to be as satisfied with this arrangement as I was.

Only a few people knew where we were. Andy checked in the first night to make sure Temple had arrived in Florida safely. J. Emmett Hogan strategically timed his calls so that we'd be out. He sang little snatches of songs for me on the answering machine; among my favorites, a show tune— *"When you walk through a storm, hold your head up high . . .";* a romantic ballad— *"The way you wear your hat, the way you sip your . . .";* and the requisite Springsteen— *"I'm in love with a Jersey girl—"*

Once, sounding half in the bag, he left this brief message. "Hey, in the words of some wise person I used to know—we do what we can, right?" Before hanging up he added, "You did what you could, Garner."

THE MORNING BEFORE we were scheduled to leave, we walked on the beach as usual. Temple stopped to pick up a shell and I noticed she was crying. "What's wrong?" I asked.

She waved me away. "Just so you know, I'm not going back to Dad's," she said, jutting out her chin. "I want to go home with you."

Whoa, I thought, *where did this come from?* Out loud I said, "What about the wedding?"

Temple turned and threw the shell far out into the ocean. "I don't care," she said. "They don't need me to get married."

"Maybe not. Only think how disappointed your dad would be. He's counting on you."

"So?" Her lovely face contorted. "When was he ever there for *me?"*
He wasn't, I thought, and yet, somehow there was no satisfaction in admitting that to her now. I watched her run away, her calves glistening and hard, like running fish—a squiggle of aqua moving over white sand, then disappearing under the shade of our umbrella.

I found her sitting crosslegged, hands over her face. "Temple." I sank down on the mat. "You made a commitment."

When she didn't respond, I went on in my best adult voice. "I know it's hard, sweetheart. Relationships are hard. But you can't just give up on them. You've got to keep trying."

Temple lifted her head. "What do you know about that?" she asked, not smart-alecky or fresh-mouthed, but with such heartwrenching solemnity I didn't know what to say. "You loved Dane, but you gave up on him, didn't you?"

"That's different."

"You gave up your writing," Temple persisted. "And just because you made a mess with this guy Larson, you're ready to give up on finding Gordon Spangler, aren't you?"

"How do you know about that?"

"I *read,* Mother," Temple sighed, adding cuttingly, "And, believe it or not, there are *some* people who actually talk to me." She picked up a shell and wrote her initials in the sand: T-Q-M. "Dad says that man Owen Larson should sue the pants off you," and her expression and inflection were so very much Andy's, for a moment it was almost as if he were sitting under the shade of the umbrella with us.

"Is that why you're angry with him?" I asked gently.

Temple pressed the letters of her name with the flat of her palm, erasing them. "I'm just tired of him always trying to get me to say things about you."

I couldn't help being curious. "You mean like bad stuff?"

"Bad, good"—Temple shrugged—"it's just . . . weasly the way he does it. I mean, I love Dad and all. I just don't think I like him much, you know?"

Now that she'd started, the words kept tumbling out. "And Candace, well, she's way too nice. Perfect, almost. Only she's not." Temple paused. ". . . you."

For the first time in days, I forgot about Owen Larson and Gordon

Spangler, about the travesty in Charlottesville, and Hogan's chipper, beaten voice on the tape. That my daughter could love her father and yet see him for a weasel, that she could admire her new stepmother for being perfect and still long for *me* . . . well, what else really mattered?

At that moment, in our small patch of shade on this tiny, sunscorched island, all seemed suddenly right with the world.

THAT EVENING AFTER our last big-deal restaurant meal, I surprised myself twice. First, with my daughter right there listening, I canceled my flight back to Newark and called Avis to extend the lease of the Mustang. "Does that mean you're going back to Virginia?" Temple asked.

"I guess I can't give up so easily after all. What about you?"

"It's only another week and a half," she said stoically, giving me a hug.

Later, I lounged on the bed, watching in the mirror as Temple trimmed her boyish hair. "Can you do that for me?" I asked suddenly.

"You want me to snip off the ends?"

"No," I said. "I want you to cut it all off."

WHENEVER I DREAMT about cutting off my hair, I'd wake up in a cold sweat, scared to death that my crown and cross—my shining glory, the thick, nettly curtain I hid behind—might really be gone. It astonished me how easy it was to finally let that go.

Temple worked for an hour trying to get it to slick back, or wisp forward, to *do something* , but even after it continued stubbornly going its own way, I didn't mind. I liked the stark, choppy ugliness of it. For the first time, I understood why Sands McColl shaved her head, what a liberating feeling it was to strip oneself down to basics . . .

Walking to the gate the next morning, I glanced away from the reflections in the plate glass windows of the airport shops. My shorn head felt strangely light, as if in addition to the knotted tangle of curls, some heavy-as-lead part of me was now gone, too.

"Love you, Mom," Temple said as they announced passenger boarding. Then, impulsively, she lifted the shell pendant over her head and placed it around my neck.

"Now a part of me goes with you," she said.

I kissed her and, remembering Lara, added, "Always."

I TOOK THE long drive back to Virginia at a leisurely pace, listening to the radio and trying not to think too much. My appetite, which after the Owen Larson fiasco had dwindled to the point of nonexistence, returned with a vengeance. The mere sight of a knife-and-fork symbol on an exit ramp set my mouth watering. I meal-rotated all the major highway chains—Cracker Barrels, Shoneys, Stuckeys—pleasantly buoyed by their bustling, family-style ambience.

For the most part, though, I kept to myself, my eyes glued to TJ's journal, as if it were a novel I just couldn't put down. After dessert and coffee, I made notes on what I'd read, dividing each sheet of paper into five neat columns:

REAL ESTATE
UNIVERSITY
GAMES
BARS AND RESTAURANTS
PEOPLE

Somewhere, I told myself, within these wide-ranging areas, TJ had hidden a clue—a tiny marker that would point me toward Spangler.

Under the "REAL ESTATE" heading I listed the Albemarle Planning and Development Corporation; Cheswick Forest; and Ashford Hills Estates, along with the bracketed code word, [*Shangri-La*]. Sterling referred to UVA's English department as *Wils Hall* in some places, *Section 8* in others. I noted both in the "UNIVERSITY" column, and added, *Did TJ share an office? Did he have a departmental secretary?*

Painstakingly, I matched Sterling's jottings with the establishments in the Charlottesville entertainment guide. Nicknames such as *Gidget, Shaft, Little Ms. Muffet,* and *the Big Cheez,* I assigned to the "PEOPLE" column. Under "GAMES," I wrote: *Go back to shop on mall—Get listings for computer software and board game retailers—Check internet cafés.* I could've added a sixth heading—"RELIGION"—but after my botched investigation into the Circle of Faith, I decided it was best to lay low from church organizations for a while.

By the time I reached Brunswick, Georgia, I'd committed most of the datebook to memory.

ALONG THE JOURNEY, I took note of a curious phenomenon. People seemed to be treating me differently. Waitresses lingered for a bit of a chat after delivering my order. Old folks I met in passing seemed compelled to tell me their life histories: where they'd come from, where they were going, their unrealized hopes and dreams. Some even showed pictures of the grandchildren who waited back home. Every stop I made, it was the same. Lethargic gas station attendants stumbled into the oppressive heat just to clean my windshield. Young couples smiled apologetically as their spaghetti sauce-stained kids played endless games of peek-a-boo with me over the wooden partition between booths. It was as if this new, short-haired version of me were infinitely more winning and accessible. Ironic that it should happen now, I thought; such irresistible charm would've come in handy, walking the true-crime beat.

In Savannah I bought a pair of sunglasses, a flax-colored linen suit, and several pale, dropwaisted sundresses that made me look and feel like Zelda Fitzgerald—golden and manically gay. That night, I tried them on in my hotel room. "Hello, I'm Garner Quinn," I said, introducing myself to the face in the mirror.

The face grimaced prettily. "Hi there," I amended, "I'm—"

TWO DAYS LATER I checked into a charming old bed-and-breakfast inn called the Eighteen-Twenty Ivy, on the outskirts of Charlottesville. "Are you here on business or pleasure, Ms."—the innkeeper's eyes wandered to the guest ledger where I'd signed my ex-husband's fiancee's name in bold script—"Kressler?"

"A little of both," I replied with a smile. "And, please, call me Candace."

The lies just rolled off my tongue. I figured, since God hadn't helped me find Gordon Spangler, all bets between us were off.

4

MONDAY, JULY 12

AFTER BREAKFAST THE next morning I put on my new linen suit and headed over to the university. On the way, I made a pit stop at the local drugstore where I bought an inexpensive pair of round, tortoiseshell + 1.00 reading glasses. They magnified my eyes just slightly, and complimented the heart shape of my face which had for years been obscured by a halo of hair. I no longer worried that someone would recognize me; I hardly recognized myself.

Wilson Hall was a newish building, all brick and glass—quiet as a hospital and footsoundingly empty. It took me forever to find the office, and when I finally did, it was locked. I spotted a young woman in cutoffs and a bright orange tee shirt about to push through an exit door. "Excuse me," I called. "I'm looking for the secretary?"

The girl turned. "Everybody's on vacation. Better try again next week."

Yeah, sure, I thought, already shifting to Plan B.

Over at the Admissions Office business appeared to be in if not full, then at least half swing. I took a steno pad from my shoulder bag, adjusted my glasses, and stepped up to the counter. "Hi, there."

An earnest-faced woman of about twenty-five asked if she could help.

"I sure hope so." I smiled. "I'm Candace Kressler, the lifestyle correspondent for *Albemarle Today*? We're doing a feature for next month's issue, which we're calling 'Seniors.' It's about people over the age of fifty-five who go back to college for their degrees?—and, well, I was hoping someone here in Admissions might be able to fill me in on how many older students you have, maybe even put me in touch with a few for a personal profile."

"That sounds great," the woman said enthusiastically. "If you don't mind waiting a little, I'll go ask who you should see." She disappeared into the inner office. *Such a breeze,* I thought, humming a zippy tune, *when you're Candace Kressler.*

Five minutes passed. Then six. And seven. When the woman returned, she looked positively crestfallen. "I'm afraid we can't give out that information unless you go through our Press and Media office first. Would you like their number?"

"I guess," and I thought, *Was there* anybody *left in the world without a press agent?* "But I sort of hoped to be able to circumvent all that."

"I'm sorry," she said sympathetically; then her small, earnest face lit up. "I bet it's interesting, isn't it, being a reporter?"

"Some days," I told her, "are better than others."

ARMED WITH A small green Chamber of Commerce map highlighted with bright yellow circles and arrows, I hopped back into the rental, heading east. Twenty minutes later I saw an elegant sign:

Ashford Hills Estates

AFFORDABLE GOLF CLUB LIVING
Sales Center Open
11 AM–5 PM Weekdays and Saturdays
(Closed Thursdays)
Noon–5 PM Sundays

Nestled in a green valley, Ford Childress's mid-range Shangri-La consisted of a maze of homesites built around an impressive southern-style inn. A row of model homes stood near the gate, each differentiated by a letter of the alphabet. Behind them, other homes were in various stages of completion. The sales office turned out to be a spotless white trailer plunked down in a rutted basin of overturned dirt. Two terra-cotta planters filled with pink geraniums provided a much-needed touch of color.

I parked the Mustang, immediately trading my sunglasses for the tortoiseshell frames. The wind had wiped my shorn caplet of hair into little peaks. Glimpsed from the narrow rectangle of my rearview mirror, it looked like burnt meringue. I ran a hand through it and slipped out of the car, carefully tiptoeing around the potholes.

The geraniums in the planter wanted watering; their petals had crumpled in the heat. I pushed open the door without knocking. A woman sat inside the trailer, eating a strawberry yogurt. She had a narrow face, accentuated by a poker-straight pageboy, and her hair, skin, nails, lips, and suit were the same shade of frosted tan.

"Hi, there," I said, "I'm looking for Tom Sterling."

"Mr. Sterling isn't here," she replied with practiced efficiency. "I'm Molly Moffat, the sales consultant. Can I help you?"

I took in the scene again—the slight, frosty Molly Moffat, ensconced behind a desk, spooning up her Dannon—and TJ's sarcastic voice fairly rang through my ears:

Little Ms. Muffet sits on her tuffet,
Eating her curds and whey . . .

"I hope so, Molly," I said, trying not to laugh out loud. "I met Tom when I was down here a couple of months ago, and well"—I gave her an embarrassed little shrug—"we got to talking and I told him I was thinking about relocating my business here from New York. He said he was in real estate. He gave me this business card." I handed her one of the leftovers I'd found in TJ's apartment.

"I'm afraid I have some bad news," Ms. Moffat said. "Mr. Sterling passed on a few weeks ago."

"Passed . . . You mean he *died?* But he was so young!"

"Fifty-one." She nodded. "Very tragic."

"How awful. I'm shocked."

"We all were," said Moffat smoothly. "Of course, if you're still interested, I'd be glad to show you around Ashford Hills, Ms.—"

"Kressler," I told her, adding, "Candace Kressler. And yes, I'd like that."

I managed a sheepish laugh. "I know this is an awful thing to say—but, to tell you the truth, I'm a bit relieved—not that Tom's dead, of course—my gracious, that's really awful. It's just . . . well, the night we spoke, he seemed rather heavily . . . intoxicated—"

"Unfortunately," said the all-suffering Ms. Molly Moffat, "he had a problem with his drinking."

"Oh." I nodded. "Now it all makes sense. See, at first when he heard I was from New York, he told me he was a writer. Then, later on, he switched and said he was in real estate."

"Tom did write books, but he never managed any of the actual sales here at Ashford," Molly added with a strained smile. "He, um . . . married into the company."

"Ahhh."

Moffat passed me a full-color brochure, with a beveled insert of her business card on the cover: *MOLLY BAYLOR MOFFAT, Sales Consultant.* "Just to give you some background," she said. "My home number is listed on the bottom."

I thumbed through the booklet. "These are lovely. Just beautiful."

"Wait till you see the interiors," Molly said, already segueing into her sales pitch. "If you have the time, I'd be happy to show you around."

"That would be great."

Moffat picked up her beeper and a set of keys. "Better turn on the answering machine," she reminded herself with a martyred sigh. "It appears I'm without an assistant again today."

"Stuck out here on your own?" I shook my head in sympathy. "Hasn't anyone come in to replace Tom?"

Molly opened the door for me, and we stepped into the torpid heat. "Tom only dropped by a couple of times a month, anyway. When the paychecks came in."

"Oh, I get it." I kept my eyes trained on the muddy ground, stepping carefully. "A no-show."

"It seems to run in the family. The daughter's supposed to be my summer help."

"Daughter? You mean Sterling's wife?"

"No, this one's the stepchild." Moffat lowered her voice, confidentially, although there wasn't another soul in sight. "I heard she had trouble, growing up. Some sort of abuse from the real father, you know how these things go. Anyway, the poor thing turned out strange. Anti-social, I'd call it. Which is so difficult," Moffat went on briskly, "when she's sitting at the front desk, taking calls. Last week she just about *killed* one of my sales—"

"No kidding."

"Oh dear, Candace," Molly Moffat apologized, "I'm afraid this mud is gettin' all over your pretty shoes."

"Don't you worry," I told her. "A little dirt never bothered me."

5

BY THE TIME we walked through the first two models, I'd pretty much charmed the polyester pantsuit off of Little Ms. Moffat. *The location was perfect,* I gushed, *and I just adore the floorplans.*

"Well, of course"— she beamed back at me—"in your business, you'd recognize quality."

Along the way I'd mentioned that I owned a small but exclusive interior design company. *We do a lot of celebrities,* I said with a casual shrug. Standing in a pool of pristine light in the custom-decorated living room of Model C, Moffat's eyes positively glowed. She knew she'd hit the real-estate sales jackpot. I was one of those rare breeds: a highly motivated, financially qualifed buyer.

"I think I prefer the four-bedroom," I said, "but in brick."

"We can do a brick front, no problem. I have some stunning photographs of the various facades, back at the office." She cleared her throat. "Of course, brick would be considered an extra."

I waved off the added expense. "You'll be able to finish the house in roughly the same time?"

"Absolutely," Moffat promised. "Four to six months." We began strolling back toward the office.

"How many of the sites have been sold?"

"Eighty-three to date. Phase One is just about completed."

"If you don't mind my asking," I said, delicately, "what's the average buyer like?"

"Oh, we have a lovely mix of people. Professionals and businesspeople, such as yourself. Very upscale. No young children."

"That's good."

"You're not married, Candace?"

It took a split-second to realize she was talking to me. "No," I said. "Not anymore, thank God."

Moffat nodded with the vehemence of the bitterly divorced; I could tell she was beginning to like me even more. "Amen. Well, then you'll appreciate that Ashford caters to singles and young marrieds, although we do have a few empty-nesters."

She opened the front door and we walked toward my car together. I asked her what the next step should be. "You just pick out your plan and sign a contract," Moffat said. "We can do it now, if you'd like. All that's required is a ten-percent down payment on the home, and in thirty days, we'll need fifty percent for whatever extras you chose. Then, once the contracts go out, there's a standard three-day waiting period for the attorney review."

I nodded. "Okay. I wish we could go over those details now, but unfortunately, I have a meeting in town. How about I call you in the morning?"

"That's fine," said Molly Moffat, although it was clear she'd rather have my John Hancock on a set of papers tonight. "I'll be here before eleven—or you can give me a buzz at home, any time."

As I slid behind the wheel, she said, "I think you're gonna just love

Ashford, Candace. I don't know whether I told you, but *Southern Living* has just classified us as a 'New Classic.' And, of course," she ran on, "the club and leisure membership is included with all the properties—do you play golf or tennis?"

"I play both," I said, and the lie melted in my mouth like butter.

INSTEAD OF EXITING directly out the front gate, I took the marginal road that wound through the development. Makeshift signs stood at intervals, marking would-be streets—*Honeysuckle Lane* . . . *Azalea Court* . . . *Whippoorwill Drive*—flowery homages to the unsullied land that had been leveled and cleared of trees, and the wildlife which had been driven away, all in the name of affordable golf club living.

Although it was nearly four o'clock a number of workers still remained on the job. I could hear heavy equipment droning in the distance, and the sound of nail guns and electric saws reverberating within the newly framed dwellings. From the looks of things, Phase One of the Ashford Hills Estates would be completed on schedule.

I turned onto *Wisteria*, taking note of the signs I passed, *Dogwood* and *Magnolia*—short streets that appeared to dead-end; *Morning Glory, Nightingale,* and *Larkspur,* which was a circle. This last name tickled my subconscious like the onset of a sneeze. I jammed on the brakes.

I'd seen those words before. Not Larkspur Circle. Larkspur *in* a circle. The name *Larkspur* circled. On a page in TJ's journal, with a number beside it. But what number? I closed my eyes and tried to remember. My mind went blank. I cursed myself for having left the datebook back in my room at the inn.

"You lost?" a voice called from behind a parked truck.

A young guy in a ripped tee shirt and jeans sauntered down the drive. He had a carpenter's belt slung around his waist, and was carrying a can of Coke. It wasn't until that moment that I realized I'd come to a standstill in front of one of the homesites. I glanced down at the marker on the curb. It said, LOT 7—Number 7 Larkspur Circle.

"Just checking out the neighborhood," I said. "Nice house."

"Nice car." The young carpenter rolled the sweat-beaded soda can over his forehead. "Kinda hot, though, for riding around with the top down, innit?"

"Yeah, well, I'm from New York, so I have to take the sun when I can get it." I'd learned from past experience that the best way to win a southerner over is to knock northern weather, culture, speech patterns, and/or eating habits.

The young man smiled broadly. "I hear ya."

I got out of the Mustang, joining him in surveying the front of the house. "Looks as though you're just about done with this one," I said.

"Just about."

"You're lucky. There's not much new construction going on up north."

"That's too bad." The guy took a swig from his soda. "You want, I could show you around," he offered. I said sure.

As coy as it might sound now, I swear I had no ulterior motive at the time. It just seemed natural to me, seesawing up the two-by-fours that served as temporary steps, dodging electricians and painters, shouting to be heard over the *tat-tat-tat* of hammers and the blare of competing transistor radios. The smell of sheetrock and semi-gloss, of grout, spackle, sweat, and testosterone, reminded me of home. For months until the night that TJ called, this had been my world, my sole contact with other human beings.

We walked on paper runners stamped with the dusty soles of work boots. "The lady whose house this is loves to cook," the young carpenter explained. "So this kitchen's got two stoves, an extra sink, a lotta extras."

I followed him into a narrow hall. "Back here's the laundry room, and a half bath, an office area."

"Hey, Rowe," one of the painters cracked, "you lookin' to put Miss Muffy out of her sales job?" *So,* I thought, *TJ wasn't the only one who made Molly Moffat the butt of his jokes.*

The carpenter led me carefully up the oak staircase. "They're working on the bedroom floors," he said, "so we'll have to stick to the paper."

"No problem." Somewhere along the way, a part of me had splintered off from this little tour. My brain still registered the familiar sights, smells, and sounds, but a single word had begun to vibrate every fiber of my being causing my body to tremble like a tuning fork.

Larkspur. The name Sterling had numbered and put in a circle.

So what? I chided myself. Molly might've been wrong. Maybe TJ actually did sell one of these places. Or perhaps someone he knew bought the lot. There were plenty of other logical explanations. Larkspur could be the name of a club, or a bar, even a person, for heaven's sake.

The list of possibilities had me so distracted, I was barely paying attention when Rowe the carpenter poked his head into the master bedroom. "Make sure you get all them dust particles off the polyurethane, Bobby," he said to a man brush-coating sealant over the floor.

"You gonna give it the flashlight test, Rowe?" The guy laughed.

The carpenter turned to me. "It's kinda a private joke. We had a guy that bought the house next door who took a conniption fit because he said there were specks of dust trapped in the finish of the dining-room floor. Can you beat that?"

"Guess it takes all kinds," I said. But my heart was flipping like a hooked fish.

I don't remember much about the other two bedrooms, whether the upstairs bathrooms were papered or tiled, what the attic looked like. The next thing I knew, I was sitting behind the wheel of the rental again, and the nice-looking carpenter in the torn blue jeans was shutting my door. "Let me know if you decide to move into the neighborhood," he said.

"I'll do that." I put the Mustang in reverse and did a clumsy K-turn. As I pulled away, I took a sidelong glance at the house next door.

The curb marker said LOT 5.

6

MY HEALTHY APPETITE went right out the window. Instead of eating dinner, I stayed in my room with TJ's journal. The entry for Thursday, April 8th read *LMM—+ $4000,* which was clearly shorthand for the check he would receive from Little Ms. Muffet. Under this, TJ had printed LARKSPUR #5 in block letters, and drawn a careful circle.

Tossing the journal aside, I opened my own notebook. I used the edge of a piece of paper to trace a straight line, then listed the following chronological events:

- Wed., June 23—I see Owen Larson at Circle of Faith
- Thu., June 24—Edenfield—meet Vicki
- Fri., June 25—Dinner with Whitley—HIT BY CAR
- Sat., June 26—ATTACKED IN TJ's APT.
- Mon., June 28—Owen Larson arrested

For almost an hour, I stared at the timeline. I had the sinking feeling there was something I wasn't seeing.

. . .

SHORTLY AFTER DARK, I put on black jeans and a sweatshirt and drove back to Ashford Hills.

Floodlights illuminated the rows of model houses, making them look flat and two-dimensional, like painted facades on a movie backlot. A full moon bleached the open fretwork of a dozen new homesites behind them. I traveled the rutted road at a crawl, with my headlights off.

The sales center was dark. I pulled behind the trailer and waited. If security was going to catch me, I wanted it to be for trespassing, not breaking and entering. When no one showed after five minutes, I slipped out of the car.

The office didn't have a patio or a porch, and there wasn't a grill in sight. I shined my flashlight toward the terra-cotta planters. Sterling's key was tucked under the geraniums closest to the door. *Thanks, old chum,* I thought. *You might've been a sneak, but at least you were consistent.*

I unlocked the door and went inside. Without the air-conditioner going, the trailer felt like an oven. I trained the beam around the room. The filing cabinets were behind Moffat's desk. I tucked the flashlight under my chin, and began searching through the drawers. Moffat kept all the pending contracts together. Eighty-three, to be exact, in alphabetical order. I'd have to open the file folders, one by one.

Several of the names jumped out at me. A Lawrence *Angler* had purchased Lot Number 43, Tiger Lily Lane. *Gordon* Dawes was the buyer for 19 Magnolia. I forced myself to concentrate solely on the addresses. Agreements had been signed for 7 Larkspur . . . 10 Larkspur . . . 11 Larkspur . . . and 14 Larkspur. It was at least ninety degrees in the trailer, and my heavy sweatshirt and jeans made it feel even hotter. If I didn't find the contract for Lot 5 soon, I thought I'd faint. I'd almost given up hope when it caught my eye.

The lot was listed as Number 5 LARKSPUR CIR.; the buyers, Arthur Wright of Charlottesville, and Nancy Koch of Lynchburg, Virginia. With shaking hands, I flipped to the last page. Mr. Wright had signed his name with an almost mechanical precision. My mind's eye called up the letter I'd read at Frank McGlynn's dining-room table—the symmetrical lines of careful writing. It was the same hand.

My flashlight had grown weak. Drenched with sweat and slightly woozy, I stuffed the folder in my bag. A heavy key ring was hanging on a hook beside Moffat's desk. I jangled through it. Slipped off the key marked *5 Larksp.* Pocketed it.

The lock snapped back into place the minute I shut the trailer door. I dropped TJ's key into the planter and ran to the car. The Mustang's engine growled angrily, then eased into a soft purr.

As I reached the gate, I noticed something in my rearview mirror—a parked car on the bluff, overlooking the development. A security guard? Another intruder? Or just my imagination?

I didn't plan to hang around long enough to find out.

LESS THAN THIRTY minutes later, I was pulling down another dark road.

In front of TJ's apartment building, a ribbon of yellow crime scene tape halfheartedly cordoned off the drive. I parked on the street, and sat motionless behind the wheel for an indeterminate amount of time. The sense of déjà vu was so intense I had to mentally will myself into the present tense; and yet, strangely enough, I felt no fear—just a dreamlike sluggishness, as if the events of this night had already been played out in some other dimension, leaving me no choice but to go through the preordained motions.

I got out of the car and walked slowly up the driveway toward the fence. *The latch will either be locked,* I told myself, *or it won't.* It wasn't. I crossed the moon-dusted patio and walked past the grill to the glass sliders. My flashlight was dead, so I used the penlight to guide Sterling's key into the lock. I thought, *Childress has either changed these locks, or he hasn't.*

The key turned easily. I stuck my hand inside, groping around for the switch. Overhead lights popped on, illuminating the room. I stepped inside, sliding the door closed behind me. No one had come to remove TJ's belongings. The boxes of odds-and-ends and books were still neatly stacked against the far wall, just as I'd left them. I crossed the room, staring straight ahead, avoiding even a sidelong glance toward the desk. The desk where—

Don't think of that now, Garner, I ordered myself. *This isn't the time to fall apart.*

I found the carton right away. Using the pointed part of my key, I sliced through the masking tape and pulled wide the flaps. The fox stoles stared up at me, splayed and glassy-eyed, as though having been roused from a debaucherous sleep. Tossing them aside, I delved down deeper until I found the shadow box.

The Plexiglas display window opened easily. I took out the gun. According to the engraved plate that had been mounted next to Sterling's book cover, this was a Colt .38, detective special. I lifted my sweatshirt and tucked it into the waistband of my jeans.

I SAT CROSSLEGGED on the Charleston bed in my pretty, lamp-lit room at the Eighteen-Twenty Ivy, TJ Sterling's journal on my lap. His last entry was for Friday the eleventh of June. *Luth. C of F—3 PM,* it read. I thumbed through a monthful of blank pages until I found tomorrow's date—Tuesday, July 13th—and in the box I wrote the words:

SHADOW GORDON SPANGLER

7

ARTHUR WRIGHT LIVED in a homely but well-tended boarding house, on an ordinary street in a quiet suburb of Charlottesville. It had been raining since dawn, and my fogged windshield made it difficult to see. Occasionally, I turned on the engine to let the defroster run, but I took care not to use the wipers. I didn't want to draw too much attention.

Five minutes after eight, the front door opened and he walked out onto the porch. In his shapeless raincoat, with his briefcase, and his Totes, he could have been just an ordinary man, on his way to work. But this man was far from ordinary. He was Gordon Spangler. I knew it— knew it with a kind of ice-cold certainty that blasted through the fog on my windows and turned the outside world crystal clear.

Spangler fidgeted with the automatic umbrella, then stepped into the murky drizzle, walking straight toward the Mustang. Surprisingly enough, I felt none of the fear that had so gripped me that day, with Owen Larson. I just slouched in my seat and watched as Spangler hustled by, too intent on avoiding puddles to even give me a second look.

He unlocked the door to a dark blue Ford Taurus and spent a full two minutes warming up the engine before pulling away from the curb. I waited until the car was halfway down the block before following.

There was no rush, I told myself. I had all the time in the world.

FROM EIGHT-THIRTY UNTIL five, Gordon Spangler worked downtown in the offices of Chadwick, Fritsch, & Durant, Certified Public Accountants. He left the building only once, at 11:15 A.M., scurrying into the Taurus with his briefcase and umbrella although the rain had already stopped. I trailed him to the bluff overlooking the Ashford Hills Estates, where he parked and proceeded to eat his lunch.

At the end of the business day I got stuck behind a slow-moving van and nearly lost him. I caught a glimpse of the blue Ford just before it turned onto University Avenue. Inching up to the cross street, I sped off after him. Spangler appeared to be headed for the Corner district. To my surprise, he pulled into a lot behind a group of commercial buildings. I waited until he'd disappeared into one of the rear entrances, then I parked my car and strolled around front for a closer look.

It was a coffee house called Charlottesville's Web. A dozen tables, all equipped with computers, lined the walls. Customers played video games or surfed the 'net while sipping designer brews and spooning pastries. I couldn't find anyone in the place over the age of thirty. Gordon Spangler was nowhere in sight.

"A man came in here a few minutes ago." I spoke softly to the girl at the counter. "About sixty, suit and tie?"

"You mean Arthur?"

"Yes." I nodded. "Arthur Wright."

"He works in the kitchen. Do you want me to get him for you?"

"No, thanks." My gaze flickered toward all the pale, gawky boys hunched over their mousepads.

I wondered if any of them enjoyed playing games of military strategy.

THE NEXT AFTERNOON, I dialed the number for Chadwick, Fritsch, & Durant and asked to be transferred to Arthur Wright's extension. "Mr. Wright, this is Candace Kressler from the Albemarle Planning and Development Corporation?"

"Oh, yes." Spangler sounded anxious. "Is something wrong? I've been assured by the bank that our mortgage should—"

"It's not that, sir. It's the floors. I understand there's been a problem with the polyurethane."

"Yes, well. I told the workers, of course. And when nothing was done, I'm afraid I felt compelled to write a letter of complaint to Ms. Moffat—"

"Molly Moffat is no longer with us. We discovered she wasn't being responsive enough to our buyers' concerns."

"That's true." Now that he had my ear, Spangler turned quite peevish. "Oftentimes, she didn't even return my calls."

"I'm sure we can remedy this situation, Mr. Wright," I told him. "Tell you what. Let's do a walk-through of your house and you can point out what needs to be done."

"That sounds . . ." He was trying to disguise his surprise. "Er . . . equitable."

"How's tomorrow at six?"

"I thought the sales center was closed on Thursdays."

I'd forgotten: this was a man who did his homework. "Under the circumstances," I said, "I'm willing to make an exception."

"All right," agreed Spangler. "Tomorrow will be fine."

IN THE STATE of Virginia you can purchase bullets without having to even flash your driver's license. I bought a box of .38 special ammunition and went back to my room to wait.

8

THE LAST GRAY light of day slanted through the bare windows—twilight settled so much earlier on these cloudy afternoons. At five o'clock, the sounds of bulldozing and hammering abruptly stopped and the construction workers all went home, leaving only heavy machinery and silence behind. I slipped quietly out of the basement where I'd been hiding since six A.M., when I used Moffat's key to open the front door of number 5 Larkspur Circle.

I'd prepared meticulously for this moment. There were only a few things left to do. I removed several items from my shoulder bag—a flashlight, a folder and clipboard, my tortoiseshell glasses, the gun. I loaded the Colt, placed it carefully in the utensil drawer next to the kitchen sink, and put on my glasses.

Spangler's blue Taurus pulled into the drive at the stroke of six. I heard him get out of the car and walk up the porch steps. He knocked gently on the door, surprised perhaps, to find it ajar. "Hello?" And once again, the innate defensiveness in his voice struck me. "Anybody here?"

His footsteps resounded through the empty living room. "Hello?" he called, still moving tentatively down the hall. "Anybody?"

I stepped out of the shadows. "Hi, there," I said.

Spangler gasped, "You startled me—I wasn't sure . . ."

"I'm sorry," I apologized. "Are you all right?"

"Yes. I didn't see a car out front."

"I left mine over at the office." Standing toe to toe as we were, he seemed smaller and more stooped than he had, at a distance. I forced myself to extend a hand. "I'm Candace Kressler."

"Yes, of course."

We shook hands briefly. A rolling tide of nausea washed over me at the touch of his moist, clammy palm. "Why don't we go in the kitchen where it's more cheerful?" I suggested. "I always find houses without furniture a bit spooky, don't you, Mr. Wright?"

"I suppose." He seemed confused. "I never thought of it . . ."

"Please." I stepped aside so he could enter the room first. "The electricians obviously still have some work to do. There's a flashlight on the counter. It looks like we may need it."

"Yes." Spangler nodded. "Especially to see the floor properly."

He was walking in front of me now, crossing from the kitchen directly into the dining room. I saw that his trousers were a half-inch too short and that he dyed his hair with Grecian Formula. He looked out of place against these bright white walls and designer tiles. "If you'll pass me the light," he was saying, "I'll show you what I mean."

With great effort, Spangler lowered himself onto his hands and knees. Then he trained the flashlight over the pristine maple floor. "Can you see those specks?"

"No," I said, barely breathing. "Not really."

He laid his cheek flat against the planking. "There. Those tiny bubbles. Dust particles that were trapped during the sealing process. You need to be at a certain angle in order to—"

But I was no longer listening. The gray light slanting through the bare windows suddenly started to undulate and spiral. Beneath my feet, the floorboards ran like maple sap. I looked down and saw the prone figure of Gordon Spangler—back hunched, arms out, face to the ground, and all at once it hit me. *He's ten small steps away from being dead.*

Ten steps. Five into the kitchen to grab the Colt. Five out. Before he had time to scramble to his feet, the gun would be drawn. I could shoot him in the head and leave him lying here on the dust-sealed floor, in his cheap suit and his rubber galoshes. Or I could take out a kneecap, and grab his tie. Yank it back so hard his head would snap, and blood streamed out from his ears . . . down his nose . . . through his thin, shoe-polish black hair.

". . . in my opinion, the men who laid the floor are responsible." Spangler, still down on all fours, continued to drone. "I told Ms. Moffat weeks ago, but she said she didn't see it." He held the flashlight parallel to the floor. "But you do, don't you?" He looked over his shoulders at me. "It's really very obvious."

"Yes." I took the flashlight from him, and snapped it off. "Yes, it is." The room now seemed absurdly dark. Suddenly, more than anything in the world, I wanted to go to sleep.

Spangler staggered to his feet. "Does that mean that you'll take care of it?"

"Yes."

"At no additional cost?"

"At no additional cost," I agreed.

I walked back into the kitchen, toward the cabinets. "There is one other thing—"

"Yes?"

"I couldn't locate your contract in Ms. Moffat's files. I'm afraid I'm going to have to ask you and Ms. Koch to sign another copy of the agreement in order for the closing to go on as scheduled." I handed him the document.

Spangler carefully read it through and signed his name. *Arthur Wright.*

"My home office is in Lynchburg," I told him. "I thought I might drop the papers by your fiancée's tomorrow. Save us all some time."

"I suppose that would be all right," he said.

"You'll tell her to expect me?"

"Yes," said Gordon Spangler. "I will."

9

"WHO IS IT?" the voice demanded from behind the locked door. Nancy Koch probably prided herself on being an extremely cautious woman.

"Nancy?" I smiled into the peephole. "Arthur Wright said it would be okay if I stopped by with this." I waved a manila folder.

I heard the sound of latches snapping and bolts sliding open. A tall, slender woman in her early fifties stuck out her head. She wore a royal blue suit, with a tailored blouse and matching blue shoes. Not a single strand of her elaborately coiffed hair was out of place. "Hi," I said. "My name is Garner Quinn."

"From Ashford Hills? Come in." Koch waved me into a small foyer. A bucket of water and a mop stood on the spotless parquet floor.

"I hope I haven't come at a bad time."

"Oh, I'm *always* cleaning," she said. *Washing floors in a dress suit and high-heeled pumps?*

Koch led me into the adjoining parlor. For the first time I noticed the S curve of her spine; it softened her appearance somehow, making her seem suddenly awkward and vulnerable. "Please," she invited, "make yourself comfortable."

All the furniture had been slipcovered in white and then plasticized. When I sat, the vinyl wheezed under me like a novelty store whoopie cushion. Nancy Koch stayed on her feet, searching for a pen. "I might as well sign the contracts right away."

"There's no rush."

My eyes traveled to a framed photograph on the mantel—Nancy in a lime green chiffon dress, standing next to Gordon Spangler. "Have you known Mr. Wright for a long time?" I asked.

She smiled. "It'll be a year in August."

"How did you two meet?"

"We attended the same church." Koch sat down in a chair without making so much as a squeak. "Now," she said, clearly wanting to steer the conversation away from such personal matters. "Where are those papers?"

"There's something else you should see first, Nancy." I handed her the folder.

Instead of opening it, Koch tilted her lacquered helmet of hair. "What did you say your name was?"

"Garner Quinn."

"Strange. I could've sworn that Arthur said it was Candace something . . ." *This was one sharp lady.* "Kissler or Kessler." Her lashless eyes narrowed at me.

"I'm afraid I lied to him," I said quietly.

Koch drew back, as if the manila envelope might explode. "I don't understand. What's this about?"

I took it from her, fanning the contents on the glass coffee table—school pictures of young Robert Spangler and little Gordy; publicity shots of Lara in her Juliet gown; a faded Polaroid of Estelle and her mother-in-law; newspaper articles; Spangler's blank, enigmatic face. It was a grisly collage.

"Do you know this man?" I slid Spangler's photograph toward her.

"No," Koch said, but there was uncertainty in her eyes.

"Look again," I urged. "Try to picture him as a man of sixty. The high forehead, the weak chin. His real name is Gordon Spangler, Nancy." Koch twisted the collar of her starched blouse.

"Did he tell you he'd been married before? That he was a widower?" Koch cowered in her chair. "Yes, but—"

"Do you know *why* he's a widower, Nancy? He's a widower because he killed his wife—killed her in cold blood as she sat down to breakfast." The woman recoiled, the curve of her spine a question mark against the stiff white plastic.

"Then he walked calmly upstairs and murdered his mother. Stuffed her in the hall closet and just shut the door." I held up Gordy's picture. "He killed this little boy, too—Gordon, Junior, his namesake. And Robert and Lara. *Look at them.* Doesn't your heart break just thinking about it?"

I pointed to Spangler. "But his didn't, Nancy. He didn't even break a sweat. He just lined their dead bodies up to form the sign of the cross— well, you probably know how religious he is—then he went to the bank and withdrew the last of his mother's money and got the hell out of there."

At the mention of the money, Koch tilted her head again, but I wasn't about to let up. "He has an old scar from an appendectomy," I told her. "He plays war games and loves fixing up houses. *You know him, Nancy.* You know you do. You might not have known about this, but you had doubts of your own, didn't you? I saw the notes Molly Moffat made in your file, how you've been wavering, wanting to back out of the deal—"

"No! I have no idea what you're talking about . . . why you're even

here." Koch rose to her full height. "I want you to go. Now. And take all this with you, understand?" She clattered into the foyer in her bright blue pumps. "Just leave me alone or I'll have you arrested for harassment—"

We both knew she wouldn't do that. "Sorry to have bothered you," I said.

I walked out the door without another word, leaving the pictures on the coffee table, along with Special Agent J. Emmett Hogan's card and his number at the FBI.

1 0

SATURDAY, JULY 17

I RETURNED THE Mustang to the rental place in Charlottesville. Leedon Whitley had been babysitting my Volvo while Temple and I were in Florida. We arranged to meet in town for the swap.

"What the hell did you do to your hair?" Whitley gaped in mock horror when he saw me. It was obvious he liked it, so I just smiled.

BY THE TIME I reached Edenfield it was already late afternoon. I parked next to the stables next to Caroline's Mercedes wagon and her stepsister's Accord. I found Caroline in the first stall, braiding the mane of the chesnut mare.

"Garner!" she cried. When we hugged, I felt the small, hard swell of her belly. "I almost didn't recognize you. Your hair is—"

"Gone."

Caroline's face darkened with concern. "Detective Whitley told us what happened. Are you all right?"

"Good as new. What about you?"

She patted her stomach. "Getting fat, I'm afraid. Here, let me just finish up with Lady Love, then we can go on over to the house for some tea."

I watched Caroline knot another little braid of horse hair. "I understand you've been staying with your parents."

"Where'd you hear that from?"

"Our mutual friend." I smiled. "The good detective."

"Yes, well, then you know I put the Cheswick place on the market. Too many bad memories, I guess." Caroline sighed. Again some highstrung intuition forced the mare into a skittery dance. I backed away. "Settle down, darlin'," Caroline cooed. "You'll have poor Garner breakin' out in hives."

She shot me a sympathetic look. "I know how disappointed you must be, not finding Spangler. Especially considering all you went through."

"That's life."

"Maybe it's better to just leave things the way they are." With a graceful flourish, she finished the last braid. "See? All done."

"I'm afraid not, Caroline."

She looked down at Lady Love's mane. "Did I miss something?"

"No," I said. "But I did, didn't I?"

The young woman's eyes came up to meet mine, slowly, and for a brief second I read the truth in them. "I was so sure that Gordon Spangler killed TJ, I overlooked the most important suspect of all. You."

The color drained out of Caroline's face. "You're joking, right? This is some kind of a joke."

"Unfortunately not." I sat down on the bale of hay. "It's the oldest story in the world. You killed your husband because he was about to leave you for another woman."

"You're talking crazy," Caroline sputtered. "I was in Charleston the night Tom shot himself."

"I don't think so. I think you had a fight with him on the phone and you got in your car and drove back Saturday night to confront him."

"No," she protested. "I left Sunday morning around six. Just ask my sister. We shared a room together at the hotel."

"What'd you do, Caroline?" I needled her. "Did you call Vicki up that night to tell her what you'd done? Did you ask her to be your alibi? You knew the poor kid would do anything for you. But she almost cracked under the pressure, didn't she?"

"I don't have to listen to this," Caroline said angrily.

I stood. "You took the back road that leads from Huntington Lane to TJ's office. Was he passed out cold when you found him? Or did he drink himself into a stupor while you fought?"

Caroline's tongue cracked like a whip. Suddenly Lady Love began snorting. Another sound from her mistress sent the mare shifting about nervously, prancing until her hooves thrashed in the air, higher and higher.

I made a run for the door, but Caroline grabbed my shoulders, and for one dizzying second her strong, athletic hands lifted me in the air; then she pushed hard, and I toppled backward onto the floor. "Caroline, please!" I screamed as she slammed the door shut.

The mare reared, her eyes shot through with blood. When I tried to move, her hooves came crashing down, dangerously close to my head. "Please," I pleaded, "she's going to kill me!"

An authoritative voice rang out through the stables. "Down, Lady. Come on, girl. Down." The latch turned and Vicki walked into the stall. "Tsch-tsch-tsch," she clucked gently. She moved sideways, shielding me with her body.

"Easy girl. It's all right. Everything's going to be okay." The mare calmed down enough for Vicki to take hold of her bridle. Very slowly, I edged myself out the door.

Caroline was slumped on a bale of hay, weeping. "Why are you doing this to me, Garner?" she asked. "You knew how he was—so mean and critical. Treating women like they were dirt. I could tell you never liked him." She looked up, with accusing eyes. "So why the hell did you have to come tramping down here, stirring everything up?"

Vicki shut the door to the stall and stood there, hovering between her sister and me. I said, "He didn't deserve to die, Caroline."

"Didn't he?" she snapped bitterly. "Want to know what he said when I told him I was pregnant? *Gee, Car, that's damn bad timing, because I don't think I want to be married to you anymore.*" Vicki tried to put an arm around her, but she shook it off.

"So good ole Caroline comes running back from Charleston, trying to patch things up, and you know what Tom's doing? He's sitting at his desk, piss-faced, writing love letters to this li'l grade-school teacher he met in one of his classes. Sending her the same kind of flowery poetry he used to send me. *'If thou regret'st thy youth, why live?'*" She wiped her nose on the sleeve of her shirt. "It made me sick!

"He said her name was Lisa Briggs, and she wouldn't give a married drunk like him the time of day. But he loved her, so he wanted to change. He'd started attending AA meetings. He was writing a novel. Don't you see, Garner," Caroline implored me, "how much it hurt? Knowing he'd do all that for *her*—"

"Yes," I said truthfully.

She caught hold of my hand. "Don't pursue it, then. We're friends—"

"My friends don't try to kill me," I said, pulling my hand away.

"What are you talking about?"

"I'm talking about the night you sent your sister to that parking garage to puncture my tire." I turned to Vicki. "What was the deal— you were supposed to follow me, give me a scare?" The girl averted

303

her face. "You didn't know Caroline planned to run me over, did you?"

"That's ridiculous," Caroline said. "I would never—"

"Never what?" I said. "Never try to shoot me, or wrap a telephone cord around my neck?"

Caroline said, "That was—"

"Gordon Spangler," I finished for her. "But see, that would've been impossible. The timing was all wrong. At that point I was on the trail of a poor innocent man named Owen Larson. He didn't attack me—although a couple of days later I had him arrested for it. Spangler didn't attack me either. He didn't even know I existed."

I sank down wearily on the hay, next to Caroline. "Only three people knew that I was trying to track down Gordon Spangler. An FBI agent named Emmett Hogan. TJ's assistant, Sands McColl. And you." I stood suddenly, yanking her shirt back so hard the buttons popped. The tiny puncture wound from the pencil was still there in the soft flesh of her shoulder.

For a long moment no one spoke; then Caroline said, "That day you told me about Lara, I realized what I had to do. I knew you'd never give up on Spangler. And once you found him, it was only a matter of time before you figured out he had nothing to do with Tommy's death. I'm sorry, Garner." She looked up at Vicki, and the young girl fell to her knees, sobbing. "I'm so, so sorry," Caroline said again, stroking her sister's dark hair.

I started for the door, and stopped. "Detective Whitley should be pulling up any minute now, but don't worry too much. I'm sure your father will get you the best defense attorney money can buy. You're rich, beautiful, and pregnant, and your husband used you like a doormat." I managed a raffish shrug. "Hey, who knows? If poor TJ's luck in court holds, the jury'll probably find him guilty of his own murder and let you go scot free."

FRIDAY, JULY 23

I ARRIVED BACK home on the morning of my ex-husband's wedding. Five minutes before Andy and Candace were to take their vows, the telephone rang.

"Thank God you're there," sighed J. Emmett Hogan.

"What's up?" I asked.

"What's up is we've got Gordon Spangler," he said. "And this time we got him for real."

"How'd it happen?"

"His fiancée, a woman named Nancy Koch, turned him in. Said she'd never heard about the case until she read about it in the papers, during the Owen Larson thing." Hogan was tapping his fingers in excitement. "So I guess, in a way, you were responsible for catching the bastard, after all."

"Yeah," I said. "I guess I was."

EPILOGUE

SHOULD AULD

ACQUAINTANCE

BE FORGOT,

AND NEVER

BROUGHT

TO MIN'?

ROBERT BURNS

EVEN ON THIS gloomy autumn afternoon, the little theater sparkled. The battered walls had been painted Williamsburg blue, the proscenium arch, milky white. I walked down the center aisle, and hoisted
myself up on stage. Out of habit, I squinted up toward the balcony, and
into the wings, to make certain I was alone. Then I reached into my
pocket, and took out the small white votive candle in its clear glass
holder. This time I even remembered to bring a match.

The wick hissed when I lit it, the tiny flame no bigger than my
thumbnail. I closed my eyes for a moment, considering the events of the
last few months. So many lives, so irrevocably changed . . .

Caroline Sterling had been indicted for the murder of her husband,
and released into the custody of her parents, pending trial. Owen Larson
married the widow he'd met at the Circle of Friends. We've spoken on
the phone several times, and to my chagrin, he just won't bear a grudge.
Sands McColl went out to L.A., to peddle a screen version of TJ
Sterling's novel. And Leedon Whitley keeps telling me I'm missing an
opportunity of a lifetime by not collaborating on his detective story with
him. On the night of their thirtieth wedding anniversary, Hogan's wife
Sue kicked him out of the house; they're presently working on their

third reconciliation. Cilda returned from Jamaica. Andy and Candace came back from their honeymoon. When school started up, Temple cut her visits back to once a month.

As far as I know, Dane Blackmoor remains in Paris.

A few weeks after he was extradited back to Jersey, I went to see Gordon Spangler in jail. He asked me if I'd heard from Nancy, and seemed depressed about the house deal falling through. Although he refused to discuss the murders, he did admit that he was surprised it took the authorities so long to catch him. "It wasn't really planned," he said, dully. "One day just led to another."

I asked if, in all that time, he ever thought of Lara, and the others.

"Not really," he replied, without emotion. "Except that first year, on their birthdays."

"How did you do it? What were you thinking of when you killed them like that?" I wanted to know.

"I wasn't thinking of anything," Gordon Spangler said. "I just kept counting."

I SAT ON the stage, thinking of Lara. I thought, too, of my own life, and for a brief moment, it was so overwhelming it drove me to the very brink of despair.

How, I wondered, could I possibly go on?

But then I heard a voice say, *You're Garner Quinn, aren't you? Bold and courageous. A perfect number three.*

And so I blew the candle out with a smile.